BOOK THREE OF
THE CODED MESSAGE TRILOGY

I0657993

T-U-L-E

RANDY C. DOCKENS

Carpenter's Son Publishing

T-U-L-E

Published by Carpenter's Son Publishing, Franklin, Tennessee

Published in association with Larry Carpenter of Christian Book Services, LLC
www.christianbookservices.com

Cover and Interior Design by Suzanne Lawing

Edited by Robert Irvin

Printed in the United States of America

978-1-946889-26-3

CONTENTS

ONE

T-U-L-E

Love brings hope back into view. That's how Luke now felt. After all this time, it had finally happened. He had proposed, and Sarah said yes.

The time between proposing and this moment seemed like a whirlwind to him. He glanced over at Sarah, his beautiful fiancée. As she walked over to talk with Natalia, her blonde ringlets bounced as her amber-colored eyes twinkled, making Luke's legs go weak. How did he get so lucky?

He thought about this and had to wonder how both of them had made it this far. It seemed like such a long time ago when that fateful piece of confetti fell as he sat waiting for his cup of coffee. Who would have thought that three simple letters—T-H-B—would lead to such an adventure, the one he and his friends had stumbled into?

Luke thought of all the things that had happened since that time. His once enemy—Viktoria, now his friend—had become an integral part of their lives, and now she was an important member of their wedding party. He chuckled and shook his head thinking back to when he first met Viktoria in an interrogation room. She was one beautiful lady with her dark hazel eyes and black ringlets, but she had also been extremely intimidating as she exhibited her Illumi-Alliance persona with that ultra-intimidating smile.

Luke looked over at Oliver, Viktoria's husband, who had gotten him into all of this in the first place. Again, this man *should* be his enemy, but had become a good friend. He was the one who had fallen in love with Viktoria and developed a code word that allowed her to snap out of her Illumi-Alliance persona and become a loving and loyal wife. The two of them were likely the only ones—or at least one of only a few; who knew entirely?—who had found a way to overcome the mind manipulation which The Six, an elite group of world leaders molding earth's future agenda, had instituted upon the world.

And Luke never understood how or why Oliver had gotten Luke's two best friends, Jeremy and Natalia, into all of this. Luke smiled to himself. Likely Oliver knew he would listen to Jeremy and Natalia when he wouldn't listen to anyone else. Jeremy being a top-notch restaurateur had greatly helped in their adventure. Without Jeremy's wealth, Natalia's brains as a brilliant architect, and the impact both of them had on influential people, they likely would have been caught a long time ago.

Xiaofeng, Natalia's mother, approached Natalia and Sarah. Natalia's beautiful Oriental eyes came from her mother while her cheekbones and tan came from her father, Matteo, who was of Italian descent. Luke smiled, thinking back to when he and Sarah had first met Xiaofeng in the Neuroscience Center in Paris; they had no idea who she was at the time. Somehow, she had been chosen for a "reintegration program" under the guise of finding a compound which would compromise those who were immune to the current mind-manipulating compound incorporated into the Invocation wafer. Everyone, on every continent, had to take the wafer at least once a month. Luke's small group had rescued Xiaofeng just before she was scheduled to enter Mercy Farewell, which was nothing but a euphemism for a place of euthanasia. Luke's smile vanished thinking back to the moment he realized he and Sarah were immune to this compound—which put them all in danger. The Six were determined to get rid of any immunes since they feared immunes would spoil their plans of controlling the world's population for their own agenda.

Luke's mind turned to Matteo next. Xiaofeng's husband had been a lifesaver for him—indeed, for all of them. Natalia getting her parents back was a miracle in and of itself. Since all children were taken to a government boarding school at the age of ten, the parents' minds were manipulated to forget their children, and the children were taught their parents had given them up for their own good to better understand and serve Community . . . well, for Natalia to reconnect with them had truly been a God-designed event.

Since *T-H-B* had been *The Holy Bible*, a book banned for nearly sixty years, at first Luke had been very much against reading it. He had felt betrayed since *T-H-B* was supposed to be the answer to life's issues: the ultimate reason behind the mind manipulation, the reason behind the upcoming Mars mission, and the meaning to life itself. He couldn't see how a religious book could answer any of those questions.

The role Matteo had played had been to give each of these six friends important insights into understanding the seemingly confusing passages in this book. He had helped Luke understand the second coded message he had received: *F-S-H-S*. Matteo helped him understand that God, being Trinity . . . well, it was important for him to be a God of love *and* a God of justice. The Holy Spirit helped God exhibit both of these seemingly opposite forces. Matteo and Xiaofeng had helped him understand that the character of Father, Son, and Holy Spirit—Trinity—was exhibited at the center of all matter. (And thus, the meaning of *F-S-H-S*.) *The Holy Bible* also predicted the return of this second part of the Godhead, God the Son. This was the reason for the mind manipulation—it was to prevent people from being able to pray for such an event to occur. So, according to the plan, those who were immune would be taken off the planet to Mars so that, even if they prayed, they would not be on Earth for such an event to happen. If The Six could find an alternative drug to work on those immune to the current drug in the Invocation wafer, then those immune would be programmed to think of Mars as their home and never know that Earth had, for most of their lives, been home.

Luke shook his head. How had such a perfect world turned so dark? Only a short time ago, he felt his life was so perfect. Now his life was in constant danger. Yet he was now also getting married! For now, he was going to focus on the latter—some happiness amid all this chaos. He looked at Sarah and smiled again. Yes, it was time to focus on her—and make her feel as special as he felt her to be.

As he leaned against the balcony railing of Jeremy and Natalia's penthouse where everyone had gathered here in Shanghai, he saw Sarah approach. He smiled. *Yes, I am a very lucky man.*

She leaned in and gave him a kiss. "We're heading over now to get ready."

Luke looked at his watch. "So early?"

Sarah laughed. "Early for you. Trust me, beauty doesn't just happen."

Luke smiled and gave her another kiss. "Hard to see how you could get any more beautiful."

Sarah gave a smile as her cheeks reddened. "Charmer." She

patted his chest. "I don't believe you, but I appreciate the lie."

Luke shook his head. "Just have fun."

Sarah turned and went back into the penthouse. Not long after, she left with Natalia, who had hired two beauticians to help Sarah get ready after the baptism ceremony. Everyone else got ready beforehand.

Around 17:00, the guys headed to the beach. It wasn't far from Jeremy's Shanghai high-rise. Luke laid his tux and change of clothes in his tent. He thanked everyone who made it to the wedding from work; this included Scott, Brian, and his boss, Larry. Brian had brought Carmella, who was a scientist in Brazil. She looked more beautiful than he remembered.

When Scott introduced Carmella to Jason and Jared, Luke grabbed Brian's arm. "Hey, buddy, how's it going with Carmella? I didn't know you were bringing her." He raised his eyebrows a couple of times. "Must be getting serious." He nudged him in the side.

Brian laughed. "Maybe. We thought we'd take this opportunity you gave us to turn it into another holiday for us. We've never been to Asia."

Luke smiled. "Glad I could help out."

Kathleen, a nurse and friend who worked with Sarah, came up and gave him a kiss on his cheek. "I'm happy for you, Luke. You be good to her now, you hear?"

Luke smiled and nodded. Ken, Sarah's boss, had walked up with Kathleen. Luke shook Ken's hand. "Thanks for being so accommodating, Ken."

Ken smiled. "Couldn't pass up a chance to visit Asia, now could I?"

Jason and Jared, also friends from work, approached. Luke gave each a heartfelt hug, thanked them for coming, and introduced them to Ken. As they talked, he noticed his new friend Maher talking with Jeremy.

He excused himself and walked over to Maher, shook his hand, and pulled him in for a hug. "Maher, thanks for coming. It really means a lot."

Maher shook his head. "Wouldn't miss it. I'm really happy for you, Luke." He pointed behind Luke. "Here comes your happiness now."

Sarah was walking out with Matteo. Luke walked over to her, took her hand, and smiled. She smiled back. They were both wearing jeans and a pullover. Matteo motioned for everyone to gather in close.

"OK, everyone," Matteo began. "Marriage may seem somewhat passé to the masses these days. Yet Luke and Sarah have decided to make this day a very special day in their lives. In addition, they have decided to add something else to their special day. Immersion, in olden times, represented purification. Today, they are going to publicly demonstrate what the Holy Spirit has done for them on the inside. The Holy Spirit is a term that may be foreign to many of you. They will be happy to explain this to you after their ceremony, if you so choose."

Both Sarah and Luke walked with Matteo across the beach and waded into the lake. He first turned to Sarah. "Sarah, it has been my honor to get to know you and see what a wonderful person you are. Because of your faith in the one true God, I baptize you in the name of the Father, Son, and Holy Spirit." He then immersed her in the lake—completely under the water—and Sarah stood back up.

Luke reached over and kissed her. The audience clapped. Luke knew most of them didn't understand what they were witnessing. He hoped what they saw would allow him a chance to explain its significance later. Luke knew the entire baptismal ceremony was a risk since the government didn't sanction belief in God. Yet he felt close to everyone, so the risk seemed low.

Sarah then stood while Matteo turned to Luke. "Luke, it has been my honor to get to know you and see how you have matured in spiritual matters. Because of your faith in the one true God, and because you now know what *F-S-H-S* means in your life . . . " Luke smiled and nodded. "I baptize you in the name of the Father, Son, and Holy Spirit." Luke felt Matteo submerge him under the water. He stood up and shook his head, water splashing everywhere. Sarah reached over and kissed him. He hugged her with a tight squeeze. "Thanks, Sarah," he said. "This was an excellent suggestion."

She whispered, "Now comes the hard part. I have to get beautiful in less than an hour."

He shook his head. "No, that's not hard at all."

He took her by the hand and they stepped through the water and waded back to shore. Matteo followed. While Jeremy entertained the guests with drinks and appetizers, Luke and Matteo went to get changed in his tent while Sarah went to change in hers. Natalia, Viktoria, and the beauticians went with her. She blew Luke a kiss. He smiled and blew a kiss back.

Both Luke and Matteo changed into their tuxedos. It didn't take long for Luke to get ready. He helped Matteo with his cummerbund, and Matteo helped put Luke's pink rose boutonniere in place.

"Luke, I'm proud of you for having a ceremony like this. So many people these days take the easy way out without giving it the proper attention and respect such a step deserves."

"Thanks, Matteo. You and Xiaofeng have been inspirations to me and Sarah."

Matteo smiled. "Well, I'm glad we can be used in such a way."

Both of them left the tent and joined the rest of the wedding party. It seemed to take quite a while for Sarah to leave her tent, but emerge she finally did. Luke took this time to talk and joke with all those in attendance.

Natalia exited first. She nodded to Matteo. "We're ready."

Matteo went to where two tiki torches had been placed in the sand. The poles were decorated with white orchids and pink roses. The wedding party formed a path from Matteo toward Sarah's tent. Luke walked to the tent to retrieve his bride. Natalia and Viktoria held back the tent flap and Sarah exited.

Luke smiled. "Sarah, you are gorgeous." He meant it—in every way. Her dress, all white and simple in design, looked beautiful at the same time. There were strategically placed sequins that twinkled from the torchlight. The uneven hem at the bottom added a flair of contemporary. Her hair, arranged in ringlets, had a small laced veil woven in at the back, and this draped down her back. She had a small bouquet of pink roses and white orchids.

Sarah looked back at Luke. He couldn't get over her smile, which seemed to show her adoration for him. "You look pretty dapper yourself, Luke. I didn't know white would make your eyes even more blue than normal." She ran her hand through his hair and smiled. The breeze off the water was likely making it look more disheveled than normal.

Luke held out his arm and walked with Sarah to where Matteo stood. The sun was setting, and the lake reflected the reds and golds of the sunset.

As he stood admiring Sarah and thankful for this moment, something caught Luke's eye. It looked like a piece of confetti floating down in a twisting, turning fashion. Another déjà vu moment hit him. *Where did this come from?* One side, apparently metallic, seemed to catch the light of the setting sun and had a noticeable twinkle. Luke tried to ignore it, but he couldn't help glancing at it. In fact, he found he couldn't keep his eyes off it.

Sarah got a curious look on her face. She followed his gaze

and she, too, watched this piece of confetti descend. It landed with the nonmetallic side up—on her shoulder. There seemed to be something written on it. Luke retrieved it from her shoulder and looked more closely. There were four letters: *T-U-L-E.*

Sarah gave him a puzzled look. He showed it to her and then put it in his coat pocket. She whispered, "What does it mean?"

Luke shook his head. "More mystery. We'll look at it later."

Luke put that mystery out of his mind and focused on Sarah. He smiled and took her hand in his. Matteo began the ceremony with brief remarks, and within minutes, Luke found himself speaking.

"Sarah, with God as my witness, I choose you as my wife to love and cherish from this day forward no matter what comes our way. I promise to love and support you all of my life." He then placed a tri-gold band on the finger that already held her engagement ring. The golden band matched the other ring perfectly.

Sarah shared a few words, then did the same for Luke, giving him a tri-gold band. They both turned and faced Matteo.

He held up his hands. "In the sight of Almighty God, you are pronounced husband and wife. May God prosper you and may you glorify him all of your days." He turned to Luke. "Now kiss your bride."

Luke looked into Sarah's eyes, leaned in, and gave a loving kiss. Not too passionate since they were in public, but passionate enough that Sarah would know his love for her, and one that roused the crowd to applaud.

Everyone joined around them and gave hugs and kisses and congratulations. A couple of bonfires were soon lit to provide more light. A band started playing. Everyone danced, ate, and talked. This went on for several hours.

* * * * *

Both Luke and Sarah danced with nearly everyone in attendance. As Luke retrieved Sarah from Ken, she looked at him and replied, "Luke, this has to be my last dance."

"Oh, a party pooper already?"

She smiled. "I've found dancing in sand makes my calves hurt." She patted his chest. "I'm willing to still talk with everyone, but let me change into something more beach appropriate."

His eyes lit up. "Oh, putting on the string bikini already?"

She gave a smirk. "Hardly. Maybe some capris and a pullover."

Luke laughed. "All right. I'll be right here."

He watched Sarah head up the beach to her tent. Jeremy came over with Oliver and the three close friends began conversing.

After some time, Natalia approached the three men. "Where's your better half?" she asked Luke. Luke turned his head sideways.

Jeremy laughed. "Get used to it, Luke. From now on, you're the worse half."

Natalia pushed Jeremy's shoulder. "Oh, stop. It's just a saying."

Luke smiled. "She went to change." He looked at his watch. "But that was some time ago. She should be done by now."

Jeremy pushed Luke toward the tent. "That's something else to get used to."

Luke laughed. "Let me go see what's taking her so long."

He hesitated at the tent door. "Sarah?" He didn't hear any response. It then dawned on him: he didn't have to wait outside anymore. She was his wife. Waiting was over. He smiled as he entered. "Sarah, need any help?"

He looked around. The tent was empty. Odd. Why didn't she come back out to him? Where would she have gone? Maybe someone else saw her. He turned to exit, but then saw it—the back of the tent blowing in the breeze. Luke walked over. His eyes widened as fear gripped him. The tent had been cut. He walked through the back end and frantically looked around, but didn't see anyone, only the beachside properties. A few flags were flapping in a light breeze. He ran back out to the others.

"Sarah! Sarah's gone!"

Jeremy turned. His smile quickly faded after seeing Luke's panicked face. He grabbed Luke's shoulders. "Luke, what's wrong?"

"Sarah's gone."

"What?" He squinted. "Are you sure? She's probably here somewhere."

Luke shook his head. "No. I . . . I think she's been taken. The back of the tent was ripped."

Jeremy hurried back with Luke to the tent. Luke pointed out the large tear in the rear of the tent. They walked through. Luke saw a figure—a man—some distance away.

"Hey!!"

The man turned and began to run.

Luke took off after him. Jeremy followed. The man stumbled in the sand and fell. Luke took the opportunity to gain on him and tackle him as the man stood to run again. They wrestled until Jeremy came up and helped Luke restrain him.

Oliver arrived and helped Jeremy hold the man down while Luke faced him to get a good look. The man looked familiar.

"Bring him over into the light. I think I know him."

Oliver and Jeremy dragged the man to where Luke could see him much better.

"Anton? What are you doing here?"

"I was too late. I warned her. I warned her."

Suddenly, Luke had a knot in his stomach, but he wasn't exactly sure why. "What are you talking about, Anton?"

"I told her not to marry you. I warned her not to marry you. Now they've taken her."

Oliver wrenched Anton's arm upward. "*Who* took her?"

Anton groaned. "Hurting me won't change anything. I came here to warn her they were coming."

Luke grabbed Anton's face with his hand. He scrunched it, turning Anton's neck in what had to be pain. "Who, Anton?!"

"The Illumi-Alliance."

Luke eyes shot to Oliver, who shook his head.

Luke knew that meant Viktoria hadn't been contacted. That also worried him, but he turned his focus back to Anton, loosening his grip a bit. "Why do they want her?"

"She's a pure immune! You're a pure immune! They can't have you two together. If you have children, it will destroy their plan."

Luke shook his head. "What? You're not making any sense."

"Immunity comes through the mother. Two perfect immunes will have perfect immune offspring. The two of you will start a cascade of widespread immunity. They can't—they won't—stand for that."

"Where are they taking her, Anton? I know you know!" Luke was in full panic.

"To Mercy Farewell."

TWO

Search for Sarah

Luke's knees went weak and he literally sat in the sand with a thud. He stared at Anton for several seconds. "What? What did you say?"

Anton cleared his throat. "I'm sorry, Luke. I tried to warn her. She didn't tell you anything?"

Luke tried to think. "She said you gave her a warning that Philippe and Simone were gathering immunes and she was likely at the top of their list because of Simone's jealousy."

Anton's eyes widened. "And that's all she told you?"

Luke nodded.

Anton looked down and shook his head. He looked back over at Luke. "I told her Simone knew she was a pure immune. That made her extremely dangerous in their eyes—and they would do anything to keep her from being with another pure immune." Anton's eyes began to water. "Believe me, I emphasized the word anything."

Luke put his hand to his forehead. He couldn't believe this was happening.

"After them killing all those people, I told her nothing was past them."

Luke's gaze shot to Anton and he leaped back to his feet. "*Them?* Wasn't it *you* who killed all those people? All those innocent people!" Luke pointed his index finger at Anton. "*You*, Anton. Not them."

"They commanded it." His tone was now extremely defensive.

Luke's anger rose, making his voice louder than he actually meant it to be. "And you do everything they tell you to do?"

Anton shot a hot gaze back at Luke and shouted, "Yes!" Spittle flew from his mouth. He stared in silence for a few seconds and then sighed. Quietly, he replied, "That's the way it works."

Luke turned several times. "There . . . there has to be something we can do." He pointed at Anton again. "Something *you* can do."

Anton didn't look up, but simply shook his head.

Luke's hands went to his head as he turned in frustration. Suddenly, he stopped. "Wait. They can't do anything without my permission. She's married. They have to have my permission to initiate Mercy Farewell." For a brief moment, he felt a flood of relief. "It's protocol! They can't do it."

Anton looked over at Luke as if sorry for someone who just doesn't grasp the gravity of a situation. "Luke, you think they care about protocol now?" He shook his head. "Their minds are made up. There's nothing anyone can do."

Luke was on top of Anton in a split-second, holding him up with his hand, this time squeezing his throat. "Well, you'd better come up with a reason."

"Luke . . . Luke," Anton croaked. "I . . . can't . . . breathe."

Luke let go of Anton and ran his fingers through his own hair. "I can't let this happen." His eyes teared as he looked at Oliver. "Is there anything we can do?"

"We can certainly try."

Ken walked up. "Anything I can do?"

Luke looked from Oliver to Ken. A new thought caught in his mind. "Do you need Sarah?"

Ken gave a confused look. "Excuse me?"

"I mean, can you complete your work for the Mars mission without her?"

Ken shook his head. "Not very well. She's the one who basically came up with the screening program all by herself."

Luke looked back at Anton. "Do you agree with Ken, or do you think it was all your brilliant idea?"

Anton shook his head and gave Luke a hurtful look. "I'm not heartless, Luke, in spite of what you think. Sarah took my initial idea and developed an efficient protocol for screening who can physically take the strain of the Mars mission. She refined the protocol quite substantially from my original design."

Luke looked between Anton and Ken. "There. Then do you feel you can make a compelling argument?"

Ken nodded, still looking a little confused. "I know *I* can. If they want this Mars mission to go without a hitch, they need Sarah."

Anton gave a shrug. "Maybe. I'm not disagreeing, mind you. But Simone is one tough person to get to change her mind."

Luke put his face next to Anton's. "Well, maybe you'd better start thinking of how to do just that."

Oliver finally let go of Anton. "Luke, I'll take Anton and Ken with me. If they're unsuccessful, I'll think of something else."

Anton rubbed his wrists and shoulder. "And what do you think you can do?"

Oliver gave Anton a stare. "You just worry about you."

Anton took a step back from Oliver, apparently feeling just as uneasy with Oliver not restraining him as he did when restrained.

Luke nodded. "OK, the four of us will head back to Paris."

Oliver shook his head. "Luke . . . you should stay here."

Anton nodded. "If you're there, it could make things worse."

Oliver grimaced. "As much as I don't want to agree with this guy, in this instance, I do."

Luke's jaw dropped. "What? You expect me to just stay here while my wife is in severe danger?" He shook his head. "No, I can't—I won't."

Oliver put his hand on Luke's shoulder. "I completely understand, buddy. But it's more about what's best for Sarah right now and her best chance. Anton and Ken are her best chance right now." He looked Luke in the eye. "Believe me, I will do everything in my power to bring her back—no matter their success."

Luke ran his hand over his mouth. He shook his head. "I don't like it." He gave a long sigh. "But if Philippe and Simone see me right now, it will only make them more determined." He threw up his hands. "OK. I concede." His eyes watered again. He grabbed Oliver's shoulder. "If anything happens to her . . . " His throat constricted. Luke could not finish his sentence.

Oliver put his hand over Luke's. "She's family to me, too, Luke. Rest assured, I will not leave family behind."

Luke nodded. Oliver gave him a quick, heartfelt hug, then motioned for Ken and Anton to follow.

Luke heard Ken say, "Oliver, fill me in," as Viktoria joined the three of them as they left.

Jeremy put his hand on Luke's shoulder until the others had walked out of sight, then waved Natalia over. "Luke, go with Natalia back to the penthouse. I'll dismiss everyone else for you."

Luke nodded. "Thanks, Jeremy." He turned with Natalia, but then turned back to Jeremy. "Ask Maher up also, will you? He's sort of the odd man out over there."

Jeremy gave a weak smile. "Sure. I'll bring him up with Mom and Dad."

THREE

THE PUZZLE

Maher brought cups of tea to where Luke and Matteo sat. "Natalia has prepared you something warm to drink."

Matteo took his cup. "Thank you, son."

Maher smiled and nodded. He handed the other cup to Luke and patted his shoulder. "I added a little something extra to yours."

Luke took a sip and tasted the rum. "Thanks, Maher. Went light on the tea, I see."

Maher laughed and sat next to Luke. "I put things in the priority that seemed necessary."

Luke smiled. "Maher, I'm not sure you've been introduced to Natalia's dad." He pointed to Matteo. "This is Matteo Mancini." Luke gestured to Maher. "Matteo, this is Maher Cohen."

Maher stood halfway and shook Matteo's hand. "My pleasure, sir."

Matteo smiled. "Mine as well." He put his hand to his chin. "Cohen, huh?"

Maher nodded. "It's a Jewish surname."

Matteo nodded. "Yes, yes. The person in the cell next to mine was named Cohen. Great man. Very bright."

Maher's eyebrows raised. "You were in prison?"

Luke set his cup down. "Yeah. Matteo was in the same prison as your father. We were able to get him out, but that was some time before we knew about your father."

"Father?" Matteo leaned forward slightly. "Was Joe Cohen your father?"

"Well, that was the name most called him, but his real name—"

"Was Jehoshaphat Cohen." Matteo smiled as he sat back in his seat and raised his hand ever so slightly. "You're Mahershalalhashbaz."

Maher nodded. "So, you . . . you knew my father?"

"Oh, absolutely. We talked often." Matteo pointed toward Maher. "He talked about you a lot. He kept saying if he ever got out, he was going to find you."

Maher's eyes watered. "That would have been nice." His voice got low. "But I guess that will never happen now."

Matteo slowly shook his head. "No, I guess not. I'm so sorry, son."

Maher gave a slight nod and blinked rapidly to keep his tears at bay.

Matteo became excited. "Oh, oh. I have something for you."

Maher looked up, perplexed. "What? For me? We . . . we just met."

Matteo was waving his hands. "Yes, yes. I had almost forgotten. When I was rescued, Joe gave me something to give to you." Matteo shrugged. "Of course, I never knew if I would meet you, but it shows God knows all." He shook his head. "Anyway, he gave me a piece of paper with writing on it to give to you."

Maher leaned forward. "What was it? What did it say?"

Matteo shook his head. "I don't know. It was for you. I didn't feel right looking at its content."

"Where is it now?" Maher looked from Matteo to Luke.

Luke shrugged. "Matteo, do you still have it?"

Matteo smiled and nodded. "I put it in a curio box in our bedroom."

Maher ran his hand over his mouth and held his chin. He looked at Luke. "My father left me something . . . " His eyes watered. "I wonder what it is."

Luke knew he had to retrieve it. He couldn't let Maher wait for such a gift as this. "Let me go get it." He turned to Matteo. "Where in your bedroom is it? May I go get it?"

"Oh, sure. It's on the dresser just behind the picture of Natalia and Jeremy."

Luke patted Maher's knee. "Hang tight, buddy. I'll be right back."

Luke bounded out the door and took the elevator to the basement level. He then took the journey all lab employees took every day, except he was all alone at this hour. He walked through the empty lab, down the stairs to the living area, and down the hallway to the first bedroom on the right. The bedroom light went on as soon as he entered. He was surprised at how spacious the bedroom looked. He smiled. Quite the contrast to Matteo's old jail cell, for sure. He saw the picture of Natalia and Jeremy and walked to the dresser. A small, octagonal wooden box lay just behind the picture. The piece of paper, the only thing in the box, was neatly folded in a perfect square, and secured in a way that kept the paper folded together.

As Luke left the room, he noticed one of the other bedrooms was lit. He cautiously walked to that bedroom door and slowly opened it. He shook his head as a lump developed in his throat and his eyes began to water. The room was decorated with pink and white balloons and streamers. On top of the dresser lay a mound of presents and cards. He wiped a few tears from his cheeks. Yes, this was supposed to be a very joyous night. This only reminded him of his heartache. He had to be strong. Oliver and Viktoria could be quite persuasive. They would not let anything bad happen to Sarah. He had to believe that. He bowed his head and said another short prayer asking God to watch over Sarah and give Oliver and Viktoria the wisdom—and the means—to rescue her.

He looked back at the piece of paper in his hand. He gave a weak smile. This was a chance to have happiness come out of tonight's sadness. A message from Maher's father had to be special. He wiped the rest of his tears and hurried back to the penthouse. He couldn't wait to see what Maher would discover.

When Luke got back to the penthouse, everyone was sitting around the bar having one of Jeremy's notable concoctions. They all eyed him expectantly as he approached.

Natalia waved him over. "Maher just filled us in. We're all anxious to hear what Maher's father said to him."

"Wait a minute." All eyes turned to Xiaofeng. "Let's all go over to the sitting area and let Maher first read in private. He can share what he feels is appropriate."

Luke approached Maher and handed him the folded paper. "I hope it's all you want it to be."

Maher smiled. "Thanks, Luke."

Luke joined the others where they had gathered. He had just sat down when Maher motioned for all of them to come back.

"Hey, everyone. I think I need help to decipher this." He looked at Matteo. "Did my father say anything when he gave this to you?"

Matteo put his hand to his chin. "Well, let's see. He said

you would understand, as you like puzzles, and . . . and this explains all of Édouard's fears."

"Édouard Mauchard?"

Matteo nodded. "While Édouard didn't believe like his father, he became paranoid with those beliefs."

Luke pointed to the piece of paper Maher held. "So, what does it say?"

Maher shook his head. "It doesn't say anything."

Luke turned up his brow. "What do you mean?"

Maher shrugged. "It's like Matteo said. It seems to be a puzzle." He spread the paper on the counter as everyone gathered around to look. He looked back up at them. "So, can anyone

```
101026       4            0            6            8
311201      101          201          204          909
108310     13002        53006        23000        43012
020103    0269422      1268401      2295420      0262402
100131   231272119    231425123    431178228    431481006
012623  10572132106  10534064110  30563030026  21501241019
102131 2400044131407 2601864282604 2901514253410 2500864076402
THB0307030059216343750 07F008930649132225S014030694255223HS022113844192118
       5632206000615921057100101624232261308007314889103600258462ELUT
      061323 4266813113233  8065503153163  1069030110113 025332
      120682  61168013312    22118236921    60211005402  101160
      011603  111702163      101782230      400861093    045433
      203256   4426113        3327221        9013522     415040
      210223    61053          62230          60043      061126
      621230     104            701            302        616001
      676203      3              1              5         684341
```

tell me the answer to this?"

Everyone stared at the paper and then looked at each other with blank expressions.

Xiaofeng looked up at Maher. "It's a pretty design, at least."

Everyone laughed. Matteo wrapped his arm around her shoulders. "You're always the positive one, my dear."

Maher shook his head. "Matteo, that was all my father said? Are you sure?"

Matteo nodded. "I'm sorry, Maher. But, yes, that's all he said. There wasn't really time to say much more."

Maher nodded and stared back at the paper.

Luke touched Maher's arm. Their gazes locked. "Luke, does any of this make sense to you?"

"Maybe." Luke pointed at the letters on the paper. "These are letters I have been receiving. Some of you are aware of this, some of you not. But . . . these pieces of confetti have drifted in front of me at various times. Three so far. They have these letters on them—" He pointed to each as he identified them. ". . . T-H-B, F-S-H-S, and the third one just today before our vows: T-U-L-E." He shrugged. "I have no idea why the T-U-L-E is spelled backward on this piece of paper, and I have no idea what the numbers are supposed to mean."

Maher gave a short laugh. "Well, my dad did call it a puzzle."

Matteo patted Maher's shoulder. "But one he knew you could solve."

Maher looked up with a weak smile and nodded.

FOUR

Deciphering the Puzzle

Luke stared at the ceiling as he lay in bed. Who was he trying to kid? There was no way he would get any sleep not knowing how Sarah was doing. Maybe he should have insisted on going with Oliver. He shook his head. *No, they were right. My presence would probably just add fuel to the fire.* But the not being there . . . the not knowing . . .

"Ugh." He threw the covers back and sat up. He felt tears starting to come. The thought of Sarah not being in his life was unfathomable. He shook his head. No. He was not going to wallow in self-pity before he knew her fate. That would be admitting defeat. He wasn't going to go there.

Luke got up, donned a pair of sweatpants and a T-shirt, and went to the kitchen area. He put on a pot of coffee and sat at the counter. The piece of paper Maher received from his father lay on the counter. He turned it around and looked at it. *A puzzle, huh? What better way to take my mind off things?*

He stared at the paper through squinted eyes to look at the

shape without the detail. It looked like two arrows pointing upward flanking a wavy line. But then, there was this rectangle on the far left side all by itself. What was its purpose? He shrugged, got up, and prepared a cup of coffee. Apparently, this would be a long night whether he wallowed in pity or tried to solve this puzzle. At least the puzzle would be more productive—maybe.

He first decided to concentrate on the elements he knew. He tapped on *T-H-B* with his finger. He definitely knew what that stood for. It was what got him started down this treacherous road in the first place. *The Holy Bible*. He stopped and put his hand to his chin. That should mean this puzzle is about something that is in, or is related to, the Bible. He laughed to himself. Well, that certainly narrowed things down.

He then looked at the "F," "S," and "HS." Thanks to Matteo's help, he now knew they stood for *Father, Son*, and *Holy Spirit*. But here, they were separated by these triangles of numbers. Was that significant? He assumed so, but how? Then there was the letters he had received last night at his wedding: *T-U-L-E*. He shook his head. He had no idea what those letters meant, but here they were written backward. He stared at the puzzle for quite some time; various options were going through his head. He sat up. *Maybe they aren't backward after all.* Luke took his finger and started at "T-H-B," and when he came to the end of that line, he ran his finger backward on the second line. That kept "T-U-L-E" in the same order as on the piece of confetti.

He took another swig of coffee. He felt like he was on to something. So, if this was continuous, it would not be two lines but one. Then the triangles and rectangles would also be in one straight line. He nodded to himself. They were all connected as one continuous stream. He felt elated, but then his shoulders drooped. OK, even if that was so . . . so what? *A continuous what?*

He looked up as he heard footsteps coming from the hall. Maher walked into the kitchen and stopped in his tracks, eyebrows raised.

"Oh, Luke. I didn't expect anyone else to be up."

"Couldn't sleep either?"

Maher shook his head. "No, I can't get that puzzle off my brain." He looked over and smiled. "I see you can't either."

Luke shook his head. "No, this is just a distraction for me."

Maher patted Luke on his shoulder. "Understood." He pointed to the puzzle. "Any progress?"

Luke cocked his head with a half shrug. "Pour yourself a cup of coffee and pull up to the bar. I'll show you my revelation."

Maher's eyebrows went up. "All right. Sounds intriguing." He poured a cup—left it black—and sat across from Luke. "OK. Hit me with your wisdom."

Luke explained what he had just discovered about the puzzle being one continuous line rather than two.

Maher nodded. "OK. That makes sense." He looked back at Luke with eyebrows raised in anticipation of more.

"That's it."

Maher stared at him for a few seconds.

"Maher, that was my revelation. Sorry. That's as far as I got."

Maher cocked his head. "Well, it's a start."

Luke pushed on Maher's shoulder. "Oh, stop. Now you're just being condescending."

Maher gave a small laugh. "No. No, that's an important start."

Luke laughed. "Now you're trying to butter me up."

Maher waved his hands. "No. No, that helps us to put this in better context. So . . . " He wiped his hands across the paper as if that would help him to decipher it better. "We have a rectangle, followed by four triangles, another rectangle, three triangles, and then a final rectangle."

Luke nodded. "And that means . . . ?"

Maher shrugged. "No idea." He tapped his index finger. "OK, let's look at the triangles. They're all the same size."

"Yeah. Each one is an isosceles triangle with the base being fourteen numbers across and each eight numbers high."

"OK." Maher glanced up at Luke. "So, that makes an area of fifty-six. Each triangle is composed of fifty-six numbers." He tapped his chin. "That's divisible by 2, 4, 7, and 8."

Luke smiled. "OK, Mr. Math Genius. What does *that* give us?"

Maher gave a smirk. "Well, I don't know. I'm just throwing things out there. Are any of those numbers common across these shapes?"

Luke looked at the piece of paper again. "Well, every rectangle and triangle is eight numbers high."

Maher nodded. "OK, that seems significant. That would mean each rectangle could be composed of six eight-digit numbers and each triangle composed of seven eight-digit numbers."

"Any idea how to divide the rectangle up into those numbers?"

Maher propped his chin in his hands and glanced up at Luke. "No, not really." He stared back at the puzzle. He seemed transfixed for a long time.

Luke refilled his cup and came back to the counter. He slowly sipped his coffee as he too stared at the puzzle.

Maher suddenly sat up. "Wait."

Luke looked up. "What? Did you get a revelation?"

Maher bobbled his head. "Maybe. You stated the design is really rectangles and triangles in a continuous line."

Luke nodded. He had no idea where Maher was going with this.

"What if the whole thing is continuous?"

Luke felt confused, but was interested in learning more. "What do you mean?"

"Take a pencil and go from one end to the other without ever taking the pencil off the paper to form one continuous line."

Luke looked at the puzzle again. After several minutes, a path emerged in his mind. "Oh, I see it." He traced his comments. "After T-H-B, go up and down through the rectangle and then go up the side of the triangle and then back diagonally all the way through each pyramid. Then you go through each one and reach the end of the last rectangle."

Maher nodded with a smile. "At least we now know how to string the numbers together." He looked around. "Any idea where more paper is located?"

Luke glanced around. "Uh, I think there is some in my room." He swung around in his seat and headed that way.

As he entered his bedroom, he heard Matteo and Xiaofeng stepping from their bedroom. He glanced at the clock next to his bed. His eyes widened as he looked at the time: 06:54. He had been up all night. He smiled. The puzzle had helped him keep his mind off his sadness, his uncertainty.

He came back to the kitchen and handed Maher the paper. "Where's Matteo and Xiaofeng? I thought I heard them come out of their bedroom."

Maher nodded. "They've already gone upstairs. They said to make ourselves at home."

Luke laughed. "Talk about the early birds."

Maher grinned. "They must love what they do."

"Oh, I'm sure they do. After being in prison for so long, I bet they feel they have a lot to catch up on."

Maher nodded, and he started writing down numbers on his piece of paper. He then turned it around for Luke to peruse.

Maher had a list of eight-digit numbers for each rectangle and each pyramid.

"OK. Now what?"

"Well, we need to understand what these eight-digit numbers represent."

Luke pointed to *T-H-B* on the paper. "Well, the puzzle starts with these three letters, which represent 'The Holy Bible.' So, I presume they represent something about the Bible."

Maher nodded. "Makes sense. But what?"

Luke stood. "That, my friend, is your dilemma . . . while I fix us some breakfast."

As Luke prepared eggs and toast, he noticed Maher pull out his phone. "Need to call someone?"

Maher looked up. "What?" He smiled. "Oh, no. I was pulling up the Scripture app you sent me." Luke saw him look from his phone to the puzzle and back several times over several minutes. Luke was curious but held his question. After a while, Maher looked at Luke and pointed to his phone. "In the beginning, before the text, the app lists all the books of the Bible. It seems there are sixty-six of them."

Luke put a plate of food in front of Maher and filled his coffee mug once more. He sat back in his seat. Maher took a bite of food and kept working.

"So, what are you finding?"

"I was looking at the first two digits in each number. None of them go higher than sixty-six, so I think the first two numbers likely represent a book of the Bible."

"Really?" Luke leaned over for a closer look; Maher pushed the paper closer so Luke could see. "That's interesting. Looks like you've almost solved it."

"The Bible seems to be broken down into books, chapters, and verses. So, I'm wondering, if the first two numbers represent the book of the Bible, then maybe the next two represent the chapter."

Luke nodded. "Then the next two, the verse?"

Maher nodded. "I think so."

"What about the last two numbers?"

"Must be the end verse."

Luke's eyes widened. "Oh, that makes sense. Book, chapter, start verse, end verse."

Maher nodded.

"Now I'm getting excited," Luke said. "So, the next step is to identify the Scriptures and then read them, right?"

"Seems to be."

Luke washed their breakfast dishes while Maher finished translating the numbers into Scripture references. Once complete, Luke made his own copy. They went over to the sitting area and started reviewing the various Scriptures and taking notes on what they read.

✶ ✶ ✶ ✶ ✶

Luke became engrossed in his reading. He jumped when he saw a hand waving between his face and his phone.

Jeremy laughed. "Wow. I've never seen you so wrapped up in something. What gives?"

Luke saw Natalia with Matteo and Xiaofeng in the kitchen. He glanced at his watch. *Wow. Lunch time already.* He smiled. He had no idea he had been studying, reading, and thinking all morning. "Maher cracked the code for the puzzle his father left him. All the numbers were Scripture references. He and I have been reading through them."

Jeremy patted Luke on his shoulder. "That's great, Luke." He turned to Maher. "Congratulations, Maher. I can't wait to hear what you find out."

Maher grinned. "Neither can we."

Jeremy turned back to Luke, now more somber. "Heard anything from Oliver?"

Luke shook his head and sighed. He dropped his hand and now held his phone in his lap. "No, not yet."

Jeremy patted his shoulder. "Hang in there, buddy. You know Oliver always comes through."

Luke nodded and blinked several times to hold back the tears that were trying to form.

Natalia came over and put a sandwich in front of both Luke and Maher. Natalia kissed Luke's cheek. "God will come through, Lukey. I know he will."

Luke gave a small, forced smile and nodded. "Thanks, Natalia."

She squeezed his shoulder lightly and walked back upstairs with the others, leaving Luke and Maher to their study.

FIVE

MAHER'S DECISION

Luke, startled awake, looked around, discombobulated. Realization of being in his bedroom in Shanghai slowly dawned. He remembered reading in bed. He must have fallen asleep with his phone on his chest. It buzzed, startling him again.

Luke picked it up and realized it was Oliver calling.

He sat up. Then he shot up like a rocket, finding his feet. "Oliver? What's going on? It's been three days."

"Hi, Luke. Yeah, I'm sorry. Things have been . . . rather intense to say the least."

He started to pace. "How's Sarah? Is she OK? She is OK, right?"

"Luke, calm down. You'll see her sometime tomorrow."

"Can I talk to her now?"

"I'm sorry, Luke. She isn't with me right now. But you will see her tomorrow evening."

Luke ran his fingers through his hair and nodded his head. "OK. OK."

"Luke, I know this is hard. But it's almost over."

Luke plopped back onto his bed. "Just get her here, Oliver. Just get her here."

"That's what I'm doing, buddy. We'll see you tomorrow." They ended the call.

Luke sat there for several minutes, almost numb. Then it dawned on him, and he had a moment of total relief and joy—Sarah, Oliver said, would be safe. And yet . . . what was Oliver not telling him? There was *something* in his voice. Why wasn't his tone more one of joy? It was hard to be elated when Oliver didn't sound elated.

Luke took his shower, dressed, and went to the kitchen. He desperately needed coffee.

As he turned the corner to make a fresh pot, he saw one already made. He turned and saw Maher riveted in his reading. He turned back, poured a cup, and took a swig.

"There you are. I saved you some breakfast."

Luke shook his head. "Thanks, but I'm not hungry." Luke went over to the sitting area where Maher was. He dropped into a chair.

Maher squinted his eyes. "Hey, you OK?"

Luke shrugged. He gave a weak smile. "I just talked with Oliver. He said Sarah will be back by tomorrow night."

Maher sat up and leaned forward. "Luke, that's great." He paused. "So . . . why aren't you excited?"

Luke took another sip. "I . . . I don't know entirely. It was just Oliver's tone." He shook his head. "Something's not right."

Maher cocked his head. "But the important thing is, she's coming home, right?" He tapped Luke's knee. "Right?"

Luke smiled and nodded. "Yeah, Maher. You're right."

Maher sat back. "OK. Now, tell me what you've read." He smiled. "It'll keep your mind occupied."

Luke sat back and sighed. "I'm not sure I have much to tell. Yeah, I've read a lot, even more than just the references you copied down . . ." He shook his head. "I think all of these references are connected somehow. The passage in Leviticus seems to show each triangle as one of the Jewish festivals." He shrugged. "That's about all I've got so far."

"I've heard many of the stories stated in what the app you gave me calls the Old Testament. This is the first time I've heard any of them classified as prophetic and some of them supposedly fulfilled."

Luke turned his head sideways. "Supposedly? You don't think the Scriptures are true?"

"You do?"

Luke nodded. "I do now. The Holy Spirit helps me understand what I read is really true."

Maher shook his head. "How do you know for sure?"

Luke put his hand to his chin. He had to think of a good analogy. He looked back at Maher. "Maher, how did you know to come to my wedding?"

Maher smiled. "You invited me."

Luke nodded. "But what if you didn't believe me?"

Maher squinted. "But I did believe you."

"What if you didn't? How would you know I was telling the truth?"

Maher shook his head. "I wouldn't. Not unless I came."

Luke gestured to Maher. "You just answered your own question."

"I don't follow."

Luke leaned forward with his elbows on his knees. "Maher, you want to know if God is real? And if the Scriptures are really true, right?"

Maher nodded slowly.

"The only way to know is to experience the Holy Spirit. The only way to do that is to believe you aren't perfect, you never could be, and never will be perfect. In other words, you are a sinner."

Maher's head jerked back slightly. "Well, that seems a little harsh."

Luke shook his head. "No, just realistic. If God requires perfection, and we can never achieve that, then we fall short of his standard. That's what sin—falling short of God's requirements—is."

Maher slowly tilted his head from side to side. "Well, OK. Let's say I buy that."

Luke gave a slight smile. That was Maher saying he believed it, but wasn't going to admit he did. "God required payment for our sin, but there was nothing we could do to meet his requirement. Therefore, he made the payment for us because he loves us and knew we could not save ourselves."

Maher turned his head slightly, but didn't respond.

"You have to believe in his payment and trust in him for your future since you cannot trust in yourself."

"That's it?"

Luke nodded.

"But how do I know?"

Luke cocked his head and smiled.

Maher gave a weak smile back. "We're back to your analogy."

Luke nodded. "Come on, Maher. You know it makes sense. Undoubtedly, your father believed it. It would seem he wanted you to as well. Why else would he leave this elaborate puzzle to solve?"

Maher looked down at his hands and his cell phone for several seconds. Luke waited patiently. He knew what Maher was thinking. He had been there. Yeah, it made sense, but it was still a huge leap. A leap into the unknown. A leap of faith.

Maher looked up. "So, what do I do?"

Luke smiled. "Just talk to him." He pointed to the other

chair. "Just assume God is sitting right there in that chair. Talk to him."

Maher took a deep breath and breathed out slowly. "God, I've heard many stories about you and what you did for your people. I always thought them as stories with no real purpose but to make me stay out of trouble." He chuckled. "I guess that didn't work." He turned somber. "Yet, I now realize it was all true. I'm now finding out you had a purpose. I don't understand it all yet, but I want to. I do know I can never stand up to your requirement of perfection . . . "

Maher paused and gave a short huff. "I'm not sure if I could even stand up to a requirement of just plain good." He shook his head. "But I now understand you paved the way for me. All I have to do is believe it and accept it. I don't know where such a step takes me, but I want to take it—I do take it. Thank you for your payment. And I trust you, and only you, for my future."

He looked up; Luke patted him on his knee. "Congratulations, Maher." He smiled. "How do you feel?"

Maher paused and tilted his head. "You know, it's odd. I feel different and not different at the same time." He smiled. "It feels right, though."

Luke nodded. "I felt the same way."

Maher held up his phone, referring to the Scriptures. "Let's get back to studying. I have a feeling it may make more sense now."

Luke laughed. "I have a feeling you may be right."

SIX

SARAH RETURNS

Luke kept looking at his watch. Oliver had been vague about what time he would arrive with Sarah. After lunch, Jeremy, Natalia, Matteo, and Xiaofeng stayed downstairs to be part of her arrival as well. Luke and Maher had been studying Scripture in the morning, but with everyone now present, the anxiety in the room felt palpable, and Luke couldn't focus on anything else.

He stood and started pacing.

Natalia grabbed his hand as he walked by, giving Luke a warm smile. "Be patient, Lukey. Oliver will come through. He always does."

Luke smiled back weakly and nodded. He didn't really doubt Oliver would come through, but the waiting put him on edge. He looked at his watch again: 16:45. He pounded his right fist into his left hand. Any type of movement was helpful at this point.

Jeremy came back from the kitchen and handed him a warm drink. "Try this. It may help."

Luke could smell the mocha flavor. It reminded him of the

mocha-flavored drink Sarah loved so much. It made his heart ache more. He smiled and nodded to Jeremy all the same. "Thanks."

Jeremy patted him on his shoulder and sat next to Natalia.

Matteo spoke up. "Are we preparing for a wake or a home-coming? Why is everyone so gloomy?"

Xiaofeng patted his hand. "I think everyone is just anxious. That's all."

"But she's coming home. Luke, certainly that makes you happy," Matteo said.

Luke smiled and nodded. "Of course, it does. But . . . something just doesn't feel right. Something seems off."

"Well, I think we should prepare for a celebration." Matteo stood. "Come on, Xiaofeng. Let's prepare some goodies for everyone when they get here."

Natalia followed them to help. After a few minutes, she came and pulled Luke into the kitchen area. "Come on, Lukey. This will take your mind off things."

Xioafeng smiled. "Plus, you can impress Sarah with your cooking talents." She held up her finger. "With my guidance, of course."

Luke smiled. "Of course." He gave a small laugh. "I couldn't do it any other way."

Soon Jeremy and Maher joined them. One person mixed ingredients, one rolled dough, two decorated, one put the pans in the oven, and Xiaofeng supervised all of it. In no time at all, everyone was talking and laughing.

Matteo looked up from his mixing. "Now, this is the way things should be."

Everyone nodded. Footsteps were heard on the stairs. Everyone turned. All laughter stopped.

Luke wiped his hands on a dishcloth and walked toward the stairs. He could barely believe his eyes. There stood Sarah—as beautiful as ever. Yet, she looked extremely tired. He held out his arms and she walked into them. Tears flowed from both of them.

"Oh, Sarah. I have missed you so much. I love you."

"I love you, too—so much." She gave Luke an even tighter squeeze.

Luke laughed; he was suddenly full of joy. He pulled away and softly wiped the tears from her cheeks with the pads of his thumbs. She did the same to him.

"Sarah, are you OK?"

She nodded. "Yeah, just . . . just tired."

Everyone else quickly surrounded them and gave Sarah hugs. They all expressed their extreme happiness to see her.

"Thanks, everyone. It's really great to be back. If it's all right, I'm going to lie down for a while. It's been . . . exhausting."

Everyone nodded. Luke came up and put his arm around her shoulders. "Let me help you."

She smiled. "I was hoping you'd say that."

Luke smiled back and walked with her to their bedroom. That was a nice thought: *their* bedroom. The last time they were here, they were in different bedrooms. They could now finally be together.

When Sarah saw all the balloons, presents, and cards, she put her hand to her mouth and her eyes watered again. "Oh, that is so sweet."

Luke nodded. "Yeah, they really went all out for us."

She nodded and began to undress. Luke helped her out of her clothes and into bed. He sat next to her, stroking her hair and rubbing her back.

Sarah smiled and gave a contented sigh. "Where have you been all my life?"

Luke replied softly, "I'll always be here from now on."

Luke badly wanted to ask his new wife what had happened,

what she had been through. But his better instincts took over; he knew he needed to respect her need for rest.

Sarah closed her eyes and was asleep in minutes. Once she began breathing regularly and deeply, Luke pulled the covers over her shoulders and left the room.

Everyone sat in the sitting area talking. Oliver and Viktoria stood as Luke entered. He walked over and gave each of them a hug.

"Oliver, Viktoria, thank you so much." He shook his head. "I . . . I can never repay you for this."

Oliver put his hand on Luke's shoulder. "Luke, no repayment is needed." He gestured for Luke to sit. "There is some information I think you need to know, though, Luke."

Once they all sat, Oliver continued. "Luke, I have some general news and some specific news which is somewhat private, but I feel all of you need to know so it doesn't become awkward. Sarah looks to all of you as family, so that is why I think you should know."

Luke nodded. "OK. I knew something was off when I talked to you. So, what happened?"

Oliver leaned forward with elbows on his knees. "First of all, I have to say Ken and Anton really made a profound case for the release of Sarah. Ken went over everything Sarah had done and what she still needed to do and why she was the one who needed to do it. Anton backed Ken up on everything he said. But . . . "

Luke's stomach did a flip. "Uh-oh. I knew that word was coming."

Oliver nodded. "Unfortunately, no matter what Ken or Anton said, Simone and Philippe were adamant in their resolve and wouldn't release her." He looked toward Viktoria.

She nodded. "I also did everything I knew within my Illumi-Alliance contacts to get her released." She shook her head. "All to no avail."

"Yeah," replied Oliver. "So much so she almost got cited for insubordination."

Luke's eyes went wide. "You didn't, though, did you?"

Viktoria shook her head. "No, all is fine."

Luke let out a long breath. "Good. I would feel pretty bad about causing that." Luke cocked his head. "But if they refused to release her, how did you get her out? Did you break her out?"

Oliver shook his head. "No. They had so much security around her—that proved impossible." Oliver looked at Viktoria and back to Luke. "It was . . . Anton who actually came through."

"Speaking of Ken and Anton, where are they?"

"Uh, Ken left to go back to Houston. Anton stayed in Paris."

Luke nodded. "OK. So what did Anton do?"

Oliver paused. "Luke, you're not going to like this. No one did. But . . . but it was the only way." He held up his palms. "Before I tell you, remember we all debated this and we all take responsibility. We just could not find any other option."

Luke leaned forward still more. "What, Oliver? What? *What happened?*"

Oliver took a deep breath and let it out slowly. "Anton helped Simone and Philippe realize their only concern about you and Sarah was having children . . . "

Natalia gasped and put her hand to her mouth. "No."

Luke looked from Oliver to Natalia. "What?" Obviously, Natalia realized something.

Natalia just looked at Luke with her eyes watering, shaking her head.

Luke looked back at Oliver, his eyes wide.

"Simone and Philippe agreed to have Sarah sterilized so she could never have children."

The words hit Luke like a ton of bricks. He fell back into his seat, stunned. "What? How . . . how could they? They . . . they had no right." His eyes filled with tears, but he managed to blink most of them away. He was hurt, but . . . Sarah. Poor Sarah. He put his hand to his forehead and shook it from side to side. He whispered, "How could they?"

Natalia switched seats and sat next to Luke. She put her arms around him and gave him a tight hug. "I'm so, so sorry, Lukey. I'm so sorry."

After several seconds, Luke released the hug, cleared his throat, sat up straighter, and wiped the tears from his cheeks. He looked back at Oliver. "So, how did they do it? Will she recover OK?"

Oliver nodded. "Yeah, I think she will be fine—physically, at least." He sat back and sighed. "They did it chemically. I didn't even know they had such a chemical. They gave her several injections. It isn't supposed to be harmful to her, except for destroying all viable eggs, supposedly. But she did have a lot of cramping, which I was told was not necessarily uncommon, but I don't know if this is something routinely used."

Viktoria cleared her throat. "That's . . . that's why we waited a few days. So most of the cramping would subside before we brought her back. She didn't get much sleep due to the side effects."

Luke nodded, but didn't know what to say.

Xiaofeng got up and passed a tray of cookies; it was an effort to try and lighten the mood. Luke had one to be sociable, but he had no appetite. He tried to make conversation but found it hard. After about an hour, he excused himself and headed to the bedroom.

As he entered, he could hear Sarah breathing rhythmically, softly. She had been through so much. He first sat on the bed and just watched her. He pulled her hair away from her face, reached down, and kissed her cheek. She stirred slightly, but returned to her soft breathing.

Luke undressed, showered, and laid down next to Sarah. He had longed for this time, when he could do just this, and feel no guilt in doing it. But this was not the way he had envisioned their time together. Still, he was thankful for it. As he lay next to her, Sarah stirred, scooted up to him, and put her head on his chest. He wrapped his arm around her and held her. She fell into a deep sleep once again. Her hair still smelled of honeysuckle, which now mixed with her cherry blossom perfume. He found it intoxicating, sensual. He laid back and eventually fell into a semi-restful sleep as well.

* * * * *

Luke awoke to the sound of the shower running. He looked at the clock next to the bed; it was only three o'clock in the morning. He turned over and decided to wait up for Sarah, but fell back asleep in a matter of minutes. He awoke to the feel of kisses. He opened his eyes and saw Sarah's face silhouetted in the darkness. She had apparently put on more perfume. He breathed in its intoxicating aroma. She leaned into him with a kiss and pressed her body into his. He kissed back, but this time held nothing in reserve. Luke yielded to his desire, holding nothing back, determined to make Sarah feel like the most special woman in the world . . . Before morning, she would know how much he really loved her.

SEVEN

TULE DECIPHERED

Luke found himself slowly waking. He stretched, then remembered Sarah was in bed with him. Yet he could not find her with his arm. He looked over. Her side of the bed was empty. He turned and saw her sitting on his side of the bed, looking at him.

She smiled. "Good morning."

He scooted up and leaned against the headboard. "Hey there. What are you doing?"

"Oh, just watching you sleep."

"That entertaining, huh?"

She chuckled, leaned in, and gave him a kiss. "Just waiting to continue last night's performance."

Luke smiled. "Oh, is that so?"

She leaned onto him, looking into his eyes. "Uh-huh."

"What if I'm not in the mood?"

She gave him another kiss. "I think I can change that."

Luke chuckled. "Yeah. I bet you can."

He wrapped his arms around her and gave her a passionate kiss. She leaned in and reciprocated. He relinquished all inhibitions and yielded to the moment. Time went into stasis; Luke entered pure bliss . . .

He had no idea how long he was in this altered state, but he hated to come out of it. Sarah ended it by pulling him up and leading him into the shower. After a lengthy time together getting clean, they dressed and headed back to reality.

* * * * *

Natalia looked up from what she was reading. "Well hello, you two." She smiled. "Welcome back to the real world."

Luke poured two cups of coffee and handed one to Sarah. "Well, it wasn't by choice, believe me." Luke took a sip. "What brings you down here?" He looked around. "Where is everyone else?"

Natalia laughed. "Working. It's the afternoon, after all."

"Really?" Luke looked at the clock: 13:07. "Wow." He smiled. "Time does fly when you're having fun." He looked at Natalia with a squint. "So, you were left here to spy on us?"

Natalia laughed and waved her hand. "Oh, stop. I was waiting to talk to Sarah."

Sarah's eyes widened. "Oh? About what?"

Natalia turned more serious. "Well, those who attended your wedding will be leaving tomorrow. I just wanted to know if you felt up to having everyone over, open gifts and such." She held up her hands. "If you don't, don't feel obligated. I'm sure everyone will understand."

Sarah stared at her coffee for several seconds. She looked up at Luke and then back to Natalia. "Well, it would be a good opportunity to let them all know what's going on and where we stand. We may not have a better opportunity."

Luke nodded and put his arm around her. "That's true, but are you really up to it?"

Sarah gave a slight nod. "Yeah, I think I am." She turned to Natalia and smiled. "Let's do it."

Natalia smiled back. "OK. I'll let Mom know." She chuckled. "She seems to thrive on such things."

Sarah nodded. "I can see where you get your drive and determination." She sat on one of the bar stools. "Natalia, can I ask you a personal question?"

Luke sat down as well. It looked like things were about to turn serious.

"Sure, Sarah. What is it?"

"Why have you and Jeremy not had children? I'm sorry if that's too personal. But now that I can't, I . . . I was wondering why others who can, don't."

Natalia remained quiet for several seconds. "Well, I've never really thought about it, to be honest. Both Jeremy and I have been so busy with our careers, we haven't really considered that chapter of our lives." She began tapping her fingertips together. "Yet, after all we've learned, I'm not sure I want to have a child and have him or her be taken away after ten years." Natalia shook her head. "I don't know if I could bear it." Her eyes watered. "After seeing all Mom went through . . . " She choked up and cleared her throat. "I don't think I could go through that and remain sane."

Sarah reached across the counter and took Natalia's hand. "That's what I thought. I've been thinking the same thing. While I'm disappointed the choice has been taken away, I'm not sure the outcome would be any different."

Luke had not thought about that, but she had a point. Who would want to give up their child after bonding to him or her? Without the memory reprogramming, it likely would never have been possible.

Sarah looked over at Luke. "Sorry, Luke. I haven't had this conversation with you."

He rubbed her shoulder. "It's OK. To be honest, I haven't thought that far into our future. While it's certainly disappointing that the choice is gone, I can't say I disagree with your point."

Sarah nodded. She sat up straight and put her palms on the counter. "OK, then. It's upward and onward." She smiled. "Onward to our wedding reception party."

Natalia smiled. "OK, let's get started."

While the two of them made plans, Luke stared at Sarah. He admired her so much. Yet, despite what she said, he knew she would forever be disappointed her choice had been taken away. He only hoped it would be something she wouldn't let eat at her. Sarah was certainly a strong and independent woman. But she had a vulnerable side as well. He wanted to be able to protect that side of her.

* * * * *

The girls decided to have the party at the penthouse, so all the gifts and cards had to be moved. Luke didn't think the gifts were that many—until he had to move them. After two trips, Matteo met him at the door with a lab cart.

"I thought this would come in handy."

Luke wondered why this idea hadn't occurred to him. "Thanks, Matteo. How did you get so smart?"

Matteo pointed at his head. "See the white hair? Wisdom."

Luke laughed. "Can't deny that."

Matteo went with him to the penthouse and helped place all the gifts on a table just as Natalia directed. Luke then went back and got dressed for the party. He barely saw Sarah since Natalia and Xiaofeng had her directing so many details. She seemed happy, so Luke felt content.

* * * * *

Everyone began gathering around dinner time. Jeremy had the mocha-mint drink that Sarah liked so much available for all the guests as they arrived. Appetizers and then cake followed. The levity in the room was infectious. Luke had rarely seen Sarah so . . . happy. He had to admit, this was really the therapy she needed.

Before long, Viktoria announced, "OK. Time to open presents."

This woman, Viktoria, was quite the conundrum. One minute she was an Illumi-Alliance soldier with absolutely no sense of humor. Then, when she was simply Oliver's wife, she became a totally different person. That's when Luke would get a glimpse of her true personality. Despite their antagonistic introduction to one another so many months ago, she had become a good friend.

Natalia directed where everyone should sit. Jeremy brought the gifts and cards over one at a time so Sarah could open them and everyone could ooh and ahh. There were plaques, tchotchkes, linens, and other homey things.

"Luke, here's one to you specifically."

"What?" Luke took the present from Jeremy and looked at it. He looked over at Viktoria. "This is from you?"

Viktoria gave a wicked smile and nodded.

Luke squinted at her. "Should I be afraid?" He looked at Sarah. "Maybe you'd better stand back."

Sarah pushed on his shoulder. "Oh, stop. I trust her."

"Well, stay at your own peril."

Luke slowly opened the gift. It was a fairly large square box. He had no idea what to expect. After all, this was Viktoria. He took a deep breath and opened the box. He laughed heartily in spite of himself.

Sarah looked over. "What is it?"

Luke pulled out a toilet seat. Everyone laughed. Luke and Viktoria, of course, laughed the hardest.

Kathleen looked at Viktoria. "It's certainly a very unusual gift. But why is it so funny?"

Viktoria gestured toward Luke. "You tell them, kung fu fighter."

Luke laughed. He looked at Sarah. His next statement to her was in the form of a question. "I guess now is as good a time as any?"

She nodded.

Luke sat back and looked around the room. "Sarah and I have a story to tell." He looked at Jared. "Some of you already know part of it." He looked at others. "Some of you may have heard none of it. Let me start from the beginning."

Luke went through everything he and Sarah had been through, how the memory reprogramming worked, why it was started, how it was tied to the Mars mission, and how he and Sarah were immune and therefore targets of the Illumi-Alliance. He explained how they found *T-H-B*, what it turned out to be, how the message of the Bible changed them, and how all this led to the baptisms at their wedding.

Once Luke finished, everyone was quiet. Too quiet. Luke was afraid they thought he had gone over the deep end. Brian was the first to respond.

"Luke, I have to admit, that is a lot to take in." He held up his palms. "I'm not saying it isn't true, but . . . " He rubbed the back of his neck. "It just seems . . . "

"Out there?" Luke gave a slight smile.

Brian nodded.

"Yeah, I know it seems strange. But as they say: truth is stranger than fiction."

"Maybe." All eyes turned to Jason. "I know, Luke, you told

me I bought into all of this at one time." He shook his head. "I don't have any memory of that. Yet . . . something makes me feel I can't just disregard what you are saying."

Luke nodded. "Jason, I think that is the Holy Spirit still working through you. The Illumi-Alliance can take away your memory, but not the truth in which you have believed."

Jason looked over at Jared and shrugged. Jared had a worried look on his face. Luke had wanted his words to be encouraging, but it seemed they weren't taken that way.

Maher took out a piece of paper and passed it around. Each person looked at it; for most, their eyes went wide as they stared at the paper for a brief time, then passed it on to the next person. "This is something my father—who has since died—left me," Maher said, beginning to explain slowly, as the paper worked its way around the group. He explained how the puzzle had to be tied to *T-H-B*, and thus had its ultimate meaning in the Bible.

Finally, Scott handed the paper back to Maher. "But what does it really mean?"

"Well, it took a lot of digging and reading, but it seems to point to a type of timeline."

Carmella shook her head. "But isn't that just conjecture? After all, this is from a banned religious book." She shrugged. "Is it even credible?"

Maher nodded. "I can understand your point. Actually, I had similar thoughts. But I had to consider why it was a banned book. It seems to have been banned, not because of its content, but because the actions of an elite few went against its teachings. If no one knows what the Bible says, then no one can question this elite group's agenda."

Carmella didn't say anything more, but she didn't look completely satisfied with Maher's answer.

Brian added, "So what is this timeline you think you've

found?"

Maher held up the paper. "The numbers you see here represent Scripture references. They in turn indicate each of these triangles represent a Jewish festival. These festivals were not only memorials to Israel's past, they were also prophetic. The four on the top, here"— Maher pointed across the row with his index finger—"have apparently already been fulfilled in our past."

Jared leaned forward. "Fulfilled? What do you mean?"

"Well, Scripture supports God's uniqueness, of him being somehow three components, but identified as one and the same."

Jared turned to Luke. "That was what you were trying to tell me several weeks ago."

Luke nodded. He knew the others had not heard any of this. He turned to Xiaofeng.

"Xiaofeng, you gave Sarah and me a unique perspective about God. Can you explain it to everyone here? Most are scientists, so hopefully it will help them better understand."

Xiaofeng smiled and repeated her explanation about God and how he—being Trinity—was unique, unlike any human being.

Maher continued his explanation. "God was able to maintain his standard of perfection and pay the consequence of mankind's shortcoming himself on our behalf. The book of John in the New Testament calls the one who came and paid that price the Messiah. He states this Messiah was killed by being crucified; he was then raised from the dead. This fulfilled the Jewish festivals Pesach, or Passover, and Bikkurim, or Firstfruits. This was by the act of the first and second parts of the Godhead." He held up the picture again. "This is noted as the 'F' and 'S' on the diagram—Father and Son."

Jared shook his head. "All of this is hard to grasp." He

pointed. "And what is the 'HS' that follows?"

Maher smiled. "That represents the Holy Spirit, who is given to a person once he or she accepts and believes the facts I just stated."

Jared sat back. "How can I know this is all not just made up?"

Luke was afraid Maher may get impatient, but just the opposite happened. It seemed Maher had done far more studying than he had.

"Well, Jared, it seems Scripture points to this festival, called Shavuot, as a time of paradigm shifts. It seems to be the time God set up his covenant with Israel, the time the Messiah was born, and the giving of the Holy Spirit to all believers." He shrugged. "If nothing else, it would at least be consistent with such a change in how God works with us."

Jared wiped his mouth with his hand. "That's a lot to take in."

Jason nodded. "So, what are the next letters?"

Maher shook his head. "We're not sure yet what they represent. However, I think I know what the event is describing." He looked at Luke. "I haven't had the time to discuss this with you, Luke, but I think it is tied to what I told you about my parents' marriage."

"What?" Jason looked from Maher to Luke. "What marriage is he talking about?"

Maher recapped everything he had told Luke earlier in Hawaii. "Scripture calls the Messiah the bridegroom, and those who accept him and trust in him for their future his bride. As in ancient times, it was the bridegroom's father who decided when the wedding would take place. Once his decision was made, the bridegroom headed with his groomsmen to where his wife-to-be was staying. She had been preparing herself, with her bridesmaids, for his coming. Usually, a shout or trumpet blast announced his arrival. The bride was received, taken to the bridegroom's house, and the wedding feast commenced."

Luke leaned in. "Maher, that really does sound similar to what you told me. So, God will do this for us?"

"These Scripture references seem to support that. He will come quickly and we will be taken from this earth. He will take us to a place he has prepared for us."

Jason laughed. "Well, if that is true and I am currently trapped in not remembering what I once believed about all of this, then . . . well, that will certainly be the ultimate liberation event."

Maher laughed. "That's very true, Jason. Actually, before all of this is over, you are likely not the only one who will be in that position."

"So, I'm not unique?"

Maher shook his head. "No, I don't think so."

"Wait." All eyes turned to Luke. "Jason, repeat that thing you just said."

"What? That I'm not unique?"

Luke shook his head. "No, no. What you said earlier."

Jason put his hand to his chin. "What did I say?"

He looked at Jared, who shrugged, eyes wide. "Something about being liberated."

"Oh, yeah," Jason said. "I said it would be the ultimate liberation event."

"That's it!" Luke looked at Maher. "That's what *T-U-L-E* represents. The Ultimate Liberation Event." He pointed to Maher. "You said it, Maher. There will likely be many people like Jason. They can't remember their decision to believe, but this will liberate their minds and they will be part of The Receiving."

Maher nodded. "That makes sense."

Carmella shifted in her seat. "I'm sorry, but there is nothing about this that makes *any* sense."

Luke looked at Carmella with a slight smile. "I know it sounds incredible. It is very different from everything we grew up believing. But you have to admit, there is an elegance about it."

Carmella bobbled her head. "Well, I've read many novels with an elegant story line, but that doesn't mean they are real or applicable to my life."

Sarah leaned forward. "But what about everything else we've told you today?"

Carmella shrugged. "I'll admit it is a little strange, but strange doesn't equal a worldwide conspiracy."

Luke held up his hands. "Well, we don't expect anyone to make a decision today. We just wanted everyone to understand what we've found out." He gave a large smile. "You're all our friends—close friends—so we want you to know what we know. We're available to talk about any of this at any time."

Scott appeared to be holding back a laugh. "Well, if information overload was your goal, you succeeded."

Luke smiled. "Just wanted to fill all that empty void up there."

Scott laughed. "That and some." He stood, seemed to pause, then gestured to Luke. "It is getting late and our flight is early tomorrow. We'll see you in about a week, I presume."

Luke stood and nodded. Everyone else stood. There were handshakes and hugs around the room.

Luke stood with his arm around Sarah. "We want to thank all of you for your gifts and, more importantly, the gift of your presence."

Sarah nodded. "Absolutely." She turned to Kathleen. "Tell Ken I said thank you to him as well."

Kathleen nodded and gave her a hug. "I will. We'll see you soon."

All of Luke and Sarah's coworkers left. Sarah helped Natalia and Xiaofeng clean up.

Maher rubbed the back of his neck. "Did we go overboard with the information?"

Jeremy shrugged. "You presented what you felt was necessary." He turned his head. "I have to say, I was unaware of a lot of that. But I followed it pretty well."

Matteo nodded. "Yes, but you now have the help of the Holy Spirit. Luke's friends don't as yet. It's likely harder for them."

Luke let out a long breath. "Well, we can only pray the Holy Spirit can use what they heard today to help them eventually see the truth."

Viktoria came over and put her hand on Luke's shoulder. "Have faith, Luke. If God can help you see a toilet seat as a weapon, he can help your friends see the truth of your words."

Luke chuckled. Although she meant it to be humorous, truer words were never spoken.

EIGHT

SIMONE'S PLOT REVEALED

Philippe took another bite of his duck confit and took a sip of his pinot noir. "What's troubling you, Simone?" This meal was her favorite, so for her to just pick at it meant something was definitely troubling her.

"Philippe, did we do the right thing?"

"Simone, don't let your jealousy get the better of you."

He saw her gaze shoot to his. "That's what you think this is about?" Her nose flared. "I'm not a petty teenager, Philippe. There's more at stake than jealousy." She plunked her fork onto her plate. "She could still destroy *everything*—even without children."

"I thought you agreed with René."

Simone gave a smirk. She pointed to herself. "I'm going to commit career suicide and go against your brother?"

Philippe raised his eyebrows. "I would have backed you up. It would have been two against one."

Simone gave a wry smile. "Maybe you can go toe to toe with your brother and come out unscathed." She shook her head. "No one else can." She shrugged. "Besides, he did have some good points. She really is needed to get our Mars mission on track." She pointed her finger at Philippe. "But as soon as her job is done, Sarah goes into stasis."

Philippe stared at her and shook his head.

"What?"

"I don't think I'll ever figure you out."

Simone grinned. "That's good. The more interesting I am, the longer you'll keep me around."

Philippe took her hand. "Simone, I've always found you interesting."

Simone's cheeks reddened. She pulled her hand back and cut another bite of duck. She smiled. "That's nice to hear." She ate another bite, then pointed her fork at Philippe. "Now, we need to discuss your brother."

Philippe had his fork halfway to his mouth. He stopped and put his fork back on his plate. "What about my brother?" *This woman is more than interesting,* Philippe thought. *Unpredictable* would be a second, perhaps better, description.

Simone leaned in. "Philippe, you can't let him have the upper hand. You're a better leader than he will ever be. He should be supporting you, not you supporting him."

Philippe sat up straighter. "We both have equal equity in the company."

"But who does everyone look to for the final decision?"

Philippe cleared his throat. "My father had to give different responsibilities to each of us. We have equal control but different responsibilities."

"We have to change that perception."

"He has good intentions."

Simone put her silverware down and took a sip of wine. "Philippe, good intentions are not going to accomplish this Mars mission. We need someone to make the hard choices." She paused. He looked into her eyes. "That someone is *you,*

Philippe. You."

"What do you have in mind?"

A smile swept across Simone's face. "Ever heard of memory reprogramming?"

NINE

THE RECEIVING

Once back in the living quarters under the lab, Matteo and Xiaofeng said good night and headed to their bedroom.

"I'm going to make some tea," Sarah said, turning to the others. "Want some?"

Viktoria shook her head. "I'll decline. Thank you, Sarah. I think I'm going to head to bed myself."

Oliver nodded. "We'll see you in the morning."

Sarah turned to Maher. He nodded. "Sure. That sounds good."

Luke smiled. "Count me in." He pulled out a barstool for Sarah. "Here, you sit and I'll make it."

Sarah patted the stool next to her. "Here, Maher. Sit and tell me about the rest of your puzzle."

Maher sat and pulled out the paper. He spread it out before them. "You mean, what comes after . . . " He turned to Luke. "What did you call it? The Receiving?"

Luke nodded as he put the kettle on. "It seemed appropriate based on the Jewish wedding concept you presented."

Sarah nodded. "I like that concept. The receiving of the

bride by the bridegroom makes it sound so personal."

Maher nodded. He pointed at the triangles on the bottom of the puzzle. "These seem to represent the fall Jewish festivals: Rosh Hashanah, Yom Kippur, and Sukkot."

Sarah propped her head in her hand. "But what do those represent in our future?"

Luke brought the kettle to the counter, poured each of them a cup, and set the pot on a trivet. "Looks like you've really been studying, Maher."

Maher looked up and smiled. "Well, I was slightly less distracted than you, I think."

Luke patted him on his shoulder. "Good point."

Maher held up his palms. "I can't claim to be totally sure of all this, but from what I have been able to read, it would seem our future will be pretty incredible."

Sarah's eyes brightened. "Well, fill us in."

Maher cleared his throat. "Well, it would seem that sometime after The Receiving, the triangle of Rosh Hashanah starts."

Sarah looked confused. "Why is that important?"

Maher cocked his head. "Well, we used to call it the Jewish New Year, but it would seem the passages in this triangle represent it as a remembering of God's covenant with Israel. Three of these verses give examples of when Israel asked God to do just that. Then, of course, the Messiah being conceived in a human woman by the Holy Spirit was another remembrance of his promise to them. Now, after The Receiving, after he collects his bride, God again turns his attention back to Israel. Yet, the Scripture points to a series of many atrocities which will happen to the earth, but he also brings his people back to their homeland."

"Is that really necessary?" Sarah took a sip of tea. "It seems so . . . so drastic."

Maher shrugged. "Apparently that's what the world needs, I guess."

Luke leaned in. "But doesn't that lead to something wonderful? I remember reading about peace and prosperity."

Maher nodded. "Yes, after this grim time, it leads to the next triangle of Yom Kippur. This has always been a time of repentance. It seems that is what God now does. He saves Israel from total annihilation and brings forgiveness to them and their land. And that leads immediately to Sukkot."

"God tabernacles with his people," Luke interjected, knowing this part.

Maher looked at Luke and nodded. "Yes, this seems to be the time of great prosperity, peace, and wonderment you were talking about earlier. It seems to last for one thousand years."

Sarah gasped. "Wow. A thousand years? Really?" She shook her head. "But . . . but why?"

Maher smiled. "Well, I guess you can ask him when we get there. But it seems to be a time when mankind, even without evil influence, still works against God."

Sarah put her hand to her mouth. "Are we all really so wicked we would do that?"

"Apparently, apart from the Holy Spirit, we're not as great as we think we are."

Luke poured them all more tea. "So much for being truly wonderful."

Maher shook his head. "Oh, but it will be. And what comes next will be sublime."

Sarah turned her head. "What do you mean? Wasn't that the last triangle?"

Maher nodded. "Yes, but this last rectangle takes us back to the beginning, when everything was perfect." He tapped the rectangle on the paper. "This is known as Jubilee. It was a time when things were returned to their original state. All property returned, all debts annulled. People could start over. That seems to be what happens here." Now he tapped the first rectangle. "It's tied back to this, the Sabbath."

Luke leaned forward. "Why is that?"

"Well . . . it seems the Sabbath was the culmination of creation, a rest." He pointed back to the last rectangle. "This seems to be the final rest. A rest when all is made right again. We reach perfection, a perfect rest where all evil is eliminated, and we will forever be with our one true trinitarian God in a new Heaven and new earth. It seems to be the culmination of all that is joyous."

Sarah sighed. "Now, that's a hope to hold on to."

Both Maher and Luke nodded.

Luke sat back. "How do we let people know about all of this?" He shrugged. "I mean, look at how our friends reacted when we told them about everything that's already happened. They thought we were demented." He laughed, scratched his head as if thinking, then turned again to the paper. "Telling them the rest of it . . . " He gave a small chuckle. "They will certainly have us committed."

Sarah put her hand on his shoulder. "There has to be a way, Luke. It can't be God's purpose to let us be the only ones who understand this."

Maher looked from one to the other. "What about your friend, Oliver?"

Luke shook his head. "What do you mean?"

Maher shrugged. "Well, from what you've said, he seems to be pretty crafty with the Internet, viruses and such. Maybe he could post our findings and keep us from being traced." Maher stood—pacing, thinking—as he talked. "We could provide regular posts . . . you know, to lead those who read it down a logical trail . . . then, help them find what we've discovered." He turned back and looked at them expectantly.

Sarah shrugged. "But won't the memory reprogramming nullify all of it?"

Maher smiled and shook his head. "T-U-L-E."

"What?" Sarah looked confused once again. "What do you mean?"

"The Ultimate Liberation Event. We have to get people to *make* the choice, not necessarily remember it. We'll leave that for the Holy Spirit. We do our part, the Holy Spirit will do his."

Luke nodded. "Yeah, we can't guarantee the outcome, only our obedience."

Maher sat down and grabbed each of their hands while displaying a broad grin. "Precisely."

TEN

MATTEO'S FIND

Luke laughed. "Oliver, I've never seen you so speechless."

"Well, it's . . . it's incredible." He shook his head. "Never in my wildest dreams did I think obtaining *T-H-B* would yield such information."

Maher's eyes widened. "So, you'll do it?"

Oliver nodded. "Absolutely. This information has to get out. To keep this from everyone is . . . "

"Criminal."

Oliver looked at Viktoria, who had interjected that one word. He nodded. "Yes, criminal."

Sarah walked over with a fresh pot of coffee. "It has to get presented correctly, though."

"What do you mean?" Luke held his cup for Sarah as she filled it.

She held up the pot to offer coffee to anyone else. "Well, just think back to last night. People who know us have a hard time accepting the truth of what we know. How are total strangers going to accept it?"

Oliver held up his cup and Sarah filled it. "Well, the truth has a way of making itself known."

Maher jumped in. "True. But Sarah has a point. There will always be doubters, but we need to present this in a way most will see as a logical series of events."

Oliver nodded. "I see your point. But once we get a critical mass to accept this, it will go viral and the Illumi-Alliance will have a hard time suppressing it."

Viktoria patted Oliver's hand. "Until then, it's up to you to keep the message alive and not allow it to get suppressed before that happens."

Oliver grinned. "I think I still have a few tricks up my sleeve to help keep that from happening." He turned to Maher. "So, you just feed me the posts, and I'll ensure they get uploaded and fill the Internet."

Viktoria looked at Sarah and Luke. She breathed a deep sigh and paused like she didn't want to continue, but she did. "Unfortunately, I'm afraid the I-A will consider the two of you the most likely suspects when this starts."

"I-A?" Sarah looked confused.

"Oh, Illumi-Alliance. Many on the inside call it that for short." She shrugged. "It sounds less ominous."

Sarah nodded, but she gave Luke a worried look. He put his arm around her shoulder and rubbed her upper arm. "Well, that may give us the needed break for this to be successful."

Sarah gave him another quizzical look. He smiled and shrugged. "Since we won't have any direct tie to these posts, they'll look, but not be able to connect us."

Oliver nodded. "Good point, but I would still advise caution. Maybe the two of you should get back to your normal routine for a few weeks. That could provide the needed distraction to get this off the ground."

Sarah nodded and gave a weak smile. Luke could tell she felt nervous. Yet, who could blame her after all she had been through with the I-A already?

All turned when they heard footsteps bounding down the stairs. Jeremy had a huge grin on his face. Matteo followed him, carrying something in his hands.

"I think we have it."

Luke looked at Jeremy. "Have what?"

Matteo sat a covered petri dish on the counter; it contained a white powder. All looked at the dish and simply stared.

Viktoria seemed to be the first to put the unsaid pieces together. "So, this is the compound to reverse the effects of the chemical in the Invocation wafer?"

Matteo gave a solemn nod.

Jeremy beamed as he patted Luke on his shoulder. "Your wish has finally come true, Luke."

Luke was elated but stunned at the same time. He had complained to Jeremy many times that their work had seemed too slow. Now that it was very possibly a reality, it was hard to grasp. "Are . . . are you sure?"

Matteo nodded again. "The animal tests seem to confirm it."

Luke looked up at him. "So, what do we do now?"

Viktoria picked up the petri dish and looked at it more closely. "Now, we test it." She looked at each of them. "*I'll . . .* test it."

Luke's head jerked back slightly. "How?"

Viktoria looked at him, her eyes squinting.

"I just mean, how do you know how much to take?" Luke asked. He looked back at Matteo. "Do we have enough to mass produce?"

Matteo shook his head. "We have quite a ways to go before we can claim that." He raised his eyebrows. "I'm not sure we will ever get to mass production. That would require a lot more equipment and infiltration and that, unfortunately, would draw more attention to us from the I-A."

Viktoria nodded. "That's why I need to be the one to try this. If we go that route, and I can be immune, I can help divert attention away from here." Her eyes watered. "You have no idea how long I've waited for a miracle like this."

Luke looked at Viktoria. He had never seen her so emotional. As an I-A officer, she usually expressed no emotion—except disdain for others. Yet, right now, in this time and space, she seemed the most human of all of them. Viktoria never ceased to amaze Luke.

Jeremy took the petri dish from her. "Viktoria, I don't want to burst your bubble. But we don't really know what dose to give."

Viktoria looked at Sarah. "Can you tell us? Can you give an educated guess?"

Sarah cocked her head with a grimace. "It's not that easy. With several assumptions, I can come up with a guess, but it could be way off."

"You give your guess to Matteo." She turned to him. "You synthesize enough for Oliver and me to try this out several times until we get the dose right." She shook her head. "It shouldn't take too long to find out. You all know this: I get rebooted almost every day."

Oliver took her hand. "Are you sure?"

She nodded. "Absolutely. To wake up and remember on my own what happened yesterday . . . that is worth all the risks."

Oliver smiled and gave her a kiss. "You're wonderful."

She returned the smile. "Just determined."

Sarah held up her palms. "OK, OK." She turned to Matteo. "Give me what you've got on this compound and I'll do my best."

Matteo nodded. "Let me get the paperwork. I'll be right back." He headed upstairs.

Jeremy sat the petri dish down. "I have to say, though, we may be able to only make enough for a small group of people." He shook his head. "We're not really set up for mass production, and I don't know how to transfer this to another lab without raising suspicion."

Sarah jumped in. "And if Simone gets her chemical ready, which *can* be mass produced, not even immunes will be safe."

Luke tapped the dish with his index finger. "Can this protect immunes against her new chemical?"

Sarah shrugged. "Hard to say. Maybe. If . . . if the new chemical isn't too far off from how this chemical works."

Now it was Luke's turn to look confused. "What do you mean?"

She raised her eyebrows. "Well, I need to see what Matteo knows about this compound and how it works. My guess . . . " She gave a small shrug. " . . . is that Simone is looking for a compound which will bind to the drug transporter so the compound in the Invocation wafer will not get pumped out of the caudate in the brain. Now, if Matteo's compound works by blocking the fullerene transporter, then it should still be helpful for everyone."

Maher shook his head. "Sorry, you lost me."

Sarah smiled. "In other words, currently immunes pump the drug out of the brain faster than it enters. Simone wants to keep the drug from getting pumped out of the brain. But if Matteo's drug prevents that drug from getting into the brain, then it should still be helpful."

Maher nodded. "Ah. Well, let's hope Mercure's solution is less brilliant than Matteo's solution."

Sarah nodded. "Since she doesn't know we've put countermeasures in place, it's likely she'll go for the quick win rather than a calculated overall win to overcome all countermeasures."

Matteo returned, waving his papers. He handed them to Sarah. After reading through a few pages, she looked up and smiled. "I think this is going to work."

ELEVEN

SARAH'S REGRET

Luke opened the taxi door for Sarah after putting their luggage in the trunk. He entered the other side, then gave the destination to their apartment building and inserted his credit disk.

Sarah leaned into him. He raised his arm and she nestled up to him. "Luke, are we really back home? It seems like a lifetime since we've been here."

Luke nodded. "Yeah, we left here single. Now, we come back married." He laughed. "Which apartment do we live in?"

Sarah raised up suddenly and looked at him. "I . . . I never considered that." She laughed and leaned back. "What do you want to do?"

Luke shrugged. "Well, my lease is up before yours, so why don't we just use yours? Besides, I have less stuff."

Sarah looked up at him and grinned. "Back to Mr. Methodical, I see."

"Just trying to be realistic. Besides, I had all the presents shipped to your address."

"And we won't have to clean out the refrigerator."

Luke looked down at her. "Ouch. Now who's being methodical?"

Sarah laughed. "Two can play your game."

Luke laughed with her. "OK, Mrs. Methodical. How do you want to do this?"

"We can move your stuff this weekend, sublet your apartment until the lease is out, and then be free and clear."

Luke gave her a squeeze. "I've taught you well, my padawan."

Sarah smiled. "Oh, so you're now using old *Star Wars* movie references? I think you've been watching too many old movies." She chuckled and pushed her finger into his ribs.

Luke jerked. "Umph. Hey now. Don't start something you can't finish."

She looked up at him and pulled his head down to hers to give him a kiss. "I can finish this."

He smiled. "That, I don't mind you finishing."

"Destination achieved."

Luke got out and opened the door for her. After retrieving the luggage, they went up to Sarah's apartment. *Their* apartment, Luke told himself, correcting his thought. Once they settled in, it almost seemed as if the last couple of weeks, except for being married, had become a distant memory. It was hard to believe it had all really happened.

＊ ＊ ＊ ＊ ＊

The next morning, Luke woke to find Sarah sitting up in bed staring straight ahead. He smiled. "Good morning."

Sarah didn't respond, but stayed in what seemed a trance-like state.

A worried look came across Luke's face as he put his hand on her leg. "Honey, are you all right?"

His touch caused her to turn toward him. He saw her tear-stained cheeks and immediately sat up, putting his arm around her shoulders. She fell onto his chest and began to sob.

"Sarah, honey. What's wrong? What's wrong?"

She sat up and wiped her tears away. Through sniffles, she forced out the words. "I'm sorry, Luke. I know I said we shouldn't bring children into the world." She nodded her head slightly. "I . . . I do believe that. I thought I'd get over this feeling, but having the choice taken away still hurts."

She looked into his eyes. He saw her bottom lip quiver. He wrapped his arms around her and pulled her into himself. "I know. I'm so sorry. So, so sorry." He kissed her on her forehead.

Luke wanted to do something to comfort her, but felt helpless to do so. He just held her. He knew nothing else to do. After a few minutes, Sarah began kissing his chest and made her way up to his lips. She leaned into him and he reciprocated. Letting her know how much he loved her was something he could do. He would make sure she knew how much . . .

They later got up together and dressed. They walked to work, stopped for their ritual coffee, and headed to their work floors.

Sarah squeezed Luke's arm. "Thanks again for being there for me this morning. I think being back and starting our lives together . . . " She shrugged. "It all just overwhelmed me again."

He patted her hand and smiled. "Anytime."

He gave her a kiss just before she exited on the fourth floor. "See you at lunch?"

She nodded and stepped off.

He stayed on and rode up to the fifteenth floor. As he exited, a flood of memories came back over Luke. It was another feeling of home with everything looking and feeling familiar. As usual, he was one of the first to arrive in his work area. He sat down, fired up his holo-computer, and looked around. Larry was in one of the pod rooms.

Luke walked over to wave hello, but Larry held up an index finger. In a couple of minutes, Larry opened the door. He extended his hand. Luke shook it.

"Luke, glad to have you back." He smiled. "I hope you're well rested. Work has started to escalate."

"Glad to be back, Larry. I assume the assignments are already logged?"

Larry nodded. "Yep. Let me know if you have questions."

Larry went back into the pod room and Luke returned to his desk. He checked his e-mail. Most were congratulatory notes regarding his wedding. There were only a few work-related ones that required a response. He then looked at the jobs that were waiting for him. His eyes widened. It looked like it would be a long week—and he would be joined to the hip with Scott and Brian once more. The three had to go over the entire Mars mission scenario and ensure all was working within expected parameters. Then, Luke had to work with them on the asteroid assignment to put plans together for a viable mission of retrieval and deployment of the asteroids. He would then have to ensure Dwayne, in propulsion, received the precise fuel requirements.

After Scott and Brian welcomed him back, they too looked at their job task lists. Luke couldn't help but laugh after seeing their eyes go wide. "Looks like we got work to do, boys."

Scott looked over. "Give us half an hour to review, and we'll get started."

Luke nodded. "OK, I'll get things set up for us." Luke had forgotten that due to memory reprogramming the two of them often had to review what they did the day before as some of their memories were overridden in the process.

It took Luke about fifteen minutes to get the simulation program set up. He went ahead and assigned the various tasks to each of them. He then went to the break room and grabbed a protein drink. When he came back, both Brian and Scott were ready.

They each monitored various parameters during the simulation. They had to start and stop several times.

Scott looked over and smiled. "Fifth time's the charm."

Luke noticed it was already 12:15. "Let's take a short lunch break and come back to see how far we can get with the simulation." All agreed with this plan.

Luke found Sarah in their usual spot in the cafeteria. Jason was just leaving as he approached.

Jason gave a short wave. "Hi, Luke. Welcome back. Sorry, have a meeting in ten minutes."

Luke waved back, sat down, and took a big bite of his sandwich. "How are things with him?"

Sarah furrowed her brow. "I think he's struggling a little. I'm hoping to be able to help him sort through some issues."

Luke nodded. "Maybe we should have the two of them over sometime."

Sarah perked up. "That's a great idea."

Luke finished his sandwich and looked at Sarah. "Actually, why don't we have a standard meeting, say, every Thursday night? Everyone and anyone can come over to just talk and discuss. Maybe that will be less intimidating, but we can still make inroads with people."

Sarah nodded her head. "Let me think about that."

Luke took a drink and pointed her way. "How's your work? Mine is already bonkers."

Sarah laughed. "Well, that's not how I would describe it, but it is certainly hectic."

Luke looked at his watch. "Actually, I should get back. It's going to be a long afternoon."

Sarah nodded. "Just text me later and let me know when you'll be getting off."

"OK." He leaned over and gave her a kiss. "See you later."

Brian and Scott were already back at their desks when he arrived. Once they started, Luke had no awareness of time because, the next thing he knew, Sarah was standing next to him.

"Hi, guys. Ending anytime today?"

They each looked up and then down at their watches. It was 17:34. They looked around; only a few others in their department were still present, and they hadn't even noticed.

Brian tapped his watch. "Is it really that late? I swear we just got started."

Scott laughed. "Well, we are at a good stopping place. Let's pick it up tomorrow."

After shutting down, all four of them walked out together.

As Sarah pushed the elevator button, she looked at Luke, raised her eyebrows, and turned to his coworkers. "Brian, Scott, any further thoughts about what we spoke about the other night, in Shanghai?"

Scott nodded. "Yeah, actually. It's freaky and fascinating at the same time. Could I read those verses for myself?"

The doors opened. They stepped in and Luke pushed the button for the first floor.

Luke smiled. "Sure. I'll send them to you."

Luke noticed Brian didn't say anything, but he didn't want him to feel uncomfortable, so he didn't push the issue. Having a positive response from Scott was a good first step.

They parted ways once they left the building.

Luke walked hand in hand with Sarah back to their apartment. It had been a good day.

* * * * *

Luke found that hectic first day turn into a hectic week which turned into a hectic month. Larry had a meeting with them at the end of the fifth week.

"OK, boys. Let me know the issue here. How far behind are we?"

Luke swiveled back and forth in his chair. "I think the main issue was, when we programmed the individual components of the mission, we didn't really take into account interdependencies between the modules. Now that we have, it all runs smoothly."

Larry turned to each of them. "So, we can get back on schedule?"

Luke gave a grimace.

Larry sighed. "What is it, Luke?"

"Even if the other sites do the same as we did, are we confident all our systems will work smoothly together across sites once integrated?"

Larry shrugged. "Why wouldn't they?"

Luke cocked his head. "Well, we thought our integration would be simple, but it's taken four times longer to get it done." He shook his head. "I'd rather be sure than sorry."

Larry shook his head. "Well, I hate to ask. But what are you proposing?"

"I think we should take three of our sites at a time and see how they work together."

Brian leaned forward. "Which ones?"

Luke rubbed the back of his neck. "I would want to be sure Hohhot and Brasilia work well with us."

He gave a slight smile while watching Brian make a fist and pull it down to his side while mouthing the words, "Yes." Larry was staring at Luke, so he didn't see the motion.

Luke shrugged. "I say that because we've had issues with them in the recent past. If those go well, then so should the others."

Larry rubbed his hand across his mouth and gave a long sigh. "Let me think about that one. I'll let you know tomorrow."

TWELVE

Hohhot

Luke felt as though there had been so many déjà vu moments of late. Here they were back on a train to Hohhot. Sarah was again leaning against him reading Scripture. But this time they were reviewing Scripture to help address questions their friends from work were asking rather than trying to investigate for themselves whether God even existed, as they had done on their first trip to Hohhot.

Luke reached down and kissed her on her forehead. "I really appreciate you coming with me."

She looked up from her reading and into his eyes. "My pleasure. But I have to say, Ken was not very happy when Larry approached him about me coming to interpret again."

"But surely he understands the importance."

"Well, yeah, or else I wouldn't be here." She sat up straighter. "When I told him I would meet with the physicians at Hohhot to be sure we are operating on the same protocol, he felt it wasn't a totally wasted trip from a medical point of view."

"So, we'll see Dr. Chan first to get the simulation under way?"

Sarah chuckled and shook her head. "No, you see Dr. Chen. I see Dr. Chan." She patted his chest. "You're confusing Dr. Chang with Dr. Chan. Dr. Chang works with Dr. Chen. Dr. Chan is head of their medical team and works with Dr. Ching, who I work with on preparation of stasis protocols."

Luke put his hands to his temples. "Oh . . . just . . . stop. I'll never keep this straight. I feel trapped in a limerick."

Sarah belted out a huge laugh. She reached over and kissed his cheek. "Just follow my lead."

Luke's eyes widened. "Like glue. I can't afford a faux pas now that we're so close to getting everything ready."

She leaned back against him again. "Don't worry. You'll do fine."

Luke felt nervous. He usually didn't feel this way, but for some reason, which he couldn't understand, he felt ill at ease. Anyway, he'd be glad to get started on the simulation. Once they started, he would be in his element and, hopefully, feel more confident and comfortable.

Once at the train station, Luke took their luggage with them, found a taxi, and headed to their hotel. He smiled to himself. This time they would be in the same room. No cold showers this trip. As they didn't have to be at the facility until the next morning, Luke ordered in and they lounged on the bed talking.

Sarah cuddled up to him on the bed and read some of the Scriptures supporting The Receiving. After reading a few, she paused.

Luke looked at her. "Anything wrong?"

She shook her head. "Not really, but do you think there is a time limit to prophecy being fulfilled?"

"What do you mean?"

"Well, this was written in the first century, and we're coming close to the twenty-second century. That's a long time to wait for a prophecy to be fulfilled."

He rubbed her arm. "I know Maher was looking at the prophecy of the Messiah's first coming. It seems from the first announcement of his coming in Genesis to his arrival in Matthew, almost four thousand years passed. So this one is still well within that timeline."

Sarah rubbed her chin. "So, do you think it will be another thousand years or so before he comes for his bride?"

Luke shook his head. "I don't know." He looked at her. "I don't think so, though." He shrugged. "Would there be anyone left who would even remember anything about him if he waits that long?"

Sarah smiled. "Well, I suppose he can make happen whatever he wants to make happen."

Luke gave her a squeeze. "Aren't you the pragmatic one tonight? Yes, that's true. Yet, it just feels like it would, or should, happen earlier."

She reached up and gave him a kiss. "Well, enough speculating for tonight. Let's get some sleep. We have an early day tomorrow."

He turned out the light and they drifted into slumber still in each other's arms.

* * * * *

Once Luke and Sarah exited the hotel the next morning, he pressed the center button of the hotel credit disk and a taxi soon pulled up. The taxi headed north out of the city once Sarah gave the destination in Chinese.

After about half an hour, the taxi pulled up to a large building and stated their arrival. Luke inserted his disk and stepped from the cab, then helped Sarah out as well.

Luke had forgotten the size and beauty of this building. It

was several stories tall and extremely wide; the entire building was made of glass, but random panes had different different colors. Luke and Sarah entered through a cobalt-colored archway into a large atrium. Next to the receptionist desk a large waterfall meandered down over large rocks and entered a small pond at its base. He remembered this beautiful sight from before: many iridescent lavender-colored lotus flowers floated in the small pool that received the water from the falls.

Luke also recognized the receptionist from their previous visit. She once again wore a lotus flower behind her ear, making it stand out against her jet-black hair draped over both sides of her shoulders. She gave a bright smile as they approached.

"Dr. Loughton. Dr. Morgan. Welcome back to Hohhot. Shall I call Dr. Chen?"

Her English wasn't perfect, but Luke was able to understand her. He smiled. "Yes, please."

She gestured for them to sit while they waited. In a matter of minutes, a man with short black hair, wearing a lab coat, approached. The man's name appeared under his left shoulder, written in Chinese characters.

Dr. Chen bowed. "Dr. Loughton. Dr. Morgan. Welcome."

Luke returned the bow. "Thank you, Dr. Chen." He extended his hand; Dr. Chen shook it.

"Dr. Chang is preparing the simulation." He gestured back in the direction from which he came and then said something in Chinese. Luke looked at Sarah with eyebrows raised.

Sarah smiled. "He said, 'Shall we get started?'"

"Oh." Luke turned back to Dr. Chen. "Yes, absolutely."

Chen gave him a curious look in return.

Luke caught himself. "Shi," he said.

Dr. Chen smiled and nodded.

Luke found Dr. Chang to be a focused and determined individual. He didn't stand when they approached, but did give a slight bow. Although seated, he looked to be tall. Luke thought that unusual compared to everyone else around him.

Luke sat next to Dr. Chang. The simulation was already on the holo-screen. Chang made the connections to the U.S. and Brazil sites. Both Larry's and Brian's video feed came on-screen as well. This would allow them to have a dynamic conversation as they attempted to troubleshoot any issues as the simulation executed.

Luke turned to Dr. Chang. "Before we start, I just want to be sure you've gone through your entire simulation and all is working seamlessly."

He glanced at Sarah. She interpreted. Dr. Chang gave a slight bow. "Shi." He then said something else. Luke looked at Sarah.

"He said they spent several weeks working out all the issues, but they're all now resolved."

Luke nodded. All the more reason to now be sure all would work in concert, he thought.

Once they began, Luke was, in one way, impressed there were not as many issues to troubleshoot as he had feared. Yet the issues they found would have been major ones if not identified before the actual mission.

* * * * *

As things unfolded the next few days, Luke was also impressed it only took three days to go through the simulation and make corrections.

On the fourth day, they gathered to be sure the entire simulation would run in concert without further issues. Once the simulation began on this day, Sarah leaned next to his ear.

"Luke, while this is running, I'm going to go meet with Dr.

Ching. I think it will only take a couple of hours to go over our protocols and be sure we're on the same page."

Luke looked up and nodded. "OK. I think I'll be fine for a while." He smiled. "They're not a talkative bunch, anyway."

She patted his shoulder. "I'll see you in a few."

As Luke watched the simulation, it seemed everything was working properly and without incident. Although the simulation went on for several hours, everyone in the room was glued to their holo-screens. Once the simulation completed the Mars landing, everyone broke into cheers and applause. Luke sat back and breathed a sigh of relief. He could see Brian and Scott doing the same. And . . . it was quick, but he saw Carmella give Brian a kiss on his cheek. Luke raised his eyebrows. Brian smiled.

And then . . . Luke jumped as the doors in front of him were abruptly opened and I-A soldiers barged in. This time, Dr. Chang did stand up, as did everyone else. Luke heard Scott say, "What's going on?" No one answered.

Everyone talked and yelled as soldiers poured into the room. Luke wished Sarah was here; he could not make out what was being said. It reminded him a great deal of when Dr. Liwei was arrested the last time he and Sarah were here.

The soldiers ordered everyone to line up. Dr. Chen appeared to be trying to understand what the soldiers wanted. And then Dr. Ching and Sarah entered. They were talking and laughing and didn't notice the soldiers at first. They stopped talking and stared at the lineup. The soldiers motioned with their guns that the two of them join the others.

Sarah looked at Luke, whispering, "What's going on?"

Luke shrugged. "Can you understand anything they're saying?"

She nodded toward the lead soldier. "He keeps asking, 'Where is he?'"

"He, who?"

Sarah shrugged. "Wait." Luke noticed her strain her attention to, what seemed to him, a choppy conversation. "He's talking about Dr. Liwei, I think."

Luke scrunched his brow. "Why? They took him last time we were here."

Sarah seemed astounded. She whispered: "They say he's here somewhere."

"Why would he be here?" Luke glanced at Dr. Ching, who had a worried look on his face. He looked at Sarah and nodded toward him.

Sarah put her hand on Dr. Ching's shoulder. "Are you OK?"

He nodded, but he didn't look that way. Luke wondered what he wasn't saying. He saw Dr. Ching pull out his phone and double click on something. One of the soldiers saw him and came over. They argued about something. Luke looked at Sarah.

She whispered to Luke: "The soldier thinks he deleted something from his phone. Dr. Ching is saying he was checking his e-mail to see if there was an announcement about what's going on."

Luke looked up as another soldier entered with someone. His jaw dropped. It was Dr. Liwei. What was he doing here? Why did he come back?

The soldier slip-tied Dr. Liwei's wrists behind him and had him sit in a chair next to Luke and Sarah. He looked up at them and gave a weak smile, a way of saying hello.

While the soldier who brought Dr. Liwei in went to talk to the soldier who seemed to be in charge, Luke kept his voice low and tried to find out from Dr. Liwei what was happening.

Luke shot him a whisper: "Dr. Liwei, why are you back here?"

"These are my friends. I had to let them know what I found

out about God. I couldn't not tell them."

"Let me guess. Your main contact was Dr. Ching."

Liwei nodded. "I hope I haven't put him or your friends in danger."

"What do you mean?"

"Well, they know I work for Jeremy. They'll likely question him."

Luke wondered if that would be an issue. Just because someone works for another person doesn't put the other person at risk. Does it? He looked back at Liwei. "What's going to happen to you?"

Liwei shook his head; his eyes looked vacant. "It's starting. What's happening to me will happen more and more. Get ready."

Before Luke could ask anything more, the guard returned and forced Dr. Liwei away. Luke had no idea where they were taking him.

THIRTEEN

UNDER SCRUTINY

Philippe walked around his desk and moved the bowl on the glass table in front of the yellow sofa to make room for Simone's computer tablet.

"What are you wanting to show me?"

Simone patted the sofa cushion next to her. "Come sit and see."

As a video came on, Philippe leaned forward. "Is this a satellite feed?" He looked at her with raised eyebrows. "Where . . . where did you get this?"

She rubbed his forearm. "Now, now. Let's focus on what's important here."

Philippe nodded. "OK. What am I seeing? I see two people entering a large building." He rested his head in his hand with elbow propped on his knee. "Now I see people coming out." He leaned in closer. "Are those I-A officers? They're bringing out someone." He looked at Simone. "Who is that?"

"OK, before we go there, look at this."

Philippe looked back at the screen. "OK, I see four people entering a building." He turned back to Simone. "What are you wanting me to understand from this?"

"Doctors Loughton and Morgan were in both places."

Philippe cradled his forehead in his hand. *Is she becoming obsessed?* He looked back at her. "Simone, are you taking this too far?"

Simone sighed. "Philippe, I haven't gone batty, if that is what you're thinking." She sat back. "Last year, Dr. Liwei was arrested at the Hohhot Aerospace Center when both Luke and Sarah were present. He got . . . displaced once he was taken." She folded her arms across her chest. "Now those two arrive again, and Dr. Liwei is again found and arrested." She pointed back to the screen. "Then they arrive back in Shanghai and enter a building owned by Luke's friend. And they arrive with another couple, one of which is Agent Komcova, an I-A officer." She leaned closer to Philippe. "Now, why would an I-A officer be casually hanging out with Luke and Sarah?"

Philippe put his hand to his chin. "That is curious." He turned to her. "But what does one have to do with the other?"

"If we follow these two, I think they will lead us to those we need to be concerned about."

"I'm not quite sure I get where you're going. Dr. Liwei is an immune, but an I-A officer is not. That was one important stipulation when the force was created. We had to be sure we could control them. I'm certain Rosencrantz made sure he could control Agent Komcova."

Simone raised her eyebrows. "I don't think Rosencrantz knows she's working with these two and their friends."

"They do have personal lives—just very controlled ones."

"Looks like, to me, she's compromised."

Philippe sat back. "Maybe we should get René's opinion."

Simone shook her head and touched his arm. "You can make your own decisions without him."

The conference room door opened and René stepped in.

"Philippe, I need—" He stopped in his tracks. "Oh, Simone, I didn't realize you were here. Sorry."

Simone smiled. "That's OK. We were just talking about you."

Philippe gave her a stare, but she ignored him. He had no idea what she was up to. Surely, she wouldn't actually tell René they were trying to usurp him.

René's eyebrows went up. "Oh, really?"

Simone nodded. "Philippe was concerned about you taking so many supplements."

René looked at Philippe and cocked his head. "Why's that?"

Philippe's mind spun. He glanced at Simone and then at René. "Oh, uh, well, you take so many . . . "

Simone put her hand on Philippe's arm. He looked at her. She smiled and looked back at René. "Yes, he's concerned you may not be taking the right ones or the right dosage."

René gave Philippe a weak smile. "Why the concern?"

Philippe shrugged. "You're my brother."

Simone closed her tablet. "I have a minor in nutrition." She gave a small shrug. "I could take a look at what you're taking and be sure they're right for you—and the right dosage."

"Really? That would be great. I'll tell Sonja and you can coordinate with her."

Simone smiled and nodded. "My pleasure."

Philippe knew Simone had a hidden agenda, but he had to admit to himself he wasn't sure what it was. "What did you need, René?"

"Oh, yeah." He laughed. "I got sidetracked." He gestured toward Philippe. "I was going to ask if you had any success on the chemical to affect immunes."

Philippe looked to Simone. "Care to share what you told me?"

Simone smiled. "We have what we think will work. We

have some . . . tests to do to confirm."

"Like what?"

"Well . . . "

Philippe stood and put his hand on René's shoulder. "I want to give you denial plausibility until we know for sure."

René laughed. "Look at you, Philippe. Protecting your older brother."

Philippe smiled and patted his shoulder.

René turned to exit, but then turned back. "Well, keep me apprised once you have your positive results."

Philippe nodded. René left the room.

Philippe turned to Simone. "What was *that* all about?"

Simone gestured for Philippe to once again sit next to her. "Philippe, René is the perfect test subject for the compound."

Philippe's eyes widened. "What?"

"I will include it as one of his supplements. If he starts to concede important decisions to you . . . we'll know it's working."

Philippe wasn't sure how to respond. Yes, they had talked about Philippe becoming the more prominent of the two, but this seemed extremely risky. "How?"

She took his hand in hers and looked into his eyes. "This is your time, Philippe. We need a reprogramming feed for whatever media René watches."

"But that's so risky. How do we keep the programmer silent?"

She smiled and patted his hand. "By ensuring he watches the same."

FOURTEEN

COMPROMISED

Luke looked around at his friends. Two he had known since college. The other four he had only known for several months. Yet he felt just as close to Oliver and Viktoria as he did to Jeremy and Natalia. Matteo and Xiaofeng were like parents to him. He smiled. It was a nice feeling. It seemed he had known all of them for a lot longer than he actually had. A lot had happened in the last eleven months. And there were only five months to go before the Mars launch. Things would only get more hectic, and more dangerous, from here.

Luke's attention turned to Matteo, who was excitedly sharing with the others. "Since the last time we met, we have been able to synthesize more than we thought."

Luke's eyes widened. "Just how much?"

"Enough to affect one local Invocation Center."

"How?"

Sarah nodded. "You don't have control over the manufacture of the wafers."

Xiaofeng smiled. "But we have something those in charge never thought of. Ingenuity."

Matteo laughed. "It was really Dr. Liwei's idea."

Luke realized they probably didn't yet know what had happened to Dr. Liwei. He wondered if this was likely the reason for him being captured once again. "What did he do?"

"He was able to incorporate the compound into a batch of chocolate that was passed out after Invocation. Almost everyone took a piece."

Natalia beamed. "Isn't that ingenious?"

Sarah nodded. "So, what happened?"

Natalia put her hand on Sarah's arm. "Get this. The local factory was so productive they filled all orders in half the time. People remembered issues from the previous day and demanded resolutions. The managers didn't know what to do. The I-A officers had to come in and shut the place down because of the arguments that ensued."

Luke shook his head. "No wonder they were looking for Dr. Liwei."

Matteo's smile turned to a frown. "What do you mean, Luke?"

"He was arrested in Hohhot." Luke shook his head. "I didn't hear where he was being taken."

Xiaofeng gasped. "No wonder we haven't heard from him." She took Matteo's arm. "Maybe we should tread more softly." She turned to Viktoria. "Did you hear anything?"

Viktoria shook her head. "I wasn't part of either of those events."

Oliver took her hand. "You don't think they suspect you, do you?"

Viktoria shrugged. "Maybe. I . . . I don't know. It just seems I'm involved less and less. Makes me wonder."

Xiaofeng shook her head. "Poor Dr. Liwei. I wonder what's going to happen to him?"

Oliver shrugged. "Likely what's going to happen to all of us, eventually. He's likely in one of the immune prisons by now."

Natalia reached for Jeremy's hand and turned to Oliver. "You really think that's our fate?"

Oliver gave a half-laugh. "Our fate is likely to be on Mars. Prison is likely an intermediate step."

Xiaofeng stood. "Enough of the doom and gloom. We all knew the risks of what we were getting involved with. I'm going to make us some tea. In the meantime, who has some positive news?"

"Maher's posts are getting wonderful comments." All eyes turned to Oliver. He smiled. "There's some group out there that keeps reposting them everywhere." He chuckled. "As soon as Maher's posts get shut down, all of a sudden they appear somewhere else. It seems to be spreading faster than the Illumi-Alliance can shut it down."

Luke was glad to hear Maher's work was making a difference. "Who is this group you are referring to?"

Oliver shrugged. "They go by Clarity of The Way." He shook his head. "I don't know who they are, but at least one of them knows how to hack. The posts seem to spread faster than the websites can get shut down."

Luke laughed. "It's good to hear something is going right."

Oliver nodded. "I think Maher is having a tremendous impact."

Xiaofeng came back with the tea. "Everyone have a cup. Then let's head upstairs. I think all of you should get some of this compound to take—just in case."

Sarah turned to Matteo. "Do you have it in capsule form?"

Matteo nodded. "Some, at least. Why?"

"Well, it looks like Ken and I will be leading the preparation of those who win the lottery for space travel. It would be nice to have some drug on hand to give to at least a few."

Matteo patted her hand. "Come with me and I'll show you

what I have."

The two of them left and went upstairs while the rest of them finished their tea.

They all had barely made it upstairs when all the glass in the lab went opaque. Xiaofeng and Matteo headed for the nearest door and exited. The rest of them stood and waited to see who the uninvited guests would be.

In a matter of minutes, in walked agents Caine and Abel.

Jeremy took a step forward. "You again? You didn't find anything here last time. Why have you returned?"

Abel waived his gun toward Jeremy. "OK, bud. Back down. We're not here for you."

Caine jumped in. "And in spite of you always being with Commando Loughton here, we'll ignore that this time."

Luke rolled his eyes. "So, just why are you two here anyway?"

Abel glanced at Viktoria. "Yeah, boss, want to explain that one to us? Why are you already with them rather than with us?"

Luke could see Viktoria's countenance change, visibly, as she went into Illumi-Alliance mode. "How dare you question me and my tactics? You report to me, remember."

Abel shook his head. "Not this time, we don't." He patted his coat pocket. "Orders."

"You dare question my loyalty?"

Luke was amazed at how Viktoria could turn into that persona even when she had all of her faculties, all of her memories. He was also amazed Abel didn't back down either.

Abel patted his pocket once again. "Not mine to question." He waived his gun. "You can come with us with dignity or get handcuffed. Your choice."

Luke kept glancing at Caine. He seemed more quiet than normal. Luke thought it odd Caine was letting Abel do all the talking.

As Viktoria took a step forward, so did Oliver. "Where are

you taking her?"

Abel smirked. "Not your concern."

Oliver's face turned a shade of red.

Viktoria turned. "It's OK, Oliver."

He shook his head but remained in place.

Caine never moved from where he stood. It happened in a flash: as Abel passed him, he shot Abel in the back, and Abel crumbled to the floor.

Viktoria turned, a smile spreading across her face. "You believed what I told you?"

Caine nodded. "I thought you were crazy, but after I thought about what you said, it really started to make sense." He looked at Abel on the floor. "But he only got more irate." He shrugged. "I'm not sure why."

Oliver came over. "What just happened?"

Viktoria smiled. "Caine is on our side now."

Caine smiled and looked at Luke. "Sorry about that comment. I had to make Abel think I was still his partner in crime, so to speak."

Luke chuckled. "Well, you had me convinced."

Oliver reached out and shook his hand. "Welcome aboard." He looked down at Abel. "What now?"

Caine put his hand on Viktoria's upper arm. "Viktoria, you must get off the radar. Do you have somewhere you can go?" He looked down again at Abel. "I can get his memory reprogrammed about today, but I don't know who exactly issued the orders. They'll still be gunning for you."

Viktoria put her hand to her chin. She slowly shook her head. "I'm pretty sure this wasn't condoned by Rosencrantz. He would have dismissed me himself. He wouldn't have gone through all of this cloak and dagger."

Oliver came up and put his hand on her back. "So, you think this was done behind Rosencrantz's back?"

Jeremy raised his eyebrows. "Trouble between The Six?"

Viktoria shrugged. "I know Rosencrantz has never trusted Dr. Mercure. There's a big personality clash there."

Caine gestured toward Viktoria. "So, what do you plan to do?"

"I think I'll reach out to Rosencrantz."

Caine's eyes went wide. "Do you think that's wise?"

"Wise or not, I think it's my best option." She turned Oliver's way. "If he's still supportive, I'll be fine. If not, then I'm no worse off than now anyway."

Oliver nodded. "OK. Just be careful."

Caine didn't look convinced, but told Viktoria, "OK. If you say so." He looked down again at Abel. "Can you help me get him back to his hotel room? I've got some reprogramming to do."

Viktoria nodded. She turned and gave Oliver a kiss. "I'll be in touch."

He put his forehead to hers. "Be careful. I love you."

She smiled. "Back at ya. Don't worry. I have plenty of the compound Matteo developed. I should be fine."

They all watched Caine and Viktoria head out, each shouldering one side of Abel. The windows turned clear once again, and everyone else headed back downstairs.

FIFTEEN

BRASILIA

Luke announced his destination to the taxi and it pulled into traffic. He was leaving the Brasilia airport and heading to the Aerospace Engineering Center on the outside of town. Luke was astounded by the modern architecture of this city. The taxi drove by the Invocation Center and he had to acknowledge to himself that this was one of the more beautiful centers he had seen. The hyperbolic structure was all glass except for the pillars that formed a type of a teepee structure. The pillars came near one another at the top of the building and then fluted outward. He made a mental note that he would have to come back at night since the Center was touted as displaying beautiful colors after dusk.

He kept his eyes peeled for the Juscelino Kubitschek Bridge, which crosses Lake Paranoa. The Aerospace Engineering building would be on the other side of the lake. His mouth went agape as the bridge came into view. Three huge steel arches rose from the water and crossed over the highway, each in the opposite direction of the previous arch, suspending the bridge over the water through the use of large steel cables. It was, Luke admitted, awe-inspiring. He shook his head. These were only two of the many modern and beautiful landmarks this city boasted.

Luke knew the Aerospace Engineering Center was one of the newest buildings in the city, but even this knowledge didn't prepare him for the wow factor. In some ways it was reminiscent of the bridge he had just crossed; this building was also composed of three arches that crisscrossed in a similar manner. But it also reminded him of what he observed with the Invocation Center. It was all glass between each of the arches. As the taxi pulled up in front of the building, a replica of one of the ships that would leave the space station and head to Mars pointed to the sky. Again he saw this pattern: the body of the ship seemed to have the arches as well. As Luke exited the taxi, he read the sign next to the monument. It stated the structure was one-tenth the size of the actual ship. He quickly did the math. This replica looked to be about three stories tall. He shook his head. The real ship would be massive.

The inside of the building looked just as impressive as the outside. The atrium, containing the welcome center and receptionist, looked like a giant terrarium—a replica of part of the rainforest. He looked up. The all-glass ceiling and walls certainly supplied the natural light for such a spectacle. A toucan flew by close to his head and landed on one of the nearby trees; at first, this startled him. But as he stared at it, he realized it was actually a hologram. He shook his head. It looked so realistic. He had to admit, their building in Houston, even though also beautiful, was beginning to look plain compared to the centers built on other continents.

He approached the receptionist desk. The woman there appeared quite attractive with her dark skin and dark wavy hair draped over her shoulders. She looked up from her holo-screen and gave a warm smile. "May I help you?"

Luke smiled back. "Yes. I'm here to see Dr. Carmella Mendez."

The woman nodded, typed something on her computer, and looked back up at him. She gestured to a small device on the counter. "Please place your thumb on the pad."

When Luke did this, a green light came on underneath his thumb. That created a déjà vu moment for him, taking him back to when he had gone through all the levels of the vault at the Paris Invocation Center, ending at the inner vault containing *T-H-B*. The woman keyed something else into her computer. "Hi, this is Maria at reception. I have a Dr. Luke Loughton here to see you." She nodded as she typed something more on her computer. "OK. I'll tell him."

She put a printed card into a plastic clip-card holder and handed it to Luke. He noticed it had his name, picture, and that he was from Houston. As she handed it to him, she smiled again. "Dr. Mendez stated she will be down in just a few minutes." She gestured to some chairs. "You can wait there for her if you wish."

Luke smiled and nodded. "Thank you." He went over to the seating area and sat on one of the chairs decorated in a leaf print on a white background. Most were decorated in that fashion, but a few were solid colors of orange, yellow, and maroon, and these were dispersed throughout the seating area. As he sat there and looked around the place, it dawned on him that these colors were the same as the flowers blooming throughout the "forest" around him.

Luke then became mesmerized by what he saw behind the receptionist desk. People seemed to disappear into, and appear from, the forest. He knew there had to be a door somewhere, but did not see it. He assumed all this was some type of optical illusion. He smiled. Some designer had way too much time, and money, on his or her hands.

In only a short while, Carmella emerged from the forest. She came over to the seating area. Luke stood and held out his hand.

Carmella shook it. "Welcome, Dr. Loughton. I hope you found your way without incident."

Luke nodded and smiled. "Please, call me Luke."

She nodded and started walking back in the direction from which she came. Luke followed. Her formality struck him as odd. He remembered her being far more personable when they had their video conference a few months back.

His mystery of the entrance was solved: they went behind a long wall which then allowed them to enter the facility itself. From the seating area, the projection on the wall made it blend in with the actual plants which grew within the atrium.

Carmella didn't speak until they reached the elevator and she pressed the button to ascend. "Brian is getting my supervisor and a few others to meet in our conference room to go over our work on the simulation and to discuss next steps."

The elevator doors opened and they stepped in along with a few other people. They exited onto the third floor.

"It will be good to see Brian again. I feel like it's been a long time."

Carmella smiled but didn't comment. He couldn't get over the apparent change in her demeanor. Maybe this was her business demeanor. But she had not been this way on the video conference, even with her supervisor present. Luke quickly reminded himself that her supervisor, Dr. Cortês, was one of The Six. Had she influenced Carmella against him?

After walking down the hallway a short distance, they came to a conference room on his right. The inside wall, all glass, was frosted up two-thirds of the way—probably to add privacy, and yet to still look modern. As he entered, he saw two people he knew and two he didn't.

Brian walked over and shook his hand. Brian then turned to introduce Luke to the others. "You know Dr. Cortês."

Luke turned and smiled. "Yes, it's good to see you again."

Dr. Cortês shook his hand and displayed a weak smile. "Welcome, Dr. Loughton."

Brian pointed to the other two in the room. "This is Dr. Hernandez and Mr. Gonzales."

Luke shook both of their hands.

Dr. Hernandez smiled. "My pleasure, Dr. Loughton. I oversee our 3-D simulator and Mr. Gonzales is my assistant."

Luke nodded. "All is in order, I hope."

Gonzales smiled and nodded. "Thanks to you."

Brian pulled out a chair. "Here, Luke. Sit here."

Everyone else took a seat. Dr. Cortês leaned forward with interlocked fingers leaning on the table. "I thought it would be good to go over the issues we encountered, compare those to your initial issues, and then alert the other three Centers of the common issues. They can then hopefully solve these on their end before we try to run through the simulation with them."

Luke nodded. "I think that's a great idea. Then, hopefully, the simulation will go more smoothly, and we would know any issues found during the simulation would be a different root cause."

Everyone nodded.

Dr. Hernandez pointed to Gonzales. "Jorge can also supply the edits we had to make and pass those along as well. It should make things go smoothly."

Luke nodded. "Can't argue with that."

Dr. Cortês sat back in her chair. "Now for the potentially controversial part."

Luke raised his eyebrows. "Oh?"

Dr. Cortês smiled. "I think Dr. Patton wants Houston to

RANDY C. DOCKENS

coordinate all of this," she said of Luke and Brian's boss, Larry. "But I would like for this second simulation coordination to be run from here. You think he'll go for that?"

Luke gave a slight shrug. "Maybe. Is there a compelling argument for it?"

Brian leaned in. "I think so."

Luke raised his eyebrows and turned his head slightly.

Brian chuckled. "No, it's not for the reason you're thinking."

Luke smiled. "And what is the compelling reason?"

"Well, if we're going to ensure each Center can work both independently and in concert, this will test whether any site, not only Houston, can achieve that." Brian shrugged. "I think it will prove to be a better test."

"Besides," Carmella said, "we'll likely do a final test with all six running simultaneously, so Houston could lead that part."

Brian nodded. "I know Larry will want to be in control of that one."

Luke agreed. "You have a good point." He shrugged. "I think Larry should go for that." He looked over at Dr. Cortês. "You want me to talk to him?"

She shook her head. "I just wanted to be sure you were in agreement." She stood. "Actually, I have to leave to attend to another matter. I'll go ahead and contact Dr. Patton and let him know we're all in agreement." She smiled. "We'll see if he also agrees."

She walked around the table. Luke stood and shook her hand before she exited.

As Luke took his chair, Carmella stood as a presentation came onscreen. "Let's go over the issues we found with our coordinated run of the simulation. I've tried to mark the ones Houston had in common with us, with Brian's—I mean, Dr. Cunningham's—help."

Luke smiled. He could tell this faux pas flustered her for a few seconds, but she recovered quickly.

Carmella smiled. "I think this can give us clues as to what we should tell the other Centers to focus on for their improvement even before we have our joint simulation with them." She turned and looked at Luke. "I know this will take some time, so I've ordered lunch to be brought in. We'll have a working lunch if that's OK?"

Luke nodded. She smiled. "OK. Let's get started."

* * * * *

Luke was surprised at how long it took to work through every issue. He remembered having a number of them, but not how many. The entire process was mentally tiring. The meeting didn't conclude until almost 16:00. After shaking everyone's hand, Hernandez and Gonzales exited.

Carmella also shook Luke's hand. "Thanks for sitting through all of that."

Luke smiled. "Sure. No problem. I think this sets us up for continued success."

She nodded. "I'll see what Dr. Cortês found out from Dr. Patton."

As she exited, Luke sat back down and looked Brian's way. "Well, you seem at home here."

Brian nodded. "I do. I really do. Any way to make it permanent?"

Luke raised his eyebrows. "That serious, huh?"

"Carmella and I make a good team. Even Dr. Cortês has recognized that."

Luke shrugged. "Well, maybe she can work out an arrangement with Larry."

Brian leaned back and crossed his arms. "You think it's that simple?"

Luke gave a slight shrug. "Can't hurt to ask, can it?"

Brian shrugged. "No, I guess not." He seemed to get lost in the very thought.

Luke chuckled. "You OK over there?"

"Hmm." Brian came back out of his thoughts. "Oh, sorry. I was just thinking."

"Hearing wedding bells?"

Brian's eyes went wide. "Uh, no." He shook his head. "I don't believe in that old-fashioned stuff."

"Oh ho!" Luke reacted with a laugh. "Was that a jibe?"

"No. But it does bring up a point."

Luke's eyebrows shot up. "And what is that?"

"Well, you've seemed to go old school on a lot of things."

"What do you mean by that?"

Brian shrugged. "Well, all of that stuff you and Sarah talked about at your wedding was just a little too far out there for me." He shook his head. "Carmella and I aren't there, and I don't think we will ever be."

Luke leaned closer to the table. "Sorry to hear that, Brian. Actually, I think we're on to something important."

Suddenly, Brian seemed to turn very serious. "You have me worried, Luke. You've gone off the reservation—and I don't think I can in good conscience allow that."

"What do you mean you can't 'allow that'?"

Brian stood. "Luke, I respect you. I really do. But you've gone too far with this faith thing. You're bordering on treason, you know."

Luke leaned back and now looked up at his colleague. "I'm sorry you feel that way, Brian." At least now he knew why he and Carmella had given him the cool treatment. It wasn't cold, but it surely wasn't warm and fuzzy either.

"Me too, Luke. One day you'll thank me."

Luke squinted and cocked his head. "Thank you for what,

Brian?"

Brian nodded toward the door.

Luke turned and immediately stood. In the doorway were two Illumi-Alliance officers. He turned back to Brian. "What have you done?"

Brian put his hand on Luke's shoulder. "It's for your own good, Luke. I can't let you destroy yourself or get others so confused you get them in trouble as well."

The officers came forward. One of them pulled out handcuffs. Brian held up his hand. "I don't think that is necessary." He looked at Luke. "You'll go with them willingly, right?"

Luke sighed. "Willingly, no. But I won't resist, if that's what you mean."

Brian headed toward the door. "I guess this is goodbye, Luke."

"Brian."

Brian turned and looked at him.

"Do you think I'll be part of the lottery?"

Brian chuckled and shook his head. "Hardly."

Luke nodded. "Just remember, if you hear of me going to Mars, just remember this conversation—and that what I told you was correct."

"Sure, Luke, sure. I'll believe that—and every other fantasy you told." He shook his head and exited.

As Luke was escorted from the building, he got quite a few looks, followed by people whispering to each other. In hindsight, maybe he should have realized that sending Brian here to be influenced by one of The Six would not have been a good idea. Still, he had hoped what he and Sarah had shared would have been received and embraced.

Luke thought he and Brian were better friends than this. And yet, it seemed Brian was just as disappointed in him as he was in Brian. In one way, it was ironic, but sobering at the same time. He found himself praying that Brian would one day remember this conversation and it would prove to be a turning point for him and Carmella.

SIXTEEN

MONITORED

Luke found himself back at the beginning: in the same room where he first met Viktoria. He looked around. Only the table, two chairs—he was in one of them—and the wall mirror were in the room. He ran his hands through his hair. What would become of him now? Was it all over?

The door swung open and in walked Viktoria and Caine. Before he could say anything, she gave a quick but imperceptible shake of her head. He remained quiet. She walked around to his side of the table and placed a large envelope before him.

He looked up at her. "What's this?"

She walked to the other side of the table and paced while holding her hands behind her back as she talked. Her voice was matter-of-fact, on the verge of condescending. "Those, Dr. Loughton, are legal documents to let you know how much trouble you are in."

Caine nodded. "And every word you speak in our presence is recorded." He shrugged. "Just so you know." Luke looked at him, but didn't respond. His attention turned back to Viktoria.

"You and your wife will be under constant guard," she

began. "You will be able to do nothing without our knowledge. Windows in your apartment have been alarmed. We will be watching your apartment from across the hallway to observe anyone who comes and leaves. We will tail you to and from work. Additional security cameras have been installed at the Aerospace Engineering Center. We will be watching you from the security office so as not to frighten other workers." She walked over and tapped the envelope. "Read where you can and cannot travel while at work. All privileges will be taken away if you violate any of the parameters stated in this document." She turned and looked at him. "Read everything in the envelope. Understand?"

He slowly nodded his head.

Caine walked up to him with something in his hands. "And just to be certain we know where you are at all times . . . "

Luke leaned away from him. "What is that, and what are you going to do?"

Caine smiled. "Don't worry. This is just a GPS tracker. It goes just under your skin." He placed a small gun at the base of Luke's neck, toward the back, and pulled the trigger. Luke winced and rubbed the spot with his hand. He could feel a capsular something just under the skin. How degrading. He felt as though his rights were violated. He shook his head. Who was he kidding? They were *definitely* violated.

Viktoria opened the door. "We will escort you back to your apartment."

Luke stood and walked out with them and stepped into a black sedan. Viktoria sat in back with him and Caine in the front. She announced their destination and the car pulled out into traffic. The two of them said nothing, so neither did he. How could he? If everything was being recorded, how would he ever get to speak to Viktoria and find out anything?

Nothing was said between any of them in the twenty minutes or so it took for the taxi to reach Luke and Sarah's apartment complex. Both Viktoria and Caine walked with him to his apartment. They stood in the hallway until he entered. Once inside, he looked through the front door peephole. Both entered the apartment just across the hallway. Luke turned, leaned against the door, and sighed. This was going to be quite an adjustment.

He expected Sarah to be home, but didn't receive a greeting. He walked into the living area and kitchen, but both were empty. He walked into the bedroom and saw her in bed. He decided to let her sleep and get needed rest. As he turned, he saw an envelope on the dresser, one that matched the envelope in his hand. So Sarah had been given rules to follow as well. Luke corrected his thought. "Rules" that were meant to be strictly enforced, that is.

Luke went to the living room and sat on the sofa as he opened his envelope. He pulled out a four-page document. He shook his head. Does it really take four pages to tell him what he can and cannot do? He scanned the document. It had the usual legalese mumbo-jumbo language interspersed with rules he was commanded to follow. It looked like he could travel unescorted anywhere on his floor of the office building, the cafeteria, and, since Sarah was a part of this, her floor as well. Traveling to any other floor would require an escort. He shook his head and made a grimace. That would be most inconvenient.

He was about to stuff the papers back into the envelope when he realized the envelope contained something else. He turned it upside down and shook it. A smaller envelope fell out. It had his name written on the front. He opened it. Inside was a handwritten letter. He scanned to the end. It was from Viktoria. He then read it in its entirety.

Luke, good news and bad. First of all, I was reinstated as an

Illumi-Alliance officer by Rosencrantz himself. He's convinced my arrest, and yours, was a power play by Simone Mercure and a personal vendetta against him to make it look like his facility is more inefficient than the others. Unfortunately, he could not reinstate you the same way. He had to compromise. He did reach out to René Mauchard, who has always been a personal friend, but did not receive the support he expected. An Illumi-Alliance escort was his compromise as he needs both you and Sarah to complete your function to keep the Mars mission here at Houston on schedule. Please note, Caine and I are on your side, but our hands are tied, and all communication between you and us is being monitored and recorded.

Luke put his hand to his mouth, tugged at his lips, and read the note again. So, even The Six were not in complete alignment with each other. Would there be a way to exploit that? He looked at his watch. It was getting late. This was a topic for tomorrow.

He took a shower and eased into bed while trying to keep Sarah from waking. She stirred, scooted up next to him, and went back to her slumber. He put his arm around her. At least they were in this together and could still be together. For that much he was appreciative. He said a prayer for guidance and protection, but fatigue overtook his thoughts and he fell asleep before he could even finish with an "Amen."

* * * * *

Luke stirred. An aroma woke him up further. He sat up. Bacon. He looked over and saw Sarah's side of the bed empty. He walked to the kitchen and found Sarah putting scrambled eggs on two plates.

"Aren't you the industrious one?"

She turned and smiled as she brought the plates to the table. She reached over and gave him a kiss. "I just thought with this being our first day back together, we'd do something out of our normal routine."

Luke laughed as he sat. "You mean, being arrested and having an Illumi-Alliance shadow isn't out of our normal routine?"

She picked up his plate and walked toward the counter. "Well, if you think that is different enough."

"Hey." He jumped up and wrapped his arms around her. "Hold on there." He kissed the nape of her neck, taking the plate from her at the same time and setting it back on the table. "I accept your out-of-the-ordinary."

Sarah laughed. "You mean your stomach accepts it."

He turned her around and put his forehead to hers. "Yes, that is true." He kissed her on her nose. "It's asking if I may eat it?"

She laughed. "Yes, you may."

They sat down and ate. After a few bites, Luke stopped and looked at Sarah.

She looked up. "What? What are you thinking?" She smiled. "I can see those wheels turning."

"I was just thinking about how much has changed for us in a short period of time." He shook his head ever so slightly. "This should be one of the happiest times of our lives, yet it's shrouded with so many complications."

Sarah gave her own small shrug. "At least we're still together. That's the main thing."

Luke took another bite and nodded. "You're right. I should be grateful for that." He set his fork down. "But how are we going to continue with our Bible study or talk to any of the others? Whoever is seen with us will likely be candidates for the Illumi-Alliance to follow and question."

Sarah finished her last bite and pushed her plate aside,

taking a sip of coffee. "Well, they likely already are, so I say we continue with everything just as we've been doing." She looked into his eyes. "We need to stay in as much of a normal practice and routine as possible. Yeah, it's risky, but otherwise we'll always be second-guessing ourselves."

Luke twisted the corner of his mouth and nodded. "Makes sense." He shrugged. "We can leave it up to all of our friends. We'll still invite and work with those who want to come."

Sarah nodded. "From Viktoria's and Caine's perspectives, it will look like people are just coming by. Most bring a snack or dessert of some kind, so it will just look like a social gathering."

Luke chuckled. "Which it is. Just our conversations go deeper than most."

Sarah smiled as she stood. She put their dishes in the sink. "Ready to go?" She turned. "Our shadows are waiting."

SEVENTEEN

René's Surprise

Philippe walked down the hall toward his office while reading the daily news on his phone. Suddenly, something felt strange. He looked up. Sonja's desk had been moved to his side of the building. She was readjusting her desk knickknacks as he neared his office door. "What's going on, Sonja?"

She looked up with raised eyebrows. "Of all people, I thought you would know. Your brother just stated I should work more closely with you from now on."

Philippe squinted, as though confused, but didn't say anything. He turned to enter his office.

"Oh, Dr. Mercure is in your office waiting for you."

He glanced back at Sonja and nodded, trying to cover up his confusion as much as possible. He felt like he was in the middle of a prank.

As he walked in, Simone sat on the yellow sofa reading something on her tablet.

"What's going on? Any idea?"

She looked up and smiled. "*You're* what's going on. I told you. You should become more prominent—and it's happening."

He sat down on the sofa next to her and turned sideways to face her better. "Simone, I'm still not following."

She patted his knee. "The compound is working on your brother. He apparently has decided you are the more important of the two of you, and so Sonja should work more for you than for him." She gave a bright smile. "Congratulations."

He cocked his head. "There's something you're not telling me."

"I'd rather let your brother tell you his plan."

"His plan?"

She nodded. "I only know because I gave him his supplements this morning. He was all chipper and gung ho. I . . . I don't want to spoil the surprise."

He knew Simone was up to something, he just couldn't figure out what—or, for that matter, figure her out.

She pointed to her tablet. "Did you read the news I sent you?"

He shook his head. "Haven't had a chance to catch up yet."

She nodded. "Well, let me fill you in." Her smiled turned to a frown. "Rosencrantz reinstated Agent Komcova into the Illumi-Alliance. But, both Dr. Morgan and Dr. Loughton are under constant surveillance."

Philippe put his hand on her shoulder. "Simone, I know you say you don't, but it almost seems you have a personal vendetta against these people."

"What?" She shook her head. "No. No, Philippe. I just think we should be observant of those around them as they seem to attract the resistant crowd."

The door to the conference room opened and René poked his head in. "OK time to talk?"

Philippe nodded and motioned for his brother to step in.

Simone closed her tablet and smiled. She stood. "I need to

leave and get back to the university anyway."

René held up his palm. "No, no. Please stay, if you can."

Simone nodded and returned to a seat on the sofa.

René began to pace. He looked excited. Philippe realized he had not seen him this energetic in a long time. René must be about to tell him the news Simone had mentioned, Philippe assumed.

"René, you obviously have something to say, so just say it." He gestured toward the chair opposite him. "Please, sit and let me know what's on your mind. Does this have anything to do with Sonja's move to my side of the room?"

René sat and nodded. He smiled, but then stood back up and paced again. "Philippe, I'm very excited about this. You may think this is a rash decision . . . " He stopped and looked at Philippe. "But I assure you, I have given this a lot of thought."

Philippe chuckled. "OK, René. You've built up the suspense. Just tell me."

"I've decided to go on the Mars mission."

Philippe's jaw dropped. This was not the news he had expected. "You . . . you've what?" He shook his head quickly. "What would make you even consider that?"

René held up his hands. "Just hear me out. We're creating a new world on Mars. Don't we want to be in control of that world as well?"

Philippe put his hand to his chin. He had not thought that far ahead. He had been so focused on his father's vision and how to enact it that he hadn't considered who would actually govern the colony. It did in fact now seem like a gap in their plans—but one that René had apparently given thought to. "Well, I suppose, but . . . " He gestured to René. "You really want to do this?"

René nodded. "Plus, it will give more credence to the mission and quell a lot of the rumors about its purpose." He smiled. "This will ensure we keep total control. You here, me there."

Philippe stood and put his hand on René's shoulder. "René, you can be so unpredictable sometimes." He looked into René's eyes. "If that's what you want to do . . . "

René nodded.

Philippe shrugged. "Then, OK."

René smiled. "Thanks, Philippe. I was hoping you'd be supportive. Now, about my office . . . "

Philippe held up his hand. "Oh, nothing to worry about. You're my brother. It'll be here when you decide to return."

René shook his head. "No. No, we need to make plans. You'll need someone to help you run things here."

Philippe cocked his head. "You have someone in mind already?"

René put his hands on his hips and displayed a large grin. "Isn't it obvious?"

Philippe shook his head ever so slightly.

René pointed toward Simone. "Dr. Mercure, of course."

EIGHTEEN

SCOTT'S ANNOUNCEMENT

Luke finished his water bottle and sat it back on his tray. He looked up and saw the increased number of cameras installed in the cafeteria's ceiling. All that work for him and Sarah. No, it wasn't all just for them. The leaders were wanting the two of them to lead the Illumi-Alliance to other potential suspects.

He looked over at Sarah, who was finishing her salad. "Sarah, are you sure we should still host our Bible study tonight?"

Sarah looked up with eyes slightly wide. "What makes you ask that?" She put her fork down. "I thought we already discussed this."

"Yeah, I know." He sighed. "I just don't want to get anyone else placed under surveillance like we are."

Sarah put her hand on his. "Luke, I understand that, but better to be under surveillance with a secure future than the alternative."

Luke gave a weak smile and nodded. "You're right." He patted her hand. "You usually are."

Sarah pushed her tray aside. "Who's coming from your area?"

Luke smiled. "I think Scott is a definite. He seems pretty gung ho." His smile dissipated as he shook his head. "Larry, unfortunately, is on the fence." He shrugged. "So, I don't really know if he will or not. Brian is still in Brasilia." He sighed, followed by a small chuckle. "He tried to act happy I was still working, but his surprise and disappointment came through at our last teleconference."

Sarah patted his hand. "Don't mark him off. He could still turn around."

Luke gave a small smile and nodded. "So, who's coming that you invited?"

Sarah gave a small shrug. "Both Kathleen and Ken also are on the fence." She smiled. "I think my cupcakes with chocolate-peanut butter frosting may be the lure to get Ken there, though."

Luke laughed. "Whatever works, right?"

Sarah nodded. "I think Jason and Jared will be there, also."

Luke's head jerked back slightly. "Really? The last time I talked to Jared he still seemed very hesitant."

Sarah shrugged. "Well, Jason told me they have started reading Scripture together."

Luke's eyes widened. "That's awesome."

Sarah nodded. "Certainly a step in the right direction." She looked at her watch. "Oh, I have to get back. We're doing a mock run-through of putting people into hyperstasis."

"When do you think that will actually start?"

She shook her head. "I haven't heard an exact date yet, but it will be soon."

Again, Luke could only manage a small smile. "I guess my dream of us walking glove in glove on Mars may actually come true."

"I'm not willing to count a dream as prophecy—not yet anyway." She stood and blew him a kiss. "I'll see you at home."

Luke nodded. She left as he stayed at the table a bit longer. He just wanted to be by himself for a short while. He looked at his watch. A very short while. He knew he and Sarah would likely be forced to be on the Mars mission even if not part of the trumped-up lottery. Yet, as long as he was with Sarah, did he care? He half smiled. The astrophysicist in him thought that would be kind of cool.

"Sorry to disturb your meditation."

Luke jerked slightly. "Larry. Anything wrong?"

"We're ready for the final simulation. I need you and Scott to man it from Houston."

Luke squinted. "Wouldn't you want to start first thing in the morning?"

Larry chuckled. "Yes. But it's always an inconvenient time somewhere."

"Good point." Luke stood and followed Larry back to their floor. He sighed somewhere deep inside himself. Of all days, this would happen on the day when everyone was supposed to come over. He hoped he wouldn't be late.

* * * * *

Once the simulation started, Luke was pleasantly surprised that all he and Scott had to do was monitor the progress. It was, so far, going flawlessly.

Scott looked over and smiled. "I guess we did good."

Luke chuckled. "Yeah, I think we did. I'm amazed at how well it's working."

Scott nodded. "Hopefully, the real thing will go as smoothly."

"How long do you think this will take? You still coming over?"

"Yeah. I'm looking forward to it." He looked at his holo-screen and then back at Luke. "If we don't have any issues, then we could be done by 18:00, I would think."

Luke nodded. That would give them just enough time to get to his apartment, he reasoned, before everyone would arrive.

* * * * *

Despite Luke's hopes, 18:00 came and went. Luke texted Sarah to let her know both he and Scott would be late. He hated leaving her to get everything ready by herself. Hopefully, she would understand.

By the time the simulation ended and a debrief was held, it was 19:05. Home being only a short walk should allow them to make it by 19:30, Luke reasoned. He texted Sarah, and Scott followed him out. Viktoria kept her distance, farther than normal, as they walked home. Scott didn't seem to notice, but Luke knew he would have to tell everyone so they could make their own decision about the risk of continuing with these meetings.

Luke looked at Scott. Scott seemed very chipper. "Well, you're certainly in a good mood after putting in a long day," Luke said.

Scott grinned. "I was going to wait and tell everyone, but I'll go ahead and tell you. I did it, Luke. I put my faith in the Messiah. I've decided to put my future in his hands."

Luke stopped and grabbed his arm. "Scott, that's . . . that's awesome." He gave him a quick pat on the back of his shoulder. Luke shook his finger at Scott. "I kept thinking something was different about you today."

Scott laughed. "I feel different. Lighter, somewhat. If that makes any sense."

Luke laughed with him and nodded. "Believe it or not, it makes perfect sense."

When they arrived at the apartment, Luke was surprised at the number who had joined the gathering. As he closed the door, he looked through the peephole and saw Viktoria enter the apartment across the hall.

As he turned, he saw Ken munching on a cupcake. He smiled. It appeared Sarah's tactic had worked. Kathleen, along with Jason and Jared, also were present. Larry, it seemed, had opted out.

He walked over to Sarah and gave her a kiss. "Sorry for being late."

She smiled. "No problem. We're just socializing at the moment."

Luke walked over to Scott, who had grabbed a plate of refreshments. "Hey, Scott. No pressure, but do you want to tell everyone about your decision?"

Scott smiled and nodded. "Sure. I'd like that."

After a few more minutes of small talk, Luke asked everyone to sit down. Some sat on the sofa, some on the ottoman, and some on the floor. He decided to go over the first three chapters of John, and the discussion went well and was lively.

After the study of John closed, Luke gestured to Scott.

Scott amazed him. As soon as he started, it seemed everyone became transfixed by his story. Apparently, hearing the impact God had on a person's life was quite powerful. Luke couldn't tell if anyone thought differently, but they certainly seemed to respect what Scott shared.

Luke ended their session with prayer. "Feel free to stay longer." He paused, then cleared his throat. "One final thing for this evening. Sarah and I need to let you know something that has occurred, and is occurring. We don't want to be perceived as hiding anything from you."

Several looked at each other and then back at him. Obviously, they didn't have any idea what Luke was referring to.

Luke took a deep breath. "I was arrested by the Illumi-Alliance when I was in Brasilia. Both Sarah and I are now tailed constantly by Illumi-Alliance officers when we're outside our apartment."

Jaws could be seen dropping around the room. Scott seemed to be the only one not surprised.

Kathleen was the first to speak up. "What on earth for?"

"Apparently, Brian and Carmella told Dr. Cortês, and they felt our talk about the Scriptures and what we shared at our wedding was treasonous."

Several had worried looks on their faces. Luke could tell most felt uncomfortable. The question was: by how much? And how would this knowledge affect them?

Sarah jumped in. "We want you to know this because if we continue to meet it could raise the suspicion of the Illumi-Alliance. We feel it is a risk worth taking because this information is so important and affects your eternity. Yet we want you to make your own decision."

Luke nodded. "As this is the first meeting since we've been under scrutiny, it will appear just as a casual get-together." He gestured toward Sarah. "We feel that learning more about Scripture together is important. You have to decide that for yourself. We have a standing invitation on this night every week. We hope you continue with us."

No one said anything. The only one who looked confident was Scott. Maybe he could help the others come around. Several of them stayed longer for small talk. It appeared most enjoyed just being together outside of a work setting. Ken had another cupcake before he left. Sarah packed up two more that he could take with him.

Scott, the last to leave, gave Luke a quick, heartfelt hug. "Thanks, Luke, for everything. Without you, I never would have known I was looking for something different." He smiled.

"I'll definitely be here next week. I still have a lot of questions."

Luke patted his shoulder. "Wonderful. I look forward to discussing things with you." He smiled back at Scott. "We can learn from each other."

Scott laughed. "We'll see about that. Let's each write out questions and see if the other can answer them. Then we'll seek the answers together."

Luke bumped his fist into Scott's shoulder. "Deal."

After Scott left, Luke closed the door and turned to Sarah. "You think we scared them off?"

Sarah gave a small shrug. "I don't know. It looks like Scott is definitely on board. I guess we'll find out next week by who shows up."

NINETEEN

CLANDESTINE POSTINGS

A week later, only Scott showed up. He had many questions. Some Luke felt confident in answering. Others, he told Scott he would have to investigate.

"Scott, I can't believe all the reading you've done already," Luke told him near the end of the evening.

Scott grinned. "Inquiring minds want to know."

Luke laughed. "Yeah, I just wish the others did, too."

"Luke, they're scared."

Luke nodded. "And rightly so. But still . . . "

"I know." Scott shut off his phone and put it in his pocket. "I've talked to some of them. They're still interested." He bobbled his head, as though only somewhat sure of that. "To a certain degree."

Scott paused. Luke looked at him expectantly.

"I think I have a plan."

Luke's eyes widened. "Yeah? What is it?"

"Well, no one's following me." He smiled. "Yet."

Luke chuckled and nodded.

"So, I thought I'd keep this appointment with you and then

have the others come to my place and then share with them what I learned. It will help me reinforce what I learn and help them, hopefully, come around."

Luke put his hand on Scott's shoulder. "Scott, that is brilliant. Best idea ever."

Scott laughed. "I thought so."

Luke pushed on his shoulder and laughed. "Mr. Modest. But, hey, it is a great plan. Then they don't have to worry about being observed with us. At least for a while."

Scott stood and headed for the door. "I'll let you know next week if I get any traction on my plan."

After Scott left, Luke stopped what he was doing and said a prayer for him.

* * * * *

The next couple of weeks became a time of adjusting to a new norm. Viktoria and Caine followed Luke and Sarah everywhere. Yet that turned into a blessing in disguise. Ever since Viktoria started taking the compound Matteo synthesized, her memories didn't get reprogrammed. She became a conduit of information from everyone else. There were a few places along the walk between his apartment and office without any surveillance; Viktoria knew these provided small windows of opportunity. That's where she would pass along notes from Oliver, Maher, and Jeremy. With Caine on their side, Viktoria didn't have to hide things from him.

Luke also used this method of exchange to pass along questions he and Scott were wrestling with. Viktoria got them to Maher and then passed answers back.

* * * * *

One morning when they were in the area of no cameras, Luke passed more questions to Viktoria.

"Luke, I just want you to know: you're helping all of us by this."

Luke turned up a brow. "What do you mean?"

"The questions you and Scott have, we all have. We all get to read the answers Maher provides back to you."

Caine nodded. "We're all benefiting." He shook Luke's hand. "Thank you."

Before Luke could reply, Viktoria shoved a piece of paper into his pocket and pushed him along. "We have to get moving. We've been out of camera too long."

As they walked, Sarah looked at him and smiled. She didn't say anything, but she, like Luke, was proud that in spite of their circumstances, God was still using them. Once at his desk, Luke read Viktoria's note. Jeremy wanted him and Sarah to meet him and Natalia at Continental Drift that evening. He texted Sarah to wait for him at her office before leaving for home, but left out any details.

Neither he nor Sarah had time to meet for lunch. That also seemed to be a new normal for them. The work for both of them had become more and more hectic. The launch date for the Mars mission was fast approaching, so they felt an urgency to get everything, and everyone, prepared for it.

At the end of the day, Luke stopped by Sarah's office. She was leaving the medical department as he arrived.

She smiled. "Well, your timing is getting better."

He kissed her cheek. "I guess you didn't get my text."

"Text?" She pulled out her phone. After viewing the message, she gave a sheepish grin and sighed. "Sorry. It's just been so busy today."

"That's OK." He held out his arm and she took it. "I thought I'd better come down early since I never heard back from you."

She squeezed his arm. "So what's up?"

"I got a note from Jeremy. He wants us to meet him at Continental Drift."

Sarah's eyes widened. "Now?"

Luke nodded. "Something wrong?"

She sighed. "No, not really. It's just . . . I'm very tired."

He started to say something, but Sarah jumped back in. "I know this is likely important, and we haven't seen them in a long time."

He smiled and rubbed her shoulder. "You're a trooper."

As they descended to the lobby, Luke pressed his taxi app. As they stepped from the building, the taxi pulled up. Once in, Luke gave the destination and sat back as Sarah nestled up to him.

After about a minute, she glanced up. "I found out today the lottery is being announced tomorrow."

Luke looked down at her. "Really? How many are being chosen?"

"I think twenty-five hundred on each continent."

Luke's eyes widened. "Wow. That's fifteen thousand people."

"During the mission, the majority will go into hyperstasis. Some will remain awake."

"It's starting to feel surreal. Preparing for such an event is one thing. Having it *happen* is quite another."

Sarah nodded but didn't look up at him. They remained quiet for the rest of the ride.

"Destination achieved."

Luke inserted his credit disk and they stepped from the taxi. As they entered the restaurant, the maître d' recognized them, giving a broad smile.

"Dr. Loughton. Dr. Morgan. A table is waiting for you in the back of the first floor."

Luke nodded and they headed into the bar area and walked

through toward the back. Luke recognized Jeremy as they approached and then saw Natalia. They all gave hugs.

"Lukey. Sarah. My, it's good to see you again." Natalia smiled and gestured for them to sit.

A waiter brought drinks and several appetizers. Jeremy picked up his glass and held it in front of everyone. They all toasted. "To friendship." Each responded in kind. Jeremy pointed to the food. "I thought you might be hungry."

Luke put food on his plate. "Jeremy, I received your letter. What's going on?"

Luke looked around and saw Viktoria and Caine sitting at a table with clear sight of them. In one way, it was comforting to know it was Viktoria tailing them. Yet Luke had to admit he wondered what she actually reported back. He turned back to Jeremy.

Jeremy followed his gaze and patted his arm. "Just be thankful it's Viktoria—our Viktoria."

Luke nodded. "It's still weird, though."

Jeremy nodded. "But she's been a big help relaying information between us."

Luke couldn't argue with that point. Yes, it would be much worse if any other Illumi-Alliance soldiers were the ones watching them.

Jeremy put his hand on Luke's shoulder. "I want you to know your correspondence to Maher is helping way more people than just the two of you."

Luke nodded. "Yeah, Viktoria mentioned that."

Natalia shook her head. "But it's even more." She smiled. "Maher and Clarity of The Way are posting your questions—and his answers—to help everyone who reads his posts."

Sarah leaned in. "That's great. But why?"

Natalia gave a small shrug. "*Everyone* has the same questions. We're all new to this, so providing answers to your questions is helping everyone learn and grow."

Sarah looked from Natalia to Jeremy. "And who exactly is this Clarity of The Way?"

Jeremy smiled. "Maher introduced me to one member of the group. He went by the name of Paul." He shrugged. "I'm not sure if that is his real name or not. Somehow, I kind of doubt it. Yet he seemed very personable and really sincere in getting this information out."

Natalia poured more water for everyone. "Actually, Lukey, this is crucial. Listen to this: Paul told us his group is the one who sent you those pieces of confetti."

Luke cocked his head. "My guess was Oliver. Well, at least the first one."

Natalia nodded. "Yes, but they planted the idea through an anonymous contact." She smiled. "You see, they had their eye on you for a long time—just like Oliver had."

"Why?"

Jeremy chuckled. "Isn't it obvious? They too were looking for immunes who could help them advance the cause. They recruited Oliver, and he, you. Now they're helping Maher."

Natalia added, "Isn't it amazing how God orchestrated this whole thing?"

Luke nodded. "Yes it is, but how? How did they get these pieces of paper to fall right where they wanted them so I would find them?" He shrugged. "After all, the piece of confetti could have landed anywhere."

Natalia smiled. "Nanites."

Luke scrunched his face. "Nanites?"

"Makes sense," Sarah said.

Luke turned to Sarah with the same confused look. "It does?"

Sarah nodded. "Nanites are now being used in all sorts of things. We're using them to help wounds heal faster." She raised her eyebrows, looking at Luke. "And they're programmable."

Luke looked at Jeremy, still not sure how all this worked. "So . . ."

Jeremy smiled. "So, they infused the paper with nanites. They then spent several months learning how to control them so they could make the paper float through the air and land exactly where they wanted it to."

Luke tried to process all this. He felt somewhat like a pawn. Yet, would he have changed anything? Probably not. In spite of the circumstances, he was in a much better position with a secure future.

Luke's attention turned back to Jeremy. "Is that what you invited us here to tell us?"

Jeremy nodded. "Partly. The other part is to ask if you have subleased your apartment."

Luke shook his head. "No, not yet. Why?"

"Would you mind Maher using it?"

Luke's head jerked back slightly. "What for? He isn't still living in Hawaii?"

"Apparently he barely escaped an arrest by an I-A soldier. Paul stated they have been moving him around to various locations so no one can track his location. Since your old apartment would not be in his name, it seemed like a logical solution."

Luke put his hand to his chin and thought. It could get him into further trouble, but he would likely wind up being sent to Mars no matter what he did. Besides, if Maher was helping so many people, he certainly wanted to be a part of that.

He looked at Sarah. She nodded.

He turned back to Jeremy. "That would be fine."

Jeremy patted his arm. "Great. Thanks, Luke." His expression suddenly turned very serious. "Just one thing."

Luke raised his eyebrows.

"You can't visit him. Even though he's close, we can't afford for his cover to get blown."

Natalia nodded. "Even though Viktoria and, now, Caine are on our side, we don't know what gets reported or how much say they have in what gets reported. For all we know, the I-A have people watching them as well."

Luke nodded. "Understood."

He hated he wouldn't be able to see such a good friend who would be living so close, but Jeremy was right. The cause was too important for personal desires.

Jeremy stood, shook Luke's hand, and kissed Sarah on the cheek. Natalia hugged Sarah and kissed Luke's cheek. Jeremy smiled. "I hope we can meet again soon. Please stay and have dinner if you want." He looked at Sarah and winked. "Besides, you still have several free dinners left."

Sarah smiled and nodded. After Jeremy and Natalia left, Luke turned her way. "What do you want to do?"

She put her head on his shoulder. "Can we just go home? The appetizers were enough for me tonight."

Luke smiled. "You hear the bed calling?"

She nodded. "Loud and clear."

He helped her up and they left. Their shadows followed. A taxi was waiting. As the taxi took them home, Luke thought about what Natalia had said. It did seem God had coordinated a lot of things.

Sarah patted his chest. "You OK?"

He nodded as he rubbed her upper arm. "Yeah, just thinking." He looked down at her. "Strange how Maher has become our Bible guru."

"Well, he did seem to pick up quickly on the information his father left him. I'm sure Clarity of The Way is also helping."

Luke nodded. If they were the ones coordinating all that

had happened, they must know more than he and Sarah did. Yet they also could be like Oliver—needing someone immune to take things to the next level. He smiled. It seemed Maher was doing just that.

TWENTY

LOTTERY

After dropping Sarah off on the fourth floor, Luke rode the elevator up to his work floor. He entered to a flurry of activity going on around him. Normally, he was one of the first few to arrive—but this was not the case today.

He found Scott. "What's going on? Why is everyone here so early?"

Scott laughed and patted his shoulder. "Clearly, you don't read much."

"Oh, the lottery is being announced today."

"Ah, so you do know your current events."

Luke smiled and gave Scott a silly grimace. "I just haven't gotten excited about it."

Scott brought his voice down to a whisper. "You know something. What is it?"

Luke matched his volume. "I won't be chosen by the lottery, but I'll be on the Mars mission."

Scott's eyes widened. "How on earth do you know that?"

"They need me—and you—to get the Mars mission off the ground, so they're not going to make us part of the lottery even if we entered."

Scott furrowed his brow. "OK, that makes sense. So, how do you know you're still going on the Mars mission?"

"Well, you're well aware of this: the Illumi-Alliance is already tailing me because I'm like their number one immune enemy." He shook his head. "They're not going to allow me to stay here. They think I'm too much trouble."

Scott got a worried look on his face. "Isn't there anything we can do?"

Luke shook his head, then raised his eyebrows. "Well, there is one thing."

Scott gave him an expectant look. "Sure, anything."

"I told Brian if I'm not on the lottery, but I still wind up on the Mars mission, then everything I told him would be true. Help him to see that and take that step like you did." Luke shrugged. "Maybe this will be the event to jolt him into belief."

Scott nodded, but before he could respond, Larry came into the room to call for everyone's attention.

"OK, everyone. The lottery is announced. There is an e-mail in your in-box with the link."

Everyone scurried to their desks. Luke looked over Scott's shoulder as Scott pulled up the list. It was divided by continent, and then names were placed in alphabetical order by last name.

Scott scrolled through the list. "Wow. This is a lot of people. I wonder how many are there."

"Fifteen thousand."

Scott stopped and looked up at him. "How do you know that? I haven't even gotten to the total."

Luke shrugged. "Something I heard."

Scott scrolled to the bottom. "You're right. Fifteen thousand." He looked back up at Luke. "If I didn't know you so well, I'd say you were scary."

Luke laughed and patted Scott's shoulder. "So, see anyone you recognize?"

Scott went to the North American roster and slowly scrolled. Luke pointed. "Hey, there's Dwayne Campbell from propulsion."

Scott nodded. "I wonder how he feels about that."

Luke shook his head. In a way, he thought it odd because Dwayne was certainly not an immune. Maybe they added some non-immunes who had critical positions for what the colony would need.

Scott pointed out a few others he knew from work, but Luke only knew them by name. He went back to his desk and looked through the roster of other continents to see if he recognized anyone. From Asia, he recognized Qian Chen. Again, as far as he knew, Dr. Chen was also not an immune. He sucked in a short breath. There on the list was Dr. Liwei. *So, they still have him after all,* Luke thought. When he came to the roster for Europe, one name leaped off the screen at him: René Mauchard. Luke couldn't believe it. Would he willingly go to Mars?

He looked around for Larry to see if he knew anything about why René would be on the mission, but Scott got his attention first.

"Click the other link in the e-mail. Mauchard is giving a pep talk to those chosen."

"What?" He hurried to his desk, pulled up the document on his holo-computer, and clicked the link. A video of René appeared. He seemed to be seated at his office desk. He had a bright smile on his face.

My fellow citizens. This is truly a great day. For all those chosen, congratulations. You are about to make history. And as many of you have observed, I, too, will be traveling with you. This mission is much too significant for me to not be a part of it.

I hope this also assures you of our dedication to this mission and its purpose. Some have spread false rumors about the purpose of this mission. I hope that by my going, it puts those rumors to rest. Feel proud you are advancing the footprint of mankind. You will go down in history as some of the bravest souls who ever lived. Now, let's prepare. Success to us all.

Luke looked up at Scott, who raised his eyebrows. Luke shook his head. Scott nodded. Luke knew this was somehow a smokescreen. He had to admit, though, that by René Mauchard going, it would be harder to convince people the entire purpose of the mission was to get immunes off the earth. Deep down, he knew Philippe and Simone were somehow behind this. That was the only thing that would make sense. He sighed. But who would believe that?

His phone beeped. It read: Medical Department. "Astrophysics, Loughton speaking."

"Luke, did you see the roster?" Sarah sounded panicked.

"Are you all right?"

"I'm just a little unnerved. I know several of the people on the list." Her voice grew very low. "But our names weren't on it."

Luke turned away from his desk and also lowered his voice as much as he could. "Sarah, I'm afraid that doesn't mean anything. They need us right up until the launch itself. We can't be on the official roster."

"What are you saying? You mean there's an unofficial roster?"

"I'm pretty sure of it. I just don't know how many are on it."

"Luke, what are we going to do?"

"Sarah, first of all, stay calm. Remember who's in control."

He heard her breathe in and force the air from her mouth. "OK. Yeah, you're right."

"Hang in there. We'll talk more tonight. OK?" He tried to

sound supportive.

"Yeah. Until tonight."

He turned around to hang up the phone. He jerked slightly, seeing Larry standing there. "Oh, Larry. You startled me. What's up?"

Larry pulled up a chair and sat next to him. "I just wanted to be sure you and Dr. Campbell finished all of your propulsion simulations. I saw him on the list and knew he would now be very distracted."

Luke nodded. "Yeah, Larry. We finished those some time ago." He looked at Larry more closely, trying to read him. *Is he depressed?* "You OK?"

Larry nodded. "Just wanted to be sure. That's all."

"Larry, you wanted to go. Didn't you?"

Larry leaned back and folded his arms. "Yeah. I sort of had my hopes up." He shrugged and sat up straighter, giving a slight chuckle. "Well, it was a lottery after all. I shouldn't have set the expectation."

"I'm sorry, Larry." He tried to ease the sting. "After this, it could become a more routine mission. Maybe there will be another chance sooner rather than later."

Larry gave a weak smile. "Thanks for trying to cheer me up." He stood and patted Luke on his shoulder.

Luke watched him walk away. Poor guy. He'd spent his whole career preparing for the mission. Yet, there was still a lot for him to do here to contribute. Next time he saw Larry, he'd try and remind him of that.

His mind turned to Dwayne. He should go and congratulate the guy. After all, they had spent a lot of time together on the propulsion simulation. He deserved a congratulatory visit.

Luke walked toward the elevator, but then remembered he had to let Viktoria know where he was heading. He dialed the special number he had been provided. "This is Luke. I'm headed down to propulsion." He disconnected without waiting for a reply. He wasn't going to let them dictate where he went.

He took the elevator down to the main floor and then took another set of elevators down three levels. The backside of the building lay on a large downslope that was used as a testing area for some of the space equipment, including scaled-down versions of the engines. He walked in to a huge celebration taking place.

When Dwayne saw him, he motioned for Luke to come over. "Luke, good to see you. I guess you heard the news?"

Luke smiled and nodded, patting Dwayne on his shoulder. "Congratulations, buddy. Looks like you're excited about the news."

Dwayne smiled. "Absolutely. My wife, Sherry, is ecstatic. She's wanted to go to Mars ever since she knew I was working on the mission."

Someone came by and put a glass in Luke's hand. Dwayne laughed. "Go ahead. Enjoy some champagne."

Luke shook his head. "Dwayne, it isn't even ten o'clock in the morning yet."

"Aw, go on, Luke. This is a celebration."

Luke pretended to drink some of the champagne. Dwayne smiled and patted Luke's arm. "That-a-boy."

Dwayne circled and several of his coworkers started dancing with him while others sang a song. Luke couldn't make out the words, the singers being off-key; he couldn't make out the tune either. Obviously, no work would get done here today.

He waved to Dwayne, who smiled and waved back before his other buddies dragged him back to their dance routine. Luke chuckled and shook his head. He hoped none of the managers came down here. There would likely be a few citations given.

As he walked back to the elevators, Viktoria was waiting.

She put something in his pocket as he walked by.

The ride back to his floor was uneventful, but once back at his desk, Luke read the paper she had slipped him.

Be vigilant. All prisons full.

TWENTY-ONE

Simone Moves In

Philippe walked toward his office as he talked on his phone. He could feel annoyance rise within him with each step.

"What? Yes, start this week. Well, put the physician coordinators on the shuttle with the pris— . . . I mean, the lottery winners." Philippe shook his head. "No, this week." His face reddened, and his voice became more forceful. "I don't care what *your* schedule says, *my* schedule says this week, and *mine* trumps *yours*." He disconnected without waiting for a response. He paused from his walk to his office, took a deep breath, and let it out slowly. He shook his head. He shouldn't let such petty things get to him. Yet, it was the principle of the matter. He had given a schedule, and he expected it to be followed. No lowly superintendent at the launch site was going to usurp his orders. Maybe he should make an example of the guy.

He walked a few more steps and stopped, his animosity replaced with bewilderment. He looked at the furniture now across the hallway from Sonja's new workstation. It looked like René's.

"Sonja."

She looked up from her work. "Yes, sir."

He pointed to where Sonja's desk used to be. "What is René's office furniture doing outside his office? Who authorized this?"

Sonja gave him a blank stare. "He did."

"Wh–" He stared back at the furniture and then back at Sonja. "Why?"

Sonja shrugged. "You'll have to ask him. He came in early and had it moved out."

He headed over to René's office and entered without knocking. He stopped dead in his tracks. "Simone?"

She turned from adjusting a few books and small ornaments in a bookcase. She gave him a broad smile. "What do you think?" She swept her hand across the room. "You like it?"

He closed the door and stepped forward. "Simone—"

She didn't slow down, but just kept talking. "Maybe you can help me decide." She walked back and forth, looking at the room from different angles. "Should I have the sofa here, or against the wall?" She smiled. "I was inspired by your furniture, but liked the traditional." She shook her head. "But the furniture in here felt *too* traditional. I wanted to go somewhere between the two." She glanced at him. "Do you think this does it?" She darted to the other side of the room again. "I chose most of your colors, but put them in a floral print. I think that softens it a little, yet makes it feel contemporary at the same time, don't you think?"

Philippe just stood there with his mouth open. Finally, he made his voice more forceful. "Simone."

She stopped and looked at him. "Yes, Philippe."

He let his breath out slowly. "What . . . are you doing in here?"

She cocked her head. "Doing? I just told you. I'm trying to

get everything arranged here."

He nodded slowly. "Yes. But why?"

She blinked a couple of times without moving. "Didn't René call you or text you?"

He pulled out his phone and looked at it. She came over and patted him on his chest. "Philippe, you work way too hard. You don't even have time to read your e-mail or texts."

There was a voicemail left on his phone. He sighed deeply. No need to listen to it now. It's obvious what it said.

"René gave you his office?"

She nodded. "Of course. That's what he said he was going to do, didn't he?"

Philippe opened his mouth to say something, but then stopped. She was right. That is what René had said. Seeing his father's furniture—now René's—outside this office seemed wrong. He slowly turned, looking at everything she had done to the room. The room certainly fit her and her personality better than the other furniture. He told himself he had to get used to new things. Simone was certainly different. Yet, wasn't that what attracted him to her in the first place?

Philippe's expression softened and his muscles relaxed. He came over and gave Simone a hug. "I'm sorry, Simone. The office looks beautiful. Just like you."

She smiled and gave him a kiss. "That was a very nice thing to say."

He shook his head. "I'm sorry. It's just that Dad's furniture has been here ever since I can remember. It was just a shock." He chuckled. "But this definitely suits you better."

She pulled him over to the sofa and sat. "Don't worry, Philippe. I'm not letting this stand in the way of our progress." She smiled. "The new compound has been synthesized and shipped to the site of each shuttle launch. I promised the immunes will not remember Earth, and if used properly, that is exactly what will happen."

He leaned in and gave her a prolonged kiss. She reciprocated. When their lips parted, she gave a soft sigh.

He smiled. "That's my business kiss."

She chuckled. "Well, I can't wait for a romantic one."

The door opened and René walked in without saying anything. "Whoops. Did I interrupt anything?"

Simone laughed. "Come on in."

Philippe felt heat rise to his face. Based on past arguments between them, he expected some type of retort, but René seemed to ignore their intimate moment.

René slowly strolled through the room. "Simone, I just love what you've done to this space." He nodded and smiled. "I think it really suits you."

"Thank you. That's nice of you to say."

Philippe stood. "I didn't expect you to give up your office so quickly."

René waved his hand. "Oh, I'll be leaving in a few days anyway. This gives me a chance to lend more credibility to Simone being here and helping out the company." He pointed between the two of them. "I'll let the two of you decide how much work Simone keeps at the university."

Simone raised her palms. "Oh, don't worry about that. After the launch is over and the current grad students graduate, I plan to scale back quite a bit, but still keep my footprint there."

René nodded. "Excellent." He turned to Philippe. "It seems everything is all set."

Philippe gave a slight shrug. "René, I just can't get over how excited you are about going on the Mars mission."

René laughed. "I know. I had never thought about going until one morning, when I realized it was the logical thing to do. It just made sense. Now I'm really excited about it. I think

I may travel in the North American ship, though."

Philippe's head jerked back slightly. "Why is that?"

"Well, it is the lead ship. I'm not just a European, but the leader of this expedition. I think being on the lead ship will send a better statement."

Philippe gave an approving nod. "Makes sense. I hadn't thought of it like that." He gave a quick shrug. "But you're right. I'll contact Rosencrantz immediately."

René shook his head. "Don't bother. I talked to him yesterday evening. He seemed excited about it as well." He smiled and pulled his arms in toward his chest, clenching his fists. "Being a part of history is just so exciting."

Philippe smiled. The memory reprogramming may have put the thought into his head, but all this excitement must be really coming from within René, Philippe thought. Maybe this had been his secret desire all along. That thought made Philippe feel less guilty about the whole thing.

René sat on the edge of Simone's desk. "So, tell me about the immunes. Have you solved the issue?"

Philippe nodded. "The prisons are full and those are the ones who will go into hyperstasis." He pointed with his head toward Simone. "Simone just informed me the compound to make the immunes not remember Earth has already been shipped to each shuttle for the stasis chambers."

Simone nodded. "We'll continue to monitor and search for immunes here. The new compound should solve the issue." She shrugged. "If not, we may have to institute Mercy Farewell until we have another Mars mission."

René opened his arms and delivered a huge smile. "It seems you have everything under control." He walked over to Simone, kissed her on her cheek, then turned to Philippe. "See, the two of you make a great team."

Philippe nodded. "Can't argue with you there." He smiled

at Simone.

René gave him a heartfelt hug. "Well, younger brother, I'm going to head for Houston in the morning. I'll give you a call before the shuttle takes off."

Philippe patted René's shoulder. "You be careful."

René nodded and stepped from the office.

Simone's eyes widened. "Well, his mind may have been telling him to stay, but it seems his heart was all about going. I've never seen anyone take to memory reprogramming like that." She laughed. "I think we actually made his dream come true."

TWENTY-TWO

Space Station

The next day, Luke was glad things had settled down a little at work. Those who had been chosen for the Mars mission were still excited, but now they were able to focus on the task at hand. The others had come to accept the fact they would be remaining on terra firma. Even Larry was acting more like his old self.

The morning went uneventfully. Since all the simulations were completed, work had actually slowed. But Luke felt certain this was just the calm before the storm. At lunchtime, he didn't see Sarah. He knew her work was actually ramping up, so that likely explained her absence. After eating alone, he headed back to his desk.

As he sat, he noticed three calls—all from Sarah. No voicemail. He called her back. "Hey, what's up? Everything OK?"

"Luke, can you come to the apartment? Right now."

Luke sat up straighter. "Sarah, is everything OK?" No reply. "Sarah, what's wrong?"

"Just . . . just get here as soon as you can."

"OK. Sure. I'll be right there."

He hung up. Her voice sounded very strange. Was she up-set? Did something happen at work? Why was she home *now*?

He swung by Larry's desk. He told Larry there was an im-portant issue at home he had to attend to. Larry didn't chal-lenge the request. With work being so slow today, why would he? As he headed to the elevator, he called the special number. "I have to head home."

As he entered his apartment, the first thing Luke saw was a duffle bag in the middle of the floor. He felt complete confu-sion. *What* was going on?

"Sarah?"

She walked from the bedroom. "I just had to see you before I left," Sarah said softly.

"Left? Where . . . where are you going?"

She led him over to the sofa and had them both sit. "I knew this day would come. I just didn't think it would happen so fast—out of the blue."

He shook his head. "What are you talking about?"

"Preparing for hyperstasis. It has to be done on the Space Station. I have to go to there to put all of the lottery winners . . . " She shook her head. " . . . likely the immunes from the prisons, in hyperstasis. Ken and I have to leave today." She looked uncertain, confused. "Well, actually tomorrow, but we have to be at the shuttle launch site today to prepare."

"How long will you be there?"

"Luke, it's going to take a couple of months."

His eyes widened. *Months?* Really? That long?"

"Think about it, Luke. It takes about twenty minutes to get a person into hyperstasis and there are two thousand individ-uals. Even if we worked twenty-four/seven, it would still take almost a full month to do that. If you take rest, sleep, prep time all into account, I think two months is pushing it, really."

Luke sat back. He knew she would be doing this work, but

for some reason it never dawned on him she would have to do it in space, and that it would take so long.

She gave him a hug and prolonged it. "I'm going to miss you so much."

He pulled her back and looked into her eyes. "Not more than I'm going to miss you."

Sarah's eyes began to water.

He shook his head. "Don't start that now. I won't be able to stop."

She chuckled and sniffled. "OK. I'll try not to."

He leaned in and gave her a kiss. She reciprocated. All he could think of was that he would not see her for a long while. He couldn't help himself; Luke let his passion take over. Sarah didn't resist. He didn't care if she was late. Sarah knowing his deep love for her was more important . . .

* * * * *

As they got dressed, Sarah looked at her wrist. "Oh, I need to hurry. I'm going to be late."

He gave her another quick kiss as he buttoned his shirt. "Don't worry. We'll make it. Is Ken going with you?"

She nodded. "Both he and Kathleen are going. We've practiced enough together, so things should go well." She shrugged. "I should be excited, but I'm not." She seemed forlorn, depressed. "I wish you were coming with me."

He nodded. "So do I."

"I'll try and video chat with you every day."

He put his forehead to hers. "You better. I can't go a day without seeing you."

Her eyes began to get moist all over again. Luke turned his head as though asking her to recall the promise she had just given him. She chuckled. "I'm trying not to. I really am." She looked down and turned solemn.

He lifted her chin. "Is something else wrong?"

"You really think we'll be part of this Mars mission?"

He turned up the corner of his mouth and nodded. "Unfortunately, I do."

Her eyes watered again. This time, a few tears spilled out. "So, once I leave for the Space Station, I may never be back on Earth again?"

He pulled her to himself and wrapped his arms around her. Now it was his eyes that were starting to get wet. He tried his best not to, but a few tears ran down his cheeks. "I don't know, Sarah. I just don't know. I promise you, though. We'll be together."

"That's the only way I could bear it."

He pulled back and looked at her. "Now see what you've done."

She smiled as she wiped the few tears off his cheeks. "Sorry. I didn't keep my promise."

He chuckled. "I'll forgive you if you let me take you to the shuttle site."

She nodded. He picked up her backpack and duffle bag and she opened the door. Off to the side, just an arm's length away, stood Viktoria and Caine. They said nothing, but followed them to the elevator.

Once they got to the corner where they were out of range of the video feed, Viktoria grabbed their arms. They stopped and looked at her. She turned off her earwig. Caine did the same. She gave a quick but deep, meaningful hug to Sarah.

"You take care of yourself now, you hear? I'm going to really miss you."

"Thanks, Viktoria."

Viktoria motioned for them to continue. Luke saw her fiddle with her earwig. She put her hand to her ear. "Yes, sir. I'm here. Must have been a dead spot. I don't know, sir. All is fine." She quickly morphed into her usual mode of a stern I-A soldier, as did Caine.

Viktoria and Caine followed them in a separate taxi. Sarah scooted toward Luke. He lifted his arm and she nestled her head between his chest and shoulder.

"I guess your dream of us being on Mars was a prophecy after all."

He looked down at her. It seemed she had admitted defeat. He rubbed her arm. "Don't worry. God has a purpose. We just don't see it yet."

She chuckled softly.

"What?"

Sarah raised up a little and looked at him. "You started out the doom-and-gloom guy and I was the positive one. Now our roles have reversed."

He smiled. "Shows we're there for each other."

She patted his chest and leaned back into him. "That's what I needed to hear."

They rode the rest of the way in silence. What was there to say? Luke just wanted to remember her this close to him.

* * * * *

They entered to a great deal of hubbub at the launch site. As they stepped from the taxi, Ken and Kathleen came up. Ken helped with Sarah's extremely stuffed duffle bag.

He laughed as he moved it up and down like he was mentally weighing it. "Sarah, you may have to give up some of this. They will have scrubs for us to wear most of the time."

"Well . . . " Sarah's tone sounded somewhat defensive. "They told me to bring a few personal items."

Ken continued to chuckle. "I think your definition of 'few'

is different than theirs."

Kathleen playfully gave Ken a push. "Stop it, now. I recall they sent some of your stuff back as well." She took Sarah's arm. "Don't worry. I'll help you sort through it all. That's why we're here a day early anyway." She looked at Luke. "I'll have them send the extra back to your apartment."

Luke nodded. "Thanks, Kathleen."

Viktoria and Caine walked up. For once, Caine spoke first. "I'm sorry, Dr. Morgan, but I'll have to accompany you to the Space Station. And your return."

Sarah opened her mouth to say something, but simply nodded instead. "Very well."

Luke looked at Viktoria. She merely raised an eyebrow. In any other situation, it would have been funny, but not this one. So it seemed Viktoria would remain his shadow.

Another I-A officer walked over to where they were standing. "Dr. Wilson, Dr. Morgan, Ms. Stapleton, it's time."

All three nodded. Luke gave Sarah a final kiss. She must have seen the concern in his eyes. She patted his chest. "Don't worry. I went through the same safety protocols as everyone I tested for the mission." She smiled. "It seems I can handle more G's that many pilots."

Luke laughed and gave her a final kiss. "Just be careful."

She turned and followed the others, looking back at him twice before they disappeared around a building. Caine was the last to disappear from view.

With a heavy heart, Luke turned to head back. He looked at his watch. He could head back to work for a few hours. In truth, he didn't think he could do that today. Maybe he'd just go home. But to an empty home? No, that didn't sit right with him either. He got out his phone and punched a quick-dial number.

"Hey, Jeremy."

"Luke. Hey, are you OK? You don't sound right. Anything wrong?"

"You could say that. Got a shoulder for me? I'd like to stop over."

"Sure, buddy. Anytime."

"Thanks, Jeremy. See you shortly."

He looked at Viktoria, who was standing nearby. She nodded.

Luke climbed in the taxi. "Continental Drift."

The mechanical voice responded. "Continental Drift. Arrival time, twenty-eight minutes."

Luke leaned back and closed his eyes as the taxi pulled off.

TWENTY-THREE

CLOSING IN

Jeremy had some type of drink ready for him as soon as he arrived. He had never tasted this one before. It had a citrus taste and a calming effect at the same time. He sat in one of Jeremy and Natalia's plush chairs and closed his eyes.

After a few minutes, he felt a hand on his knee. He opened his eyes to Natalia's smile.

"Hey, Lukey. Want to talk about it?"

He was amazed at how her tone could be so soothing. He nodded and sat up. He told her all that had happened, and that Sarah was now heading to the Space Station for at least a couple of months. Natalia periodically looked up at Jeremy, who occasionally placed his hand on Luke's shoulder and gave a squeeze. These two really were great friends, Luke thought.

Once Luke had told them everything about this day, Natalia shook her head. "Lukey, I'm so sorry. What can we do?"

He gave a weak smile. "I think you're doing it."

She gave a sweet smile and patted his knee. "Just lean back and close your eyes for a while."

Luke did so and felt slumber overtake him. Before his mind

completely left reality, he heard Jeremy tell Natalia something . . . something that sounded like, "I put enough in his drink. He should be able to rest for a couple of hours."

* * * * *

Even before Luke opened his eyes, he could smell the aroma of cooking. Yet he couldn't place the aroma. For a few seconds after he opened his eyes, he couldn't recognize where he was, but the surroundings of Jeremy's apartment quickly came back to him. He turned his head. Someone was sitting on the sofa.

He sat up quickly. "Oliver?"

Oliver smiled. "Hey, Sleeping Beauty." A grin came across his face. "I don't think your beauty nap worked."

Luke laughed. "How did you get here undetected?"

Oliver raised his eyebrows a couple of times. "I have an inside mole."

Luke realized Viktoria, likely downstairs, had let him through. "I'm sorry, Oliver. Here I've been wallowing in self-pity, and you and Viktoria have had to deal with separation many times with her I-A work."

He shrugged. "It's not ideal, but we make it work." He leaned forward. "Actually, she's the one who let me know you were here."

Luke's eyes widened. "Really? How?"

A wicked grin came across his face. "I could tell you, but I'd have to kill you."

Luke shook his head and chuckled. He held up his palm. "Then, by all means, keep it to yourself."

Oliver laughed and slapped Luke on his knee. "I've missed you, buddy."

Luke nodded. "Same here. So what brings you by?"

"Well, I wanted to give everyone an update." He waved Jeremy and Natalia over.

Jeremy came over with drinks and Natalia set out some appetizers. Luke smiled. These were what put off the incredible aroma that helped waken him. The two of them sat on the sofa across from Oliver.

They all looked at Oliver expectantly. First, he munched on an appetizer. "Mmm. These are great, Natalia."

She smiled. "You can thank Jeremy."

Oliver took a big, final swallow, wiped his hands, and then opened and clasped them. "The good news is, Maher and Paul make a great team. Their posts are getting a lot of attention." He laughed. "And not just from the I-A." He pointed at Luke. "The questions and answers you and Scott are providing are having a great impact. Many readers are responding to those."

Luke grinned. "That's great, Oliver. Much better than my expectations."

Oliver nodded. "It shows that despite the efforts to reprogram people, most people are still hungry for the truth."

Luke repositioned himself in his chair. "So . . . what's the bad news?"

Oliver raised his eyebrows. "As you would expect, the I-A has quadrupled its efforts to find the source of this 'insurrection,' as they put it."

Natalia squinted. "What exactly are they doing?"

"They question every immune they find. They incorrectly assume all of this is from the hands of immunes. We have way more responders to Maher's messages from non-immunes than immunes."

Jeremy set his cup down. "You think that's what slowed down their progress?"

Oliver nodded. "I think so." He cocked his head. "Yet, I think they're getting close. I've already had to house Paul with

Maher. They almost caught Paul, but with the help of others from Clarity of The Way, we were able to get him to safety."

Luke sensed a hesitation. He could tell Oliver hadn't yet said everything. "What are you not telling us, Oliver?"

Oliver sighed. "They may be close to us as well."

Natalia's eyes widened. "What do you mean?"

Oliver pointed to Luke. "The I-A is already tailing Luke and Sarah. They know we're friends with them. So far, that hasn't necessarily meant anything. Yet, once they figure out who Maher is and then discover we're connected to him . . . " He shrugged. "It's just a matter of time, I'm afraid."

Natalia took Jeremy's hand. "I knew it would likely happen, but now it seems too surreal."

Jeremy nodded. "Yeah, we've made plans—as certain as we can. I think Natalia's parents are safe. They'll run the restaurant in Shanghai. I've talked to Marta Pentapolous about running the restaurant in Paris. She hasn't agreed yet, but likely will."

Luke realized he hadn't thought of Marta in a long time. Against the backdrop of this difficult news, he managed a question. "How is Marta, anyway?"

Jeremy nodded. "Fine. She hasn't been too happy just making Invocation wafers after her experience at the restaurant in Paris. I've helped her take more cooking classes. Her confidence has really increased. I've even tried to talk to her about Scripture and the Messiah, but she's very hesitant at present. She's so connected to the Supreme Oracle. It's hard to be really open with her."

Natalia looked at Jeremy and then the others. "I've tried to prepare by writing out the entire process we went through to accept the truth of God and what he has done for us. If something does happen to us, I've scheduled it to get delivered to her. I just pray it will impact her the right way."

Luke nodded. It seemed Natalia and Marta had really established a bond. It was similar to what he had done with Brian.

He turned back to Oliver. "So, what do we do now?"

Oliver shrugged. "Besides trying to stay under the radar, I don't know what else to do. As I said, I don't think it's a matter of *if* it will happen, but *when* it will happen." He gave a weak smile. "I just want you to be prepared. That's all."

Luke gave a slight chuckle. "So, our next visit may be at the Martian colony?"

Oliver cocked his head and shrugged. "I want to say no, but . . . "

"As long as we're all together." Natalia held out her hands, placed together. They each put their hands on top of hers. "To Mars together."

They shared a small laugh.

Luke laughed with them, but knew it was merely a way to diffuse the tension they each had built up thinking about what could happen. Although none of them wanted to go to Mars, it would definitely be more palatable if they were all there together—and if they were able to keep their memories intact.

Luke's phone beeped. It was Sarah. He clicked the button and her face was smiling back at him from his screen. "Hi, Sarah."

Everyone else joined in. "Hi, Sarah."

Sarah laughed. "Where are you?"

Luke chuckled. "I'm at Jeremy and Natalia's." He turned the phone around for everyone to wave.

"Oliver. Hi. Good to see you again."

"Good to see you also, Sarah."

Luke turned the phone around again. "Hold on a second."

Luke pointed to the balcony. Jeremy nodded and waved him toward it.

Luke stepped outside and sat at the table with the large

umbrella on the balcony. "So, Sarah, how's everything going?"

She nodded her head. "Pretty well." She chuckled. "I had to send most of my belongings back. Expect a delivery."

He smiled and nodded. "No problem. So, you're heading to the Space Station tomorrow?"

She nodded. "About mid-morning. Some of the immunes will come with us and the rest will be shuttled periodically until they're all in hyperstasis."

"You sound apprehensive."

"My biggest concern is I will see people I know and be forced to put them into hyperstasis."

Luke nodded. "Just do what you need to do. Those who know you will understand." He knew he couldn't tell her about the conversation with Oliver; that would put too much stress on her on top of everything else. He thought he would wait a couple of weeks until she had a better understanding what was expected of her.

Off camera, something pulled away Sarah's attention. She held up her finger. "Just a minute." A brief time later, she turned back. "Sorry, I have to go. I'll try and call you tomorrow evening—from the Space Station." She blew him a kiss and ended the call.

Luke sat back in his chair and sighed. It felt as though everything was deteriorating into chaos, and quickly. He knew God was in control, but it certainly didn't feel that way. He said a prayer and felt a bit better. He had to trust God knew what he was doing. He sighed again. *Why is that so hard to do?*

TWENTY-FOUR

ON THE RUN

As far as Luke knew, all was quiet. It had been two weeks without incident. Oliver's prediction had not yet come true. He met with Scott each week and video chatted with Sarah each night.

One evening, as he ended his call with Sarah, a sudden realization hit Luke: their lives were becoming more and more like those of Oliver and Viktoria. He was sorry he had not had more compassion for his two friends.

He jerked when he heard someone pound on his apartment door. He slowly, warily walked to the door and looked through the peephole. His head jerked back slightly. It was Oliver. He froze from the shock of seeing him at his front door. Oliver pounded again. Luke jerked again and came back to reality. He opened the door just as Oliver's hand was poised to pound again.

Oliver had *fear* in his eyes. Luke had never seen that from him before. "Luke, come with me. You're in danger. We have to get all of you to safety. The I-A are on to us."

Luke looked at the door across the hall. *Did Viktoria know this?* Before that thought could continue, Viktoria's door opened and she removed her earwig, all in one swift motion.

Viktoria held her arms open slightly. "Oliver, what are you doing breaking protocol like this? I can't hide something like this."

Oliver went to her and held her shoulders. "Viktoria, all of our covers are blown." He still sounded panicked. "They didn't tell you anything?"

She shook her head as her eyes widened.

"They're on to *you* as well." He grabbed her hand. "Come with us. Maher and Paul are also in danger."

Oliver led the three of them to the stairs and down two flights to Luke's old apartment. As they approached, they heard the elevator doors open around the corner.

Oliver turned. "Luke, you get Maher and Paul. Viktoria and I will hold them off."

Luke pounded on the door. In a matter of seconds, the door opened.

"Luke? What . . . what are you doing here?"

Luke saw a man standing behind Maher. It had to be Paul. He had very tanned skin, dark hair, dark eyes. Middle Eastern came to Luke's mind.

"Maher, you and Paul need to come with us. I-A soldiers are on their way here right now."

Maher's eyes widened. "But Paul just got here."

Luke nodded. "I know. I know. But you need to come—now."

Luke basically pulled both of them into the hallway. They all turned and watched Viktoria and Oliver. Luke found he couldn't tear his eyes away. Both Viktoria and Oliver were so quick and quiet. By the time the Illumi-Alliance soldiers turned the corner, Viktoria and Oliver were already upon them. Before the soldiers had a chance to pull their stun guns,

Luke saw Oliver take out three of them like someone sliding into home plate. His jaw dropped when he saw Viktoria run full tilt, jump onto the wall, turn upside down, and at the same time grab one of the soldiers around his neck with her arms and the second with her legs. Using gravity and her momentum, she pulled both to the floor. She then used the one she had grabbed with her hands as a human shield as the other shot at her. She then shot the guy standing; he crumpled to the floor. Oliver backed her up by shooting the ones he knocked to the ground and the two Viktoria brought down as well.

Oliver and Viktoria wasted no time in heading back. Oliver motioned for them to go. "Head to the stairs at the end of the hall."

All five flew down the stairs, out the door, and to the back of the building. They stopped for a moment to catch their breath.

Between breaths, Luke asked, "What do we do now?"

Oliver put his hand on Luke's shoulder. "Call Jeremy. They're in danger, too. Have them meet us behind Continental Drift."

Viktoria motioned with her head. "We need to move. We only stunned them. They'll revive soon."

Oliver nodded. "Yeah, and be livid."

As the five of them weaved between buildings and tried to stay out of sight, Luke called Jeremy. As soon as he heard Jeremy connect, he blurted, "Jeremy, this is Luke. Get Natalia and meet us behind the restaurant. I-A soldiers are on their way to you."

"Luke? What are you talking about?"

"Jeremy, staying there is not safe. If you stay there, you and Natalia will be captured. Leave right now and meet us behind the restaurant."

"OK. But . . . Natalia isn't here."

Luke ran his hand through his hair even as he continued

their fast-walk pace. "Where is she?"

"She went to an architectural firm several blocks from here."

Luke ran his hand over his mouth out of worry and trying to think. "OK. Go ahead and meet us out back. Once there, call Natalia and set up a rendezvous point with her. We'll all go get her."

"OK. See you in a few."

Luke informed Oliver. He grimaced. "Not good. But we'll make the best of it."

They all slowed to a more conventional walk, and did so in silence for several minutes. Luke reached over to shake Paul's hand.

"Hi, Paul. I'm Luke."

Paul shook his hand and smiled. "Yes, I figured as much. Your material that we post has been really great."

"I'm just glad it could be used to help so many."

Paul nodded. Oliver held up his hand. They all stopped. They observed several I-A soldiers walk by as they crouched in the shadows between two high-rises.

Oliver motioned for them to continue. "Just keep your eyes peeled."

They were able to cut some time off by walking between buildings rather than traveling along the sidewalk. Once they got to the rear of Continental Drift, Jeremy was waiting.

Jeremy held up his phone. "I was able to reach her. There's a park right behind the building she's in. That's where we can meet her."

Oliver nodded and patted Jeremy's shoulder. "OK. Let's go."

Luke gestured to Paul. "Jeremy, this is Paul . . . "

"Samuels. I'm Paul Samuels."

Jeremy shook his hand. "Good to meet you."

Paul smiled. "Same here."

All were quiet after that, following Oliver as they slinked down alleyways and tried to stay out of sight as much as possible. A few times they had to walk down some of the larger sidewalks in the area for a short distance, but they tried to act as nonchalant as possible yet still keep their eyes peeled for I-A soldiers and street cameras.

When they came to the street where the park was located, Oliver had the others stay in the shadows while he surveyed the premises.

The park area was not large. It looked quite beautiful with its manicured shrubbery along the graveled walkway. Several benches were interspersed in shaded areas.

Luke strained to see Natalia. "Does anyone see her?"

Jeremy put his hand on Luke's shoulder and pointed with his other hand. "There."

Luke followed the direction of Jeremy's pointing; he saw a woman sitting on a park bench underneath a large tree. It was Natalia. "Call her and get her to come to where we are," Luke whispered to Jeremy.

Oliver nodded. "And as nonchalantly as possible."

Jeremy called. Luke saw Natalia answer. She slowly looked around, gazed in their direction, and then looked in other directions as well. Luke nodded. This was good; she didn't give away their location in case anyone was looking. Natalia stood and casually walked in their direction.

Luke gasped. He knew the others saw it too; he heard small gasps from them as well. I-A soldiers had stepped out from behind various buildings. They were watching them—and Natalia. It was, suddenly, the feeling of being hunted.

Luke turned to Oliver. "What do we do?"

He could see Oliver making various calculations in his mind, his head turning right and left, scanning the terrain while trying to determine the best scenario. Oliver pointed across the way. "See that gate? I don't see any soldiers there. It leads to an apartment courtyard. I know the subway is only a couple of blocks from there. If we make that, we can get into Houston itself and perhaps lose them."

Luke looked over at Jeremy. He was relaying the information to Natalia. Luke noticed she casually turned and headed toward a large oak tree in the direction of the gate. When she got there, she leaned against it. She looked like she was simply having a casual conversation. She was good, Luke had to admit. He also noticed she had already changed her dress shoes for sneakers. Luke nodded. Yes, Natalia was one smart cookie.

Oliver motioned for them to follow. They followed the outskirts of the park while trying to stay in the shadows. Luke noticed Natalia following their movement. She was making it appear as though she was looking nowhere in particular. He also noticed I-A soldiers converging into the park. Still, they were not near the gate to which the seven of them were headed—at least not yet. When they got within a couple meters of the gate, Oliver raised his hand and everyone stopped.

Oliver nodded to Jeremy, who seemed to understand what Oliver wanted.

"OK, Natalia. Head to the gate now. Once you get halfway, run as fast as you can."

Luke saw Natalia end the call in what seemed a casual manner. She readjusted her purse across her shoulder and walked calmly toward the gate. She stopped, picked up a leaf, and twirled it between her fingers. She was playing this extremely cool. No one watching would realize she was on the verge of sprinting. The soldiers stayed put. That was good. They obviously didn't suspect her, at least not in any dramatic way—yet.

And then, Natalia began walking faster and faster. The soldiers seemed to become suspicious—eyes glancing, checking their earpieces—but they were not yet advancing. Natalia seamlessly began to pick up speed and then launched into a full tilt sprint toward the gate. The soldiers now ran toward her. Luke quickly calculated the distance. She would definitely reach them before the soldiers. They all sprinted to the gate. Inwardly, though still pretty much in panic, Luke smiled. This had been a great plan. Success was only a few seconds away.

Luke turned when he heard a loud cry from Natalia. He saw her arch backward and fall to the ground. She had been stunned. But how?

"Natalia!" Jeremy screamed. He dashed in her direction.

Luke turned and saw Viktoria bend to one knee and aim her weapon. He looked toward where she was pointing and saw a body fall from the third-story balcony from the adjacent apartment complex. The hurtling body hit the grass below.

When he turned back, Maher was running behind Jeremy toward Natalia. Maher helped Jeremy pull Natalia over his shoulder. The soldiers were closing fast. The window of opportunity for success for the seven of them was dwindling quickly. Maher and Jeremy got back safely to their position, but soldiers were on their heels. Before they all got through the gate, Maher was hit and crumbled. Paul went back for him, pulling him around the corner of the building. Oliver helped to get him over Paul's shoulder.

Luke watched, amazed, as Viktoria lay on the ground with her feet slightly raised. Oliver sat on her feet and bent over. "Oliver, what are you doing?" Luke forced the words out.

Oliver seemed to throw a slight grin Luke's way, then turned back, a look of sheer determination on his face.

As two soldiers came around the corner, Viktoria forcefully pushed her legs out. Oliver catapulted into them and knocked both down. Viktoria was up in a flash and stunned them before Oliver could even stand. Both used the stunned soldiers as shields and pushed back toward the gate, stunning more advancing soldiers.

Oliver yelled over his shoulder. "Go! We'll catch up!"

Luke directed Jeremy and Paul toward the courtyard. Yet as soon as they entered, more soldiers came spilling in from the opposite side. They stopped in their tracks. Luke looked around, trying to find other escape options.

Luke noticed movement above him. Viktoria flew from a balcony above, knocking one soldier into another. Oliver came from the side, out of the shadows, and stunned them both. Again, Viktoria was on her feet in a matter of seconds. She waved to the rest of them to follow. Yet, as soon as she turned back, several more soldiers entered. Then, as with finality, Viktoria wilted to the ground. She had been hit.

Oliver shot that soldier and ran to Viktoria's side. Luke could hear his soft words: "Viktoria. Viktoria."

As Oliver bent down to her, however, he also fell, directly beside her. The gun that had shot Oliver was now directly trained on Luke. The soldier's face looked as if he was daring Luke to move. Paul and Jeremy apparently didn't see the guy; they dashed in opposite directions. Still more soldiers entered the courtyard and felled them both.

Luke stood in the middle of the chaos, hands raised. So, it was finally over. The man with the gun approached him.

Luke looked into the man's eyes—deep, expressionless eyes. "Now what?"

The man pulled his trigger. Luke felt his muscles go catatonic. A short moan escaped his lips. He was unconscious before he hit the ground.

TWENTY-FIVE

CAPTURED

Luke awoke feeling like he had been badly beaten. Every muscle in his body ached. He slowly sat up, twisting his torso to try and remove all the kinks his body felt. He noticed the others lying around him in various positions. It looked like their captors had dropped each of them in any position, with absolutely no care for their comfort.

Oliver was closest. He was turned halfway onto his stomach, and his arm was twisted under him awkwardly, preventing him from lying flat. Luke went over and shook him. He tried to reposition Oliver's arm so he could lie flat on his stomach. Oliver slowly stirred, then groaned.

He pushed himself up and sat. "Where are we?"

Luke shook his head. "No idea. You OK?"

Oliver nodded as he rubbed his wrist and tried to stretch, wincing as he attempted the feat. Looking around, Oliver pointed to those behind Luke. "You check on those, while I check on . . . it looks like Viktoria and Paul, over here."

On Luke's side were Natalia, Jeremy, and Maher. Looking back, he saw Oliver attending to Viktoria. Poor Paul looked like a human pretzel in the corner of the room. Luke turned back and shook Natalia. Life slowly came back to her. As she moved, she grimaced before beginning to awaken. Luke noticed her knee had a scrape, which had bled a bit, but it now looked dried. It must have occurred when she hit the gravel as she fell. He helped her sit up. Realization of what happened came back to her eyes.

"You OK?"

Natalia nodded slowly as she rubbed the back of her neck. "Yeah, I think so."

As she looked at everyone, she jerked around. "Where's Jeremy?" Seeing him behind her, she crawled to him, wincing as she put her left knee down. She used her right knee and left foot to scoot over to him.

Luke went over to check on Maher while Natalia checked on Jeremy. Maher, already stirring as Luke reached him, sat up. Luke put his hand on Maher's shoulder. "How do you feel?"

Maher stuck out his right arm and then placed his left arm around his torso, trying to stretch. "Oh, I feel stunningly."

Luck chuckled and patted Maher's shoulder. "Good to see your humor's still intact."

Maher nodded. "That's about all that is. I feel like I've been hit by a car."

Luke tugged on Maher's arm, requesting that he come over to where everyone else was gathering. Paul limped. "You OK there, Paul?"

Paul gave a slight grimace and nodded. "Yeah, my leg went numb from the position they left me in. I'll be OK in a few minutes."

Oliver had everyone sit in something of a circle. Luke noticed the room was empty, devoid of all furniture. The floor had a grayish tint to it, but the walls were painted a sky blue, except for the wall with the door, which was a pale yellow, and the door a brighter shade of yellow.

Luke looked at Oliver. "Anyone try the door?"

Oliver nodded. "Locked. Big surprise."

Luke nodded. "Any idea where we are?"

Oliver shook his head. Viktoria, however, nodded.

"Where are we, Viktoria?"

All eyes turned her way. "Not positive, but I think we're in one of the waiting areas for the shuttle." She nodded toward one of the walls. "These colors are supposed to help people feel more relaxed."

Maher smiled. "No wonder I feel so good."

There were a few light chuckles.

Luke looked at his watch. They had been out almost five hours. He turned to Viktoria. "I thought the effect from the stun guns were to last only a couple of hours? We've been out more than twice that long."

Viktoria nodded. "Yes, but I think they shot us again after we fell. I noticed two small bruises where the gun hit me."

Natalia grimaced. "Why?"

Viktoria shrugged. "To keep us out and get us here without incident, I'm sure."

Luke heard noise and turned. Benches were mechanically extending from the walls. Everyone exchanged glances.

Maher stood. "Well, that's weird. But I'm going to take advantage of it."

They all followed suit, but Luke had a feeling it may not be wise. He sat last, and with trepidation. As nothing seemed to happen, he began to think his fears had been unfounded. He relaxed and leaned back against the wall. Suddenly, restraints wrapped around his torso, holding him in place. The same thing happened to everyone else. Despite their struggles, no one could get free. In a matter of minutes, a long table rose from the floor. The door opened and an orderly entered pushing a cart. Luke could smell food as the cart came closer, but he couldn't make out the type of food from its aroma. It didn't smell good, but it wasn't repulsive either.

The orderly wore earbuds, evidently listening to music as his head bounced around as if moving to a beat. After he arranged the table and put food on each plate, he turned, smiled, and took the plug from his right ear. "Enjoy," he grunted. He then put the earbud back in and exited with his head still bouncing to the music. Once he exited and they heard the door lock click loudly, the restraints disappeared back into the wall.

All stood right away. Luke turned and looked where he had been sitting. He could see no sign in the wall from where the restraints had come. The benches then slowly retracted back into the wall.

Natalia took another step back. "That was just freaky."

Everyone nodded. Jeremy came up beside her and put his arms around her shoulders. "You OK?"

She gave a slight smile. "Yeah, just a little weirded out."

They walked over to the table and sat, everyone still feeling quite uncertain. When nothing happened after a couple of minutes, everyone relaxed a bit.

Oliver picked up his fork and took a bite. Everyone stared at him. He shrugged. "I'm hungry. I've tasted worse."

Jeremy let out a little "humph." He poked it with his fork. "What is it, anyway?"

Oliver chuckled. "You're a chef, and you don't recognize meat loaf when you see it?"

Jeremy's eyes widened as he pointed at his plate with his fork. "I know meat loaf. That is definitely not meat loaf."

Oliver smiled. "OK, Mister Gourmet. You tell me what it is."

Jeremy took a small bite. A grimace came across his face. "That's disgusting. That's what that is."

Oliver laughed.

Jeremy pointed to Luke. "It reminds me of the horrible food you used to eat when I first joined you at Mars City."

Luke chuckled. "That's before it even *was* Mars City."

Jeremy nodded. "True."

Luke took a few bites. It didn't taste as bad as Jeremy claimed, but it wasn't tasty either. Of course, someone of Jeremy's culinary caliber would not see this food as even average. That's why his restaurants were so successful. Luke quickly found himself wondering: What would happen to Jeremy's restaurants? He had put plans into place for their continued operation. But with no large infusions of creativity at regular intervals, would they eventually become passé?

Luke noticed most ate some of the so-called meat loaf, but no one finished.

Luke looked over at Paul as he pushed his plate away. "Savored enough?"

Paul smiled. "One can only take so much of a good thing."

Luke chuckled. "So, Paul, what happens now with the Internet posts?"

Paul's eyebrows raised. "Oh, they will continue."

"Really? How?"

"Clarity of the Way is a vast network of individuals. Although I was its leader, we have a pecking order, so to speak, for such contingencies. While no new posts may go up, at least for a while, the ones up now will continuously get reposted."

Luke thought about that. There had already been a lot of information posted, so the material already out there could help new converts get up to speed quickly. Yes, that was a good plan.

The door opened and in walked . . . René Mauchard. Behind him were two I-A officers. Mauchard walked to the table. Everyone just sat and looked at him. The officers entered and stood on either side of the door, elbows turned out in what was nearly an akimbo position, but their hands were behind their backs instead of on their hips.

René stood at the edge of the table and shook his head. "Tsk, tsk, tsk." He looked around, paused. "Agent Komcova, your actions are highly disappointing. You make Jerome Rosencrantz bow his head in shame. He had really put his trust in you." He shook his head again. "He's very disappointed and feels betrayed. Anything to say?"

Viktoria said nothing, remaining expressionless.

René turned his gaze to Luke. "And you, Dr. Loughton. You disgrace the entire mission. You could have been part of its success. Now you merely become part of the support staff rather than the elite." He gave a broad smile. "Your immunity will not help you any longer. Dr. Mercure has been extremely successful in finding a compound to combat your immunity." He shook his head. "Now all your work will have been in vain."

Luke thought about that. Well, maybe from Mauchard's perspective. But he knew he had made a difference in the eternal destiny of others. That far outweighed anything he would do with his work.

René put his hands behind him and took another couple of steps. "And Dr. Cohen. It's unclear how you got caught up in all of this, but . . . " His gaze went back to Luke. "It seems wherever Dr. Loughton goes, someone gets caught in his wake of dissidence."

Maher remained quiet, but the look Luke received from him was only one of gratitude. Maher had turned into a good friend. He was glad Maher felt the same way.

"And that brings us to Mr. and Mrs. Pangea. I can't imagine what will happen to your famous restaurants. Shows how one should choose one's friends more wisely, doesn't it?"

Natalia gave a smirk, looked at Luke, and shook her head lightly.

"At any rate, those at the Mars colony may be the winners." He chuckled and gestured toward Jeremy. "Who else will be able to boast of famous restaurants on two worlds?" He laughed again. "You could call it 'When Two Worlds Collide.'" He looked smug with his comment. Jeremy wasn't amused.

René turned to leave, apparently, but turned back after a couple of steps. "These gentlemen . . . " He pointed to the guards at the door. " . . . will take you to the shuttle launch preparation area. Once at the Space Station, you will be placed in hyperstasis." He delivered yet another smug smile. "When you awake, Earth will be a distant memory." He paused and raised his index finger. "Oh wait." He laughed. "No, it will be no memory at all. Mars will be your home and all that you will know." He gave a slight bow. "Your lives are forever changed." He turned and exited, as did the two guards.

"What a smug, arrogant twit." This came from Natalia, and everyone turned her way.

Despite everything they had just heard, Luke laughed at Natalia's assessment. "Did that just come from Ms. Positive?"

"Well, that was as positive a statement as I could manage."

Jeremy reached over and kissed her cheek. "My sentiments exactly."

She smiled and kissed him back. "Great minds think alike."

Paul looked at Luke. "He said all of our memories would be wiped out. But . . . you're immune. How will your memories get changed or reprogrammed?"

"Dr. Mercure developed a compound which now works on immunes," Luke said. He gestured to Jeremy. "But . . . here's what Mauchard doesn't know. Jeremy's lab in Shanghai has also come up with a compound, one that will counteract what Dr. Mercure developed."

Jeremy nodded. "Matteo gave Sarah a good bit of it."

Luke drummed his fingers. "Yeah, and I sure hope she still

has some of it."

Guards suddenly reentered the room and approached the seven of them. "Please follow me."

The first guard walked out the door. They followed, and the other guard took the rear, weapon drawn. They were led down a corridor, turned, and then down an even longer corridor. At the end, the door opened, and they entered a large seating area. The seats were arranged in rows, but since the shuttle stood vertical, the seats looked to be in a reclined position, although they actually were not. There was a ladder-type structure to climb to reach the last row of seats; all other seats appeared to be occupied. Once at the open row, they used a type of catwalk structure to reach their seats. The guards made sure they were strapped in tightly, then left.

Everyone remained quiet. Too quiet, Luke thought. Everyone appeared to be as young as, or younger than, him. Were these all immunes? Or were some of them the "elite" to which René had referred?

Luke heard a rumble. The seats began to vibrate. He saw Natalia take Jeremy's hand. He felt himself feel heavier, and an invisible force pushed him back into his seat.

He knew they were leaving Earth. He wondered if he would ever see it again. But his main thought was not about Earth, it was about his destination. Sarah would be at the end of this trip. He couldn't wait to see her again.

176

TWENTY-SIX

INTO SPACE

Once the vibrating and the feeling of being pushed into his seat stopped, Luke could feel himself become weightless. The restraints kept him from leaving his seat even though he was not really in his seat but floating slightly above it. He knew once they reached the Space Station, they would have artificial gravity, but it was kind of amazing, at this point, to be able to experience weightlessness.

Luke looked around. Others were not having the same pleasant experience. Some appeared to be nauseous. He hoped the nausea didn't turn to something worse. Each person on this shuttle—except for he and his friends—had supposedly been evaluated for their health status before being brought on board. He assumed that included response to weightlessness. He couldn't imagine Sarah not taking that into account. Yet, some of those in front of him looked quite green.

Luke tried to simply relax and rest; he knew it would take several hours to dock with the Space Station. He went through the process in his mind by reviewing the simulation he had done with Brian and Scott what seemed like a million times.

First, the pilot has to get the shuttle into orbit. Then, the pilot has to get the orbit of the shuttle into the same orbit as the Space Station by doing a Hohmann Transfer, utilizing two burns of the engine: once to get the shuttle farther from the earth, and then again to maintain their orbit. Next, correction bursts are done to ensure the ship is in the same orbit as the Space Station. The pilot then has to get the shuttle in front of the orbit of the Space Station and let the Station catch up with the shuttle. The last step takes the most time: the shuttle pilot has to get the craft to travel slightly faster than the Space Station and gradually slow down to match the speed of the Space Station just as they dock. The simulations worked perfectly. Luke hoped they had a good pilot.

* * * * *

Luke awoke as he felt a bump and then heard cheering. Apparently, they had docked. He looked over and saw relief on Natalia's face. Most people were smiling. Even one person he had seen earlier looking quite green was now back to his original fleshy color and looked to be in good spirits. Luke realized he was no longer floating slightly above his seat. Gravity had returned. He knew the Space Station rotated to allow centrifugal force to create the right amount of artificial gravity. It wasn't as strong as that on earth, but close.

The hatch door through which they had entered hours before opened. The Illumi-Alliance guards had them file out by row: last in, first out. This time, the orientation felt normal. They only had to stand and walk out. The Station was brightly lit, showing walls a sky blue with most doors a pale yellow. They were led down a long corridor and then asked to wait before a door which read: Medical Department. Luke smiled to himself. He may get to see Sarah sooner rather than later.

Also, next to Luke was a large window. He could see two other docked shuttles. One appeared perpendicular to their position and the other parallel, but upside down. He could see how this would be disorienting to new arrivals. Toward the bottom of the window, he could see part of Earth. It looked so beautiful. The oceans looked so blue from this angle. Clouds looked wispy and white. He could see a portion of the continent of Africa. Asia stood in darkness and the lights of its cities were visible. It was mesmerizing. He could have stood there for hours looking at it.

He felt a hand on his shoulder. He looked to his left and Natalia was smiling at him. "Isn't it beautiful?"

Luke nodded. "Breathtaking."

Jeremy stepped up beside them. "A view to write home about."

Luke chuckled. "Mood crasher."

Jeremy smiled and motioned with his head. "I think our presence is being requested."

Luke turned as the door to the Medical Department opened. Another soldier walked through. "Dr. Luke Loughton: please step forward."

Luke's eyes widened. Why was he being singled out? As he stepped forward, Jeremy put his hand on Luke's shoulder and squeezed. Luke looked at him and nodded. The nonverbal support was definitely appreciated.

The guard gestured for Luke to enter and turned to address the others. He placed a stack of what looked to be gowns on a table near the room entrance. "Each person take one, go to the changing stations, remove all clothing, and put these on." He paused and then emphasized the next words. "This is mandatory. There are no exceptions."

As Luke entered, Sarah and Ken were in conversation; Sarah's back was turned. Caine stood in an at-ease position behind them. Caine's eyes widened on seeing Luke, but he gave no other indication of acknowledgment. René Mauchard stood next to Caine and motioned for Luke to come closer.

Once Ken looked up, he stopped mid-sentence. Sarah turned and gasped. Luke gave a weak smile, unsure of what else to do. He wanted nothing more than to grab her in his arms, give her a hug and a passionate kiss. He ached for her touch. Yet he just stood there in uncertainty.

René stepped forward. "Dr. Loughton, please come and stand next to Agent Caine."

Luke stepped forward. René put his hand on Luke's chest as he approached, as if to stop his movement. Luke stopped and looked at Mauchard.

"Just so you know: the only reason you get to stand here is the stasis chambers hold two, and we have been gracious enough to allow partners to share the same chamber."

Mauchard then removed his hand. Luke continued forward without speaking. He briefly grabbed Sarah's hand and let go quickly; she looked shaken. He whispered, "It's OK." She gave a brief nod.

He stood behind Ken and Sarah, next to Caine. He whispered to Caine: "Viktoria's here."

Caine did not move or look at him. Luke did see Caine swallow—his only clue of acknowledgement. If they knew of Viktoria's involvement, did they know of Caine's?

The guard who had asked Luke to enter brought in the others. They each wore some type of gown. It looked to be a sleeveless one-piece with a tab on each shoulder strap holding it on. It all seemed very degrading.

Although Sarah was not facing him, he could tell seeing all her friends in front of the group unnerved her. Her hands were lightly shaking.

She turned to René. "Mr. Mauchard, we've already put two

thousand individuals into stasis. I thought that was the limit."

René smiled. "We've made certain . . . contingencies."

She looked from René to Ken. "Are . . . are there sufficient stasis chambers for all of these?"

Mauchard stepped forward, just inches from Sarah. She turned back to him. "Dr. Morgan, you just do your job and leave how many stasis chambers we have to me."

Sarah didn't say anything, but Luke saw the anger in her eyes as she turned to get some supplies before turning back to the group. The first in line was Paul. Without sleeves, Luke could see how muscular the guy really was. He evidently didn't spend all his time behind a computer.

Sarah took her small flashlight out and looked into his eyes. She touched his chin. "Open your mouth, but don't say anything."

Luke thought that an odd statement, but—and this was only because he was directly behind her—he saw her put something between Paul's cheek and gums. Paul looked at her, but didn't say anything.

Mauchard grabbed her hand. "What are you doing?"

Sarah looked at him. "What do you mean?"

"You did not do any type of examination on the others."

Sarah jerked her hand away from Mauchard's grip. "That's because we had already examined them." There was clear disdain in her voice as she added, "Your 'contingencies' will add a lot of time we didn't plan for."

"What's the point? They're going to Mars no matter your findings."

"Fine." Luke was surprised Sarah would use such a direct tone. "But their welfare is my responsibility, and I need to know if we have to take additional measures to be sure they arrive safely." She stared at René. "Now, if you don't mind, you're adding to the precious time we don't have."

Luke could see the fire in Mauchard's eyes, but ultimately he backed down. "Very well. Continue."

Luke heard Sarah mumble under her breath, "Like I need your permission to do my job."

Luke almost laughed, but restrained himself. Apparently, no one else heard the comment. Luke found himself loving her all the more.

After Sarah completed her physical assessment, Ken put two strips on Paul: one on his forehead and one on his chest. Luke observed several monitors on the wall turn on. It seemed these assessed Paul's temperature and other vital signs. The status light turned green.

Sarah and Ken then took the same steps for Maher.

Sarah turned to René. "This can go much faster if you allow Dr. Loughton to assist. He's just standing there anyway. If Dr. Wilson takes over for me and Dr. Loughton puts on the vital sign strips, I can then get those two into hyperstasis as they assess the next two subjects."

"But he's not a medical doctor."

"True, but he's just putting on the strips. Dr. Wilson will oversee and make the medical assessment."

René looked at Luke and then at Ken. Ken nodded his head. "Very well," Rene mumbled, gruffly.

"Thank you, Mr. Mauchard." Her tone was suddenly much more polite than before.

She gave Ken her equipment. As she briefly explained to Luke what he was to do, Luke saw her put something in Ken's coat pocket. Ken looked at her and nodded. She squeezed Luke's hand and then led Paul and Maher into the room housing the stasis chambers.

Once Viktoria was brought forward, Mauchard stopped their work. He turned to Caine. "Agent Caine. Do you recognize this woman?"

Caine went to attention. "Yes, sir. I do."

"And who is she?"

"My boss, sir."

"Do you consider her a friend?"

Caine glanced briefly at René and then at Viktoria, but then looked straight ahead. "Yes, sir. I do."

Mauchard shook his head. "Well, that was your first—and last—mistake."

He motioned as if asking someone to come forward. Luke's eyes widened. Agent Abel stepped forward.

"Agent Abel. Do you know this woman?"

Abel stood at attention. "Yes, sir."

"And who is she?"

"My boss, sir."

"And do you consider her a friend?"

"Absolutely not, sir."

"And what is Agent Caine to you?"

"An enemy of the state, sir."

Luke saw Abel glance at Caine. There was not a single ounce of softness or friendship in his eyes.

"Agent Caine. Step down."

Caine relaxed from attention and stepped forward.

Mauchard gestured toward Abel. "Agent Abel, take Agent Caine's place."

"Yes, sir." Abel then stood where Caine had stood, assuming the at-ease position.

"Agent Caine, you will meet the same fate as that of Agent Komcova." He pointed toward the group of people. "Do you know this woman?"

Caine slowly turned. Luke could see Caine's muscles visibly go lax. "Caroline?"

A woman ran forward and threw her arms around Caine. "Albert!"

Luke was stunned and felt horrible he had never asked Caine his first name. Actually, it seemed he had let his previous bad feelings about Caine before accepting the Messiah cloud his feelings about him after Caine made the right choice. Luke groaned inside. He didn't even know Caine was married. Again, another sacrifice he had not acknowledged.

Caine's eyes watered, but Luke did not see any tears fall. "Caroline, I'm so, so sorry."

Caroline pulled away and put her hand to his cheek. "It's OK. It's OK. At least we're together."

René chuckled. "Yes, you are together—for a long trip." He turned to Ken. "Dr. Wilson, get these two examined as quickly as possible and placed into hyperstasis. Such people don't even deserve this level of dignity."

Caine's wife was visibly shaken, but she also looked determined to act with dignity even though it had not been extended to her.

Mauchard then stepped from the room.

* * * * *

It took nearly eight hours to get twenty-five of the group of fifty into hyperstasis. Luke felt exhausted. He knew his job was menial, but standing for twelve hours completely sapped his energy. The guards took the remainder to a few holding rooms. They would get processed the next day.

Thankfully, they allowed Luke to room with Sarah. For now, at least, they still granted her the dignity a physician deserved and all the rights that went with such a position. He knew that would not last. He wanted to take advantage of the time he had with her.

When they were alone, he wrapped her in his arms and gave her a tight hug. It felt so good to have her in his arms again. He smelled her cherry blossom perfume. It brought back so many memories of their times together. He remembered lying in bed with her filling his senses with her perfume mixed with the honeysuckle aroma from her hair. He inhaled deeply. He pulled her from their embrace and kissed her. She kissed back.

After a prolonged kiss, their lips parted and he put his forehead to hers. "I have missed you so much."

She looked into his eyes. "Not more than I have missed you."

He smiled. "OK, we'll call it a tie."

She chuckled. "Deal."

They sat on the small green sofa in her room. It looked like the sky blue walls, pale yellow door, and green furniture was supposed to capture the essence of Earth. It was a nice try, but didn't actually deliver.

"Sarah, what were you doing today? What did you put into Paul's mouth, and the others?"

Sarah sighed and leaned back, but still held onto Luke's hands. "I discovered Simone had the hyperstasis fluid infused with the chemical she developed."

Luke shook his head. "I'm not following. How is that a concern?"

Sarah put her hand on his chest. "I guess I never really explained to you how the hyperstasis chamber works."

Luke shook his head.

"Well, you're probably not going to like it, but it really is the best way to do it."

Luke furrowed his brow. He already didn't like it based on that comment.

"In order to go into hyperstasis, one is immersed into a perfluorocarbon liquid. It is able to be a more oxygen-rich environment than air and helps protect the body better."

Luke waved his hand. "Wait. You're saying we will be *breathing* this liquid?"

Sarah nodded. "I know it sounds weird, but it is very safe. We've used it for various medical practices for many years now." She grimaced. "Yet, for some, it is somewhat difficult to initially adjust. We have a reflex to not want to breathe a liquid. You have to trick your mind . . . that it is OK to let you breathe." She took his hand. "It's better if you can do that." She shrugged. "Of course, even if you fight it, you will eventually have to take a breath, and so you will eventually breathe the liquid and your panic will subside. It's just better if you can do it not in a panicked state."

Luke shook his head. "Wow. That's a lot to process, even if one is prepared for it. How did everyone do?"

Sarah cocked her head and raised her eyebrows. "A few managed to accept it. Most, unfortunately, panicked." She gave a weak smile. "The biggest issue was having everyone get into the stasis chamber naked."

Luke's eyebrows raised a couple of times. "Hmm, sounds interesting."

Sarah laughed. "The gown just gets in the way of the wires needed to monitor one's vitals." She patted his chest. "Don't get any ideas. You'll be asleep."

"So, you force them to sleep?"

"We want them to rest comfortably and decrease their respiration, metabolism, and heart rate. That really is the best way to travel in space for a prolonged period of time with limited resources."

Luke nodded. "OK, I get that. But what does that have to do with Simone's chemical?"

"They have dissolved it into this perfluorocarbon milieu into which you will be placed. Reprogramming will be on-going the entire time. She and others are hoping by the time everyone reaches Mars, no one in hyperstasis will remember anything about Earth—and they will embrace Mars as their new home without protest."

"And you're trying to prevent that?"

Sarah nodded. "At least for some. I've been giving certain people, especially those I know, the compound Matteo synthesized. With one's metabolism slowed down, I'm hoping it will counteract Simone's compound. As a safeguard, I'm putting some of the drug into the perfluorocarbon milieu also." She shrugged. "I don't know if it will work, but it's better to try something than do nothing."

Luke nodded. "How much do you have left?"

Sarah shook her head while twisting the corner of her mouth. "Not much. Just enough for you and me, I'm afraid."

He patted her hand. "You can feel good you've done everything you could do that was under your control." He reached over and gave her a kiss. "Let me get our dinner and bring it back here. We can eat and have an early night."

She nodded. "That would be good."

Luke went to the galley, got two plates, and brought them back to their small room. After eating half of whatever the meal was supposed to be, they prepared for bed. Luke had missed having Sarah next to him. Now she was back, and he wanted to savor this night. He wasn't sure if there would be another.

She snuggled next to him. He inhaled the honeysuckle aroma from her hair. As he got closer, it mixed with the cherry blossom aroma. The combined fragrances were intoxicating. He turned her onto her back, looked into her eyes, and gave her a kiss. She reciprocated.

He let his passion swell and took it to the next level. "Let's pretend we're in the stasis chamber without the liquid."

Sarah chuckled and leaned further into him.

TWENTY-SEVEN

HYPERSTASIS

Luke turned over. It dawned on him his hand was not touching Sarah. He opened his eyes and saw her side of the bed empty. He sat up and looked around. She was sitting at the small table next to the sofa.

She smiled. "Good morning. Hungry?"

She had breakfast ready for him at the table. He went over and sat down. "Well, aren't you the early bird?"

She looked at her watch and laughed. "Actually, I'm not early. You're late. We have to be back at our posts in forty-five minutes."

Luke's eyes widened as he took the fork from his mouth. "Why didn't you wake me?"

"I was about to, but you beat me to it." She took a sip of coffee. "Besides, it's like a five-minute walk there anyway." She patted his arm. "You've got time. No need to rush."

He nodded. His mind turned to the mission. He felt Sarah's hand on his arm. He looked at her.

"Are you OK?" Sarah asked. "You look a million miles away."

Luke smiled. "Sorry. Just thinking."

"About what?"

"Last night you told me what will happen to those in stasis. But what about those who aren't put into stasis?"

Sarah took another sip of coffee. "Well, they will be kept active. There is a full gym and spa for them. There is an arboretum for them to enjoy."

Luke's jaw dropped slightly. "Wow. Who gets to enjoy all of that? Are they dignitaries or . . . who?"

Sarah shook her head and chuckled. "A few, but most of the dignitaries wanted to stay on Earth. Many of the people are the crew, and then there are those who paid substantially for the lottery to be in their favor."

Luke shook his head. "Defies the entire concept of a lottery, doesn't it?"

Sarah cocked her head and nodded.

"I guess, since this isn't really the first Mars mission, people feel more comfortable in going," Luke said.

"I think that's part of it. But nothing on this scale has been attempted before. It's still a first in many aspects."

Luke pushed his plate back. "Have you seen the ships that will take us to Mars?"

Sarah nodded toward the wall. "If you go to the very last window, you can see most of one."

"Really?" He got up and went to the small window in the back of the room. Turning his head sideways, he could see the top two-thirds of the ship. It reminded him of the replica he had seen in Brasilia, but this was more massive than even his imagination at that time. He turned back. "Impressive."

Sarah nodded. "But what's the purpose of all the arches?"

Luke smiled. "Those will turn and create the artificial gravity. There are inner arches and outer arches. That allows more room in the same amount of space. Each layer will turn at a different rate of speed to create the same degree of centrifugal force so the gravity will be constant over the entire ship." He paused. "Well, the center of the ship won't have gravity; it will be stationary." He thought for a moment, then turned and looked at Sarah. "What will be in the center?"

She raised her cup toward Luke. "We will."

Luke's eyes widened. "Why is that?"

She gave a small shrug. "If you think about it, it makes sense. The hyperstasis chambers are self-sustaining. Those in the chambers don't need the gravity, and it allows the maximum use of the ship's storage space."

"What if something goes wrong with one of the stasis chambers?"

"Oh, each and every one is monitored. The technician simply has to punch in the chamber number and the ship will automatically send it to the Medical Department."

"Technician? That doesn't sound very comforting."

Sarah smiled. "There are two technician staffs for a total of six technicians. They are all highly trained for emergency situations. About the only thing they can't take care of are surgeries. But the likelihood of the need to perform one of those is extremely low."

Luke shook his head. "I'd rather have you watching over me."

"I will. I'll be there right beside you."

"Yeah. Asleep."

Sarah laughed. "Come on. It's time to get back to work."

They walked back to the Medical Department. Ken was already there getting everything in place. Agent Abel, also already present, looked solemn as usual.

Luke patted Ken's shoulder. "Thanks."

Ken looked at him, then smiled and nodded. Luke knew he didn't have to explain himself. It seemed Ken had either taken the step of faith or was at least willing to help them out. Either way, Luke was extremely appreciative of what Ken was risking in helping them.

Once they got started, they were able to move more quickly than they had the day before. Luke knew part of the reason was because he now knew what he was doing, and the work had become so routine he hardly had to think about it. He also knew Ken and Sarah didn't have to hide administering the chemical since they had no more of it. He felt deep sorrow for most of these people; they would likely have no memory of their former lives on Earth.

Luke couldn't believe people with positions of power were so willing to take important memories away from another person without any remorse.

Once the final person was placed in hyperstasis, Luke looked at his watch. It had only taken six hours. And then he looked up . . . and saw René Mauchard approaching.

"Excellent work, Dr. Wilson. You made record time today. I'm impressed."

Ken gave a weak smile. "Thank you, sir."

René held up his index finger. "Yet, you're not completely finished."

"Sir? Don't tell me you've brought more people from Earth to be placed into stasis?"

René laughed and shook his head. "No worries, Dr. Wilson. No more are coming. This last batch of fifty was the last." He put his hands behind his back. "No, you only have two more."

"Two more? Who would that be?" Ken looked around as if expecting someone else to show up.

René turned toward the stasis chamber entrance. "Mind joining us, Dr. Morgan?"

Ken looked confused, but didn't say anything.

Sarah came through the hatch door and stood next to Luke.

René gestured to the two of them. "Dr. Wilson, here are your last two candidates."

Ken's eyes widened and his jaw dropped. "What? You're . . . you're not serious. After all . . . after all she's done for you—for this program? Why?"

"First of all, Dr. Wilson, you are not one to question my authority."

Luke saw Ken bite his lower lip. He could tell contempt was quickly filling him.

"Second. While, yes, she has helped considerably, she has also contributed to a great deal of chaos that was completely unnecessary."

Luke thought Ken was going to explode. Somehow, he held it together. Luke found himself standing there, praying that, if nothing else, this last act of the Illumi-Alliance would drive Ken to accept the truth and his Messiah.

"So, in answer to your question of why, in spite of her brilliance and aid in this mission, Dr. Morgan is just as subversive as all the others who have been placed in stasis." He turned to Luke. "And Dr. Loughton fits into the same category."

René turned back to Ken. "So, Dr. Wilson, I expect you to do your job and put these two into stasis."

Ken turned his head, as though unsure how to show his defiance. "But . . . "

Sarah put her hand on Ken's arm to stop him. "It's OK, Ken."

He turned to her and shook his head.

She gave a weak smile. "Just do your job. It's OK. I expected this." She turned to Luke, took his hand, and turned back to Ken. "We both expected it and have prepared ourselves for this outcome."

Mauchard turned to Abel. "Be sure this is carried out."

Abel stiffened as though heightening his attention. "Yes, sir. It will be done."

Mauchard nodded, turned, and left.

Ken, Sarah, and Luke stepped into the stasis chamber room. Abel followed them in.

Ken turned to him. "Agent Abel, please wait outside. They have to undress. Give them the dignity they deserve."

"I have to ensure it is done."

Ken gestured to the room itself. "There is no other exit from this room except the one you are guarding. I will let you see them in the stasis chamber after I have placed them inside it." He pointed to the hatch door. "Now, please. Stand outside."

Abel glared at Ken, but then stepped outside the room.

Ken turned and hugged Sarah. "I am going to miss you so much." He shook his head. "What they are doing here is so unjust."

Sarah kissed Ken's cheek. "I told you it's all right. Just remember this, and remember all Luke and I have told you." Her voice got quieter, and she smiled. "Make that decision we've talked about. You helping me here is one thing, but your eternal destiny is another. And it's more important."

Ken nodded. "After today, I'd be a fool not to. I will talk to Scott once I get back."

Sarah nodded. "Good. I'm so glad to hear that."

Sarah gave a capsule to Luke, which he swallowed. She did the same. No words were spoken, but Luke knew this was the compound Matteo synthesized to counteract the one Simone had manufactured. He then saw Sarah put the last two capsules into the stasis chamber fluid.

Both he and Sarah undressed. Luke felt a little weird doing so, but kept reminding himself Ken was a physician. Sarah put several strips on his body: forehead, chest, and abdomen. She then attached wires to all of them.

"These will help monitor your brain waves and vital signs. Wires are better than Bluetooth when one needs to monitor for prolonged periods of time." Sarah smiled. "Now, one last thing."

Ken held up a probe. "I guess you know where this goes?"

Luke thought about that. He could only think of one place such a long and cylindrical probe would go. "Come on. You've got to be kidding me."

Ken smiled. "Unfortunately, no."

Luke looked at Sarah. She patted his chest. "This is the best way to monitor core body temperature."

Luke shook his head, put his hands on the edge of the stasis chamber, and bent over. It was far more embarrassing than hurtful.

Ken then did the same for Sarah.

Both climbed into the chamber. The liquid felt denser than water, but being at body temperature, it actually felt extremely comfortable on the skin as they went from the coolness of the room to the warmth of the liquid. Ken adjusted the wires so there were no kinks or overlaps.

Ken pressed several buttons on the side of the chamber and then looked at the monitoring screen. "Sarah, I know you know the process here."

Sarah nodded. "I explained it to Luke as well."

"Yes, but as I stand here, it's hard to wrap my brain around breathing in this liquid," Luke said. "It just seems . . . wrong."

Ken nodded. "I know. Try not to think about it. Just do it. The faster, the better."

Luke took a deep breath and looked at Sarah.

She reached over and gave him a kiss. "Want me to go first?"

He shook his head. "No, let's do this together."

She smiled. "OK. Ready?"

He took her hand and laid back into the liquid. Once submerged, he turned to her. She held up three fingers, then two, then one. He took a gulp of the liquid. It sent a sense of panic through him. His body kept screaming *No!* . . . but he forced himself to overcome the urge to sit up and breathe air again. He forced his lungs to breathe in, and then out, as naturally as possible. In a few minutes, it became easier. It was a little harder to breathe in and out than air, but Luke felt OK. He looked over at Sarah. She smiled and gave a thumbs-up. He did the same.

He saw Sarah look toward the side. Ken was looking in. She gave him a thumbs-up as well. Ken nodded. Soon the top of the chamber closed. Luke felt it moving, receding back into the wall. The lights of the room slowly faded, and they entered darkness.

All he now saw were blinking lights. Some were red, some green, some blue. He had no idea what they meant, but it was somewhat comforting to have the glow. There was just enough light so he could see the outline of Sarah's body. She pulled him toward her. He wrapped his arms around her and she put her head on his chest . . .

Luke knew his next waking moment would likely be when they reached Mars. In one way, he was excited for the adventure. But to Luke, none of it mattered as long as Sarah was part of it.

In a matter of minutes, slumber overtook them both.

TWENTY-EIGHT

LAUNCH

Philippe slowly opened the door to Simone's office. He peeked in. She apparently hadn't heard the door open as she continued to type something on her computer without looking up. He slipped in and simply stood there watching her. His adoration for her had increased immensely. Although he knew her to be power hungry, everything she had worked on only increased his own personal power and prestige as well. He felt she really did love him. But Philippe also knew marriage would not be in the offing. He could never envision her tied to anyone—especially in such an old-fashioned institution. She was way too independent for that.

Still, deep inside, he was aware of something that yearned to be one with her in that way. He knew he loved her deeply, either way.

He saw her pause and slowly turn her head toward him.

"Philippe." She smiled. "What are you doing standing there?"

He gave a small shrug. "Oh, just admiring the most beautiful and wonderful person on Earth, and wondering what she's doing working on Bastille Day."

She gave a coy smile. "Just on Earth?"

He laughed and walked over to her, then leaned down to give her a kiss. "In the whole universe." He rubbed her back. "I'll have to remember compliments cover two worlds now."

She smiled and gestured for Philippe to have a seat. "I just had a few things to catch up on. What brings you by?"

Philippe sat and crossed his legs. Propping his elbows on the arms of the chair, he placed the fingertips of each hand together. "I just received word from René just before he began to prepare for launch."

Simone looked at her watch. "Oh, I almost forgot." She pressed a remote and a large monitor on the wall came to life. "Want to watch it with me?"

"Absolutely. Then we can go celebrate."

Simone nodded. "So, what did René say?"

"He was already on cloud nine." He shook his head. "Never would I have guessed he would be so excited about this mission." He smiled and shook his index finger at Simone. "I think you really unleashed his inner passion."

She smiled. "I'm glad it turned out so positively."

Philippe cocked his head. "Oh, absolutely. He also reported the main leaders of the insurrection were apprehended and placed into stasis, including Drs. Loughton and Morgan."

Simone smiled. "See, I told you those two were the troublemakers."

Philippe nodded. "I'll never doubt you again." He smiled and sat up straighter. "Oh, and guess who was also part of this insurrectionist group."

She raised her eyebrows. "Who?"

"I'll give you a clue. We ate there last night."

Simone's jaw dropped. "No! You're kidding me. La Dérive Des Continents restaurant was just as lively as ever." She put her hand to her chin. "But it does make sense. The Pangeas were very good friends of Loughton." She opened her hands slightly. "How are the restaurants still operating?"

Philippe shrugged. "Must have made arrangements for others to keep things going."

Simone shook her head. "Amazing. What some people are willing to give up for no good reason."

Philippe nodded. His attention turned to the monitor. The announcer was discussing how all six spacecraft would be launched in succession from the Space Station. René appeared on screen. At the bottom of the screen it read: "Prerecorded."

"Mr. Mauchard, many have been stunned at your participation in this launch. Can you tell us what persuaded you to go on this mission?"

René gave a bright smile. "You know, if you had asked me this a couple of months ago, my answer may have been different. Yet the more I thought about it, this was too much of a momentous and historical moment not to be part of it. First my father, and now my brother and I, have been pushing toward this moment all our lives. I just wanted people to know we are committed to this effort to have mankind expand its footprint into our universe. I am here to put feet to that commitment. We are not just talk, but are every bit as committed to its success as everyone else who has spent countless hours preparing for this historic mission."

Philippe looked at Simone and smiled. "That is so well said! He summarized everything very succinctly. René was always good at that."

She smiled and nodded back.

The announcer continued. "The other question on everyone's mind is why you, a Frenchman, are on the American ship?"

René smiled. "That is because it was North America which

first bought into my father's vision. I want to honor that support today. The order of launch will be the order of the continents embracing this vision. This is not to detract from all the hard work countless and very dedicated individuals from each and every continent have put into this effort. Yet, this is one way to celebrate the advancement of my father's vision."

"So, will you go through the order once again? I'm not sure our viewers know the order in which the different continents embraced this vision."

"The order is North America, followed by Europe, South America, Africa, Asia, and Australia." He smiled. "Yet, this isn't the order of arrival. Everyone arrives simultaneously. The whole globe will be united in the settlement of Mars."

Philippe and Simone watched as the announcer showed pictures of the various ships docked at the Space Station waiting to launch. He went over the design and how various parts worked, how artificial gravity would be maintained, how many would travel in stasis, and how many would be awake the entire length of travel. He then had astronomers and astrophysicists detail the flight plan and dangers the ships could potentially face. All were in agreement that something going wrong was always possible, but highly improbable.

The announcer turned to face the camera. "Now for what everyone has been waiting for."

The camera panned across Mission Control on the Space Station. Over the intercom came: "Sixty and counting." In the corner of the screen appeared a countdown clock. At various times, viewers heard systems analysts and guidance officials say "All is a go." When the clock reached ten, the intercom counted the time down to zero.

The camera panned to one of the Space Station windows. The first ship appeared to float for a brief second and then began to accelerate. The arches began to rotate and the ship quickly sped away from the Space Station.

And this occurred, like clockwork, every fifteen minutes until all six ships had launched.

Philippe reached over and took the remote, turning off the monitor. "Well, it's done." He flashed a beaming smile Simone's way. "Time to celebrate with everyone. Got your dancing shoes on?"

Simone smiled back. "I will when I meet you downstairs in fifteen minutes."

He stood and came around the desk and gave her a kiss. "Wonderful. We'll get there just in time for the fireworks."

"Ready for your speech at the gala?"

Philippe patted his coat pocket. "Got it right here."

She stood and gave him a hug and whispered in his ear, "After tonight, we'll be the two most powerful people on the planet."

TWENTY-NINE

AWAKENED

Luke felt the need to wretch. He sat up quickly. He felt his abdominal muscles contract involuntarily and liquid spewed from his mouth. He tried to breathe in, but couldn't. He coughed as more fluid came out. He did this repeatedly until he was able to breathe again. He then sucked in a deep breath of air—he felt the sense of panic slowly beginning to dissipate—and did that a few times until breathing became second nature once again.

He looked around. He was sitting in the stasis chamber with Sarah beside him. She was recovering, just as he was. They looked at each other and then began to realize there was a medical technician standing next to the stasis chamber.

"Dr. Morgan, Dr. Loughton. I am Medical Technician Barkley. Please step out of the chamber. Assistance from both of you is needed."

Luke felt somewhat awkward standing naked in front of a complete stranger. He could only imagine Sarah's discomfort. Yet she didn't seem to display any awkwardness at all.

As the technician unhooked all the wires connected to

them, and Sarah helped take all the medical strips off herself and Luke, she asked, "Are you saying we're not yet at Mars?"

"No, ma'am We're quite a distance away, actually."

The technician handed each a towel and pointed to some clothes in the corner of the room.

Sarah continued her inquiry. "So, why were we awakened?"

The technician shook his head. "I can't answer that. I was just asked to awaken both of you. As soon as you get dressed, I'll take you to Captain Abrams."

Sarah nodded but looked at Luke with raised eyebrows. He simply shrugged, unsure how else to respond. As Luke donned his clothes, he found them extremely soft and comfortable. His were a navy blue while Sarah's an olive green. They reminded him of doctor's scrubs, only slightly more dressy.

Luke used the Velcro to fit his pants to his waist. "What's up with the different colors?"

Sarah put her hair into a ponytail as she answered. "Different colors for easier recognition of job performance." She pointed to herself. "Olive for medical." She gestured to him. "Dark blue for science-related."

Luke nodded. He noticed Barkley also wore olive-colored scrubs.

The technician led them down a windowless corridor and then turned down another long corridor. Luke found his legs somewhat stiff at first, but they became more limber quickly. He noticed this corridor had numerous windows. Luke tried to slow his pace to capture the view. He saw three arches, each rotating at a different rate. They didn't appear to be moving fast, but to create the centrifugal force necessary to simulate earth's gravity, they had to be traveling faster than they appeared. He found it almost mesmerizing. He suddenly stopped and grabbed Sarah's arm.

"Sarah, look." He pointed to the farthest arch.

She looked at him, then where he pointed. "What is it?"

"Look at that window of what looks like an exercise room. The window is shattered."

Sarah gasped and turned to Barkley. "What happened?"

Barkley shook his head. "I can't say. I'm only authorized to take you to the captain."

Sarah looked back at the scene before them and shook her head. "I hope no one was in there when it happened."

Luke nodded. "But why else would they bring you out of hyperstasis?"

Sarah gave him a double take. "I sure hope you're wrong."

He rubbed her back; Luke was still trying to get used to the sense of being awake again. "So do I."

They followed Barkley down another corridor for a short distance. Barkley motioned for them to enter a doorway. Seated at a medium-sized conference table were René Mauchard and two other individuals Luke did not recognize. Luke assumed one was the ship's captain; this man was dressed in an official uniform. The other man wore olive-colored scrubs; he was obviously someone in a medical capacity.

The man in olive spoke first. "Thank you, Barkley. You may go."

Barkley bowed slightly and left, closing the door behind him.

Captain Abrams motioned for Luke and Sarah to sit.

Once they did, the Captain folded his hands, gave a warm smile, and spoke. "I know the two of you are likely disoriented and don't understand where you are and why you are here. Dr. Layne is a psychoanalyst who can help you adjust to your . . . new situation."

Luke looked at Sarah and Sarah at him.

Luke shook his head. "We're fine. We know the ship is on its way to Mars to establish a larger colony there. We were in hyperstasis, and were just brought out."

Sarah nodded. "I assume there is some type of medical emergency?"

Luke noticed confused looks on all faces. Sarah looked from one to the other. "That is why you brought me out of hyperstasis, isn't it?"

Captain Abrams looked at René, his eyebrows raised.

René leaned forward, looking confused—beyond confused. "Impossible." He looked at the captain. "It's been months. There is no way it . . . could not have worked."

Luke looked at Captain Abrams. "Is anything wrong?" Luke really wanted to laugh and tell René his master plan had not worked. But it was just as fun to see him squirm.

Abrams looked from René back to Luke. "Well, it seems we were misinformed that the stasis may have inhibited some of your memories. But that doesn't seem to be the case."

Luke smiled. "Oh, we remember everything." Luke glanced from Abrams to René and back again.

René shifted in his chair. The captain looked from René to Luke as if he had missed some secret communication. He then turned his attention to Sarah.

"Dr. Morgan, since you seem to have all of your faculties, may I now debrief you on our issue?"

Sarah nodded and sat up straighter. "Oh, by all means."

"There has been an accident."

Sarah nodded.

The captain cocked his head. "You know?"

"We saw evidence of a damaged window in one of the arches as the technician led us here."

René tapped his index finger hard on the table, his face now a shade of red. "So that's how you know. Barkley told you everything before you got here."

Sarah shook her head. "Actually, no. He refused to tell us

anything. He stated his orders were just to retrieve us and deliver us to Captain Abrams."

René sat back into his chair, fuming but quiet.

Sarah turned her attention back to the captain. "Please continue, sir. How can I be of help?"

Abrams nodded. "Yes, there was a serious accident. Commander Denning, my second in command, was in the exercise room when a tiny meteoroid hit the window." He released and relocked his fingers together. "Under normal conditions, the window should have withstood such an encounter. But an investigative team discovered this particular window had a weak spot and this tiny meteoroid happened to hit it at that precise spot. The odds of this happening would have been . . . miniscule." He raised his eyebrows. "Yet, it happened." He sat back in his chair. "The team is currently inspecting all windows, but all, so far, seem in order." He shrugged. "It was just a fluke."

Sarah nodded. "I take it the commander was injured?"

Abrams nodded. "Yes, the meteoroid went through his abdomen." He shook his head. "It was so little. No larger than a pea, really." He sighed. "Thankfully, he was near the wall that housed a portable breathing apparatus. He crawled over and got to it as the window completely shattered. He managed to pull himself through the door and seal it before getting sucked out with everything else." He shook his head. "There was one other passenger in the gym at the time. He didn't make it to the door before the window blew out completely. He was pulled out with the remaining air."

Sarah shook her head with a grimace. "I'm so sorry. How is your second in command?"

"Not good, I'm afraid. He's in critical condition. The medical technicians have been able to stabilize him to some degree, but he's bleeding internally and they haven't yet been able to stop the bleeding. Barkley says surgery is needed as soon as possible."

Sarah stood. "Then let's go. It would appear time is of the essence."

Abrams nodded. He motioned to someone outside the room. The door opened and Barkley entered. Abrams gestured to Barkley. "Dr. Morgan, Technician Barkley will direct you to the surgical suite and will assist you however you need."

Sarah nodded and turned to follow Barkley out. She turned back. "Luke, I'll catch up with you later."

Luke nodded. "Of course. This is priority."

As the two of them left, another woman, wearing dark blue clothes, entered. The captain gestured for her to sit.

"Dr. Loughton, this is Ms. Ewing. She is an astronomy technician whose main job, up until now, was to ensure there was no unexpected space debris or asteroids in our path."

Luke looked at the woman. "I take it this incident . . . took you off guard."

She nodded. "Absolutely. It didn't appear on our regular scans. It was upon us before we could warn anyone." She gave a shrug. "Although the outcome was grave for these two individuals, it could have been much worse." She glanced at the others. "It . . . it may not seem this way, but I think we were really fortunate."

Luke looked back to Abrams. "What would you like me to do?"

"Please go with Ms. Ewing and see if you can figure out why this happened and if we are in danger of any more occurrences of such a meteoroid shower in our current path. Larger meteoroids would be a huge concern. I just want to be sure our warning system is intact. And to find out what went wrong."

Luke nodded. "Sure. What about the other ships? Any damage to those?"

Abrams shook his head. "No. Although they were hit, their integrity was maintained. It seems we were the only one with damage and casualties." He cocked his head. "As I stated, an unfortunate fluke."

Luke nodded, stood, and gestured to the door so Ewing could lead the way. He was sorrowful about what had occurred, but happy to be able to keep himself busy. Hopefully, both he and Sarah would have good outcomes to report to one another later.

THIRTY

METEOROIDS

As Luke walked with Ewing, he stuck out his hand. "I'm Luke. I prefer to work informally if that's OK with you."

Ewing smiled. "Oh, absolutely." She shook his hand. "My name is Jayne—with a y." She smiled. "Just so you know."

"My pleasure. So, Jayne with a y, where are we headed?"

She chuckled. "We're not going too far from here. We'll turn right at the next corridor. This will put us on the next arch. Then, it's only a few doors down from there."

Luke nodded. "So, what do you think happened?"

Jayne shook her head. "I don't know. It didn't show up on our early warning system." She shrugged. "But even if it did, I'm not sure we would have considered it a problem. As far as we can tell, none of them were much larger than pea size. The materials used to make this ship were tested and retested, touted to be resistant to such forces."

"So, a fluke, as your captain said?"

Jayne nodded. "I think so. Yet, I'm curious why we didn't even know about it."

She came to an abrupt stop and Luke almost ran into her.

She gestured to the door. "Here we are."

Once they entered, another technician, sitting at a console, looked up. Seeing Luke, he stood. Jayne gestured to the man. "Luke, this is Derek. Derek Foster." She looked at Derek and gestured to Luke. "And this is Dr. Luke Loughton, an astrophysicist."

Derek reached to shake his hand. "My pleasure, Dr. Loughton."

Luke smiled. "Luke, please. Informality makes work go much easier."

Derek smiled and nodded.

Luke raised his hands slightly. "So, show me what you know."

Derek gestured for Luke to sit at the console where he had been sitting. Derek and Jayne stood behind him.

Derek pressed a few buttons. "Here is the video feed we have."

Luke looked. Everything looked normal.

Jayne leaned closer. "Wait for it. There. Did you see that?"

Luke looked up at her and shook his head. "I didn't see anything." He grinned. "Are you two trying to pull a fast one on the newbie?"

Jayne got a shocked look on her face. "Oh, no sir. Never."

Derek laughed. "Jayne doesn't know how to joke."

Jayne pushed on Derek's shoulder. "What do you know, anyway?"

Luke held up his hands. "OK, OK. Let's not have a war here in astrophysics." He looked up at Derek. "OK, run it again—only slower this time."

Derek reached over his shoulder and pressed a few more buttons. The monitor showed scenes almost frame by frame. "There!" Derek pressed a button and froze the screen. "You can see it right there."

Luke leaned in. "You mean that was the only one?"

Derek bobbed his head. "There were a few more, but none of those were caught on camera."

Luke kept staring at the screen. "And none were any larger than this?"

Jayne shook her head. "None that we have discovered."

Luke looked at Derek. He also shook his head.

"Well, I can see why the early warning system didn't sound. One this small would have to be contrasted against something to be detected."

Jayne nodded. "That's what we thought, but Captain Abrams didn't believe us."

Luke nodded. "I'm sure he's just concerned about the welfare of those on board."

Derek took a seat in another chair. "Is that it? They woke you just to verify that?"

Luke put his hand to his chin. Jayne looked from Derek to Luke. "Something's bothering you, isn't it?"

Luke leaned back. He reached over and pulled another chair close to him and motioned for Jayne to sit. Luke spoke slowly, choosing his words carefully. "I'm concerned because I don't think it's just a fluke."

Jayne's jaw dropped. "Why?"

"Meteoroids that small don't originate on their own."

Derek rolled his chair closer. "You think these came from an asteroid?"

Luke nodded. "But what I'm not sure about is if the asteroid is behind us or ahead of us. But first we need to be sure the early warning system is working properly."

"We had the system run a self-diagnostic, and everything looked OK," Jayne said.

He looked at her and nodded. "Let's turn the sensitivity up to high and run it again, just to be sure."

She nodded, turned to a different console, and started working.

Luke turned to Derek. "Did the other ships' early warning systems give any indication of the meteoroid shower before it hit?"

Derek raised his eyebrows. "No idea. I know we were the only ship to sustain damage, but I never asked that question."

"OK, if you will ask that question, I'll go ask Captain Abrams if I can call Houston."

Derek scrunched his brow. "What for?"

"Maybe we can simulate what occurred and see if it should have triggered the system. At least then we can better tell whether all is working properly." He tapped his fingers on the console. "See if you can have the other ships send you all of their video feed of the meteoroid shower as well. That could be helpful in preparing the simulation. Also, I want to see if Houston can scan our flight path to see if an asteroid came by here. I would feel better knowing these meteoroids were in the wake of an asteroid rather than a precursor."

Derek's eyes widened and he nodded. "Absolutely."

Luke stood to go find the captain. Derek turned to contact the other ships. Once Luke got to the door, he turned with a realization: he had no clue where he was to go. "Jayne, do you have the self-diagnostic running?"

She nodded. "Yes, sir. Need anything else?"

"Can you take me to the captain?"

She smiled. "Certainly. It took us all awhile to learn our way around."

"And maybe you can get me a map of the ship later."

"Sure. No problem. I'll have them delivered to your quarters."

He nodded. "Thanks. Uh . . . and where would that be?"

She chuckled. "We'll pass near that area. I'll show you."

211

THIRTY-ONE

PROPHECY SHARED

Luke found he couldn't meet Abrams until the next day. So he decided to go to his room. Since it had been several hours since he and Sarah went to do their assignments, he assumed she would already be there, but she wasn't. The room reminded him a great deal of the room he and Sarah shared on the Space Station.

He decided to lie down until Sarah arrived. The next thing he knew, he heard the door open; it was Sarah. As he looked at his watch, he realized he had been sleeping for nearly two hours.

"Hey, babe. Have you been in surgery this whole time?"

Sarah nodded. She looked completely spent. She plopped next to him and put her head on his shoulder. "It's been so long since I've had to do surgery like that."

"What was the problem?"

She sat up straight and looked at him. "Although the meteoroid was small, it did a lot of damage. It perforated his colon, several places in the small intestine, and the gall bladder." She shook her head. "Thankfully, it missed places that would have made him lose too much blood, but it created a constant leakage of blood internally. Then, bile and fecal content had spilled into the abdominal cavity." She raised her hands and plopped them back onto her lap. "I can only describe it as a mess." She turned her head. "I have to give the medical technicians credit for keeping him stable for that long. He was in so much pain and his blood pressure was all over the place." She raised her eyebrows. "Plus, his leg was hit with something that was sucked out with the air." She shrugged. "I'm not sure what it was, but walking may prove difficult for a time."

Luke wrapped his arm around her shoulders and rubbed her upper arm. "Sounds like it was hard for both of you. So, how is he now?"

She looked into his eyes and nodded. "Stable. It will probably be touch and go for a while. He's on a strong dose of antibiotics. It's just a matter of time, I'm afraid, before we know the outcome."

"Sounds like it will be a long recovery."

She nodded. "Very likely."

"Here." He had her lie down and then laid next to her. She put her head on his chest and fell asleep in a matter of minutes.

A short time later, he heard a knock on the door. He slipped out from under Sarah, trying not to wake her. She stirred, then resettled into slumber. He opened the door and was stunned.

"Captain Abrams. I thought we weren't meeting until tomorrow?"

"I know. But can you meet now?"

Luke turned and looked at Sarah, sound asleep. He turned back to Abrams. "Can we talk elsewhere? Sarah just finished the surgery and is sound asleep."

"Oh, sure. Let's go to the galley. I need a cup of coffee anyway."

Luke nodded and followed the captain.

"I'm really indebted to your wife," Abrams said as they started down the corridor. "It seems Commander Denning will likely pull through. Barkley was really impressed with the work she did."

"I'm sure she was happy to contribute."

As they entered the galley, Luke saw Dwayne Campbell, from the propulsion division in Houston, filling his cup with coffee. Dwayne had entered the lottery for the mission and had been "selected." As Dwayne turned, he stopped suddenly, nearly spilling his coffee. "Luke? What . . . what on earth are you doing here?"

Luke smiled. "I think the correct idiom now is: what in space are you doing here?"

Dwayne got a small chuckle out of that. "Well, pardon my verbal faux pas." He held out his hand and shook Luke's with vigor. "But seriously. I thought you were not part of the lottery."

Luke shook his head. "I wasn't."

Dwayne furrowed his brow, looking from Abrams to Luke. He shook his head. "I don't understand."

Luke patted his shoulder. "Long story. I'll fill you in later." He gestured to Abrams. "The captain wanted to discuss something with me."

Dwayne held up his palm and nodded. "Oh, sure. I'm dying to hear the story, though." He gestured to Captain Abrams. "Captain, I do need to discuss something with you also in the very near future."

Captain Abrams shrugged. "Why don't you join us? Since the two of you already know each other, might as well have a bigger discussion." He gestured to the tables. "Dr. Campbell, you find a seat. Dr. Loughton and I will join you as soon as we get our coffee."

Dwayne nodded and headed to a back table. Luke was glad

as he didn't want what he had to say to be heard by others, although no one else was in the galley at the moment.

Once they all gathered at the table and took a few sips of coffee, Captain Abrams started. "Luke . . . OK to call you Luke?"

Luke nodded. "Certainly. I prefer staying informal as well."

"First of all, I'm very puzzled . . . and troubled . . . by you, your wife, and what you're even doing here." He shook his head, glancing quickly between the two men in front of him. "I'm getting such conflicting information from René Mauchard. I thought I would just go to the source, as they say."

Luke ran his fingers up and down his cup. The warmth felt good as the galley was quite cool. He looked at Abrams. He was thinking deeply about whether to be completely honest or not. Luke resigned himself. *What do I have to lose?* he thought. What more could they do to him? Based on René's response, Luke guessed, Abrams, Mauchard, and their allies on the ship had no more of Simone's compound, or he would be acting more confident.

Luke took a deep breath. "Captain, I'm going to be totally honest with you."

Abrams nodded as if he expected nothing less.

Luke shook his head. "It's going to sound somewhat bizarre. But I'm telling you that all I am going to say here is the truth."

Both Abrams and Dwayne turned their heads, but both also continued to give Luke their full attention.

Luke focused on his coffee, but looked up frequently at either, or both, of them to take note of their engagement. "It all started about two years ago when I started noticing discrepancies in some of my gravitational calculations. I would point them out to others, but the next day, they seemed to have been resolved. And I was the only one who remembered there even *was* a discrepancy." He pointed to Dwayne. "I don't know if you remember. But there was the same issue with the amount of fuel for this mission."

Dwayne turned his head. "I do vaguely remember you coming down and talking with me about fuel, but I don't remember the specifics."

Luke nodded. "What I, and some of my friends, discovered is the Illumi-Alliance, under the direction of the Mauchard family, orchestrated this whole Mars mission to try and prevent a prophecy from . . . Scripture being fulfilled."

Abrams's head jerked back slightly. "You're talking about . . . " He looked around and his voice got low. "That book? The Bible?"

Luke nodded. He held up his palms. "I know it sounds crazy. But please hear me out."

Abrams just looked at him. He was expressionless.

"They have been spiking the Invocation wafer with some type of chemical for years. This reprograms people's memories to achieve this feat."

Abrams now changed expressions somewhat, furrowing his brow.

"Just think about it," Luke continued. "How else could there already be a colony on Mars and these six ships ready for space travel without anyone knowing about it? Tons of people had to have worked on the Space Station to get their plans this far, but everyone was surprised when it was announced." He pointed to Captain Abrams. "Did you know?"

Abrams shook his head and put his hand to his chin. "It was a surprise to all of us. I always wondered how such a thing never leaked out. But . . . mind reprogramming?"

Luke asked a simple question, but it seemed a penetrating one. "How often do you refer to notes before beginning your day?"

He shrugged. "Every day, practically."

"Why?"

"Why?" Abrams paused, looked at Dwayne, then back at Luke. "Well, to review what I need to do that day."

Luke nodded. "And why do you need to do that? You can't remember something that happened just yesterday?"

"Of course I can."

"But not everything."

Abrams slowly nodded his head. "Yes, not everything. Not until . . . I review my notes." He looked at Luke as if a light bulb had suddenly switched on in his brain. "Maybe you're on to something." He furrowed his brow again. "But what does all of that have to do with . . . Scripture?"

Luke gave a weak smile. "I'm getting there." He took another swallow of coffee. "Scripture tells of a time when the Messiah, the one who the Bible proclaims came to Earth to pay the penalty for mankind's disobedience, will return to Earth's atmosphere to gather those who have believed in him and his coming."

Abrams and Dwayne looked at each other and then back at Luke—as if they found that extremely hard to believe.

Luke held up his palms. "I did say it would sound bizarre. But hear me out."

Abrams simply gestured for him to continue.

"We call it The Receiving because it's like a bridegroom coming back to receive his bride and take her back to his home." Seeing the blank look on their faces, Luke added, "Scripture was written by Jewish authors. So most events are from a Jewish perspective."

Abrams gave a slight nod, but looked doubtful. "If that's true, why not just come back to Earth?"

Luke smiled. "He will. But there is prophecy to be fulfilled before he does that."

Dwayne looked from Abrams to Luke several times and

then spoke. "Prophecy?"

Luke nodded. "There are several Jewish festivals that are prophetic. For example, Pesach, or Passover, predicted the Messiah's death at his first coming, Bikkurim, or Firstfruits, predicted his resurrection, and Shavuot predicted the giving of the Holy Spirit."

Dwayne waved his hands. "Wait, wait. *Holy Spirit?* What on earth . . . " He grinned. "Or, in space, is that?"

Luke was glad Dwayne could approach this with some levity. It meant he wasn't totally turned off by what Luke was sharing. He smiled back. "Dwayne, it's sort of like your party when you were selected by the lottery. Who controlled you then?"

Dwayne laughed. "Probably the champagne."

Luke nodded. "Exactly. That's what the Holy Spirit does. He takes control of your life, if you let him. Except he doesn't let you dance on the table with a lampshade on your head."

Dwayne scrunched his brow. "Please don't tell me I did that."

Luke laughed and shook his head. "No, but I think it's only because no one suggested it to you."

Dwayne gave a short laugh and nodded. "You're probably right."

Abrams leaned in. He obviously wanted to turn more serious. "And Luke, you believe all this prophecy stuff?"

Luke nodded. "René and Philippe's grandfather believed this to be true as well. Their father, Édouard, didn't want to believe it, though, so he devised a plan for it not to occur if indeed it was true. René and Philippe have been carrying out their father's plan."

Dwayne leaned in. "Which is?"

"Remove the source of the prophecy, prevent those on Earth from remembering the prophecy so they can't pray for it to occur, and then remove those immune to the chemical in the Invocation wafer from the Earth so that, even if they do understand the prophecy, they will not be on Earth for the prophecy to come true."

Dwayne sat back and shook his head. "Whew, that's a lot to digest. Much less believe."

Luke nodded. "Yes. Yes it is. It took me a long time to agree with it. Yet, Sarah and I actually heard Philippe and René say, and admit, that this is the purpose for this mission." He raised his eyebrows. "Plus." He paused. "Plus, it explains all of these discrepancies which I mentioned, and . . . " He gestured toward Abrams. "Which you seem to have encountered as well."

Abrams cocked his head and raised his eyebrows. "Maybe. It's a lot to swallow." He remained quiet for a few seconds. "So, how are you on this ship if not part of the lottery?"

Luke took another sip. "They needed me and Sarah to help get the North American launch executed, so we couldn't be part of the lottery. By the way, the lottery was a ruse to get those immune off the Earth and remain subservient to the elite who would populate the Mars colony."

Luke paused, knowing it would be difficult to fully answer the captain's question without giving away the big secret. But how would he and Dwayne take that? It may get him locked up, or even in a padded cell, if the captain thought it too unbelievable. But Luke reasoned that, since he had gone this far, he might as well go the entire way. He really had nothing to gain keeping it to himself. "And just before the Mars launch happened, another chemical was developed that would work on those immune to the Invocation wafer so that, while in stasis, they are currently being programmed to forget all about Earth. And really, it's so they will better embrace being on Mars since they were abducted to be on this mission."

Dwayne pointed at him. "But it seems you still have your memories."

Abrams nodded, agreeing. "How do you explain that?"

Luke smiled. "Well, it was fortuitous that some friends of ours who are great chemists were able to synthesize an antidote to the compound. Sarah gave herself, myself, and a few others this antidote compound. It worked, apparently, because both she and I remember everything, including how René Mauchard and others forced us to be on this mission."

Abrams shook his head. "All this sounds a little too convenient. But when I think of how strangely René has been acting, it does make me wonder." He pulled out an electronic tablet. "I was given the entire roster of the twenty-five hundred people who would be on this ship." He looked at Luke. "You and your wife are not on it. Why?"

Luke raised his eyebrows. "Oh, there are about fifty individuals who are likely not on your list."

Abrams shook his head. "I don't follow."

Dwayne leaned in. "You better not be saying what I think you're saying." He pointed at the tablet. "I have that same roster. All my fuel consumption calculations are based upon *that*." He pointed back at the list on Abrams's tablet.

"There are not two thousand, five hundred people on board this ship, but two thousand, five hundred *and fifty*," Luke stated with emphasis.

"Impossible." Abrams shook his head.

Luke gave a small shrug. "All I can tell you is fifty of us were brought up on a shuttle and René told Dr. Wilson we were contingencies—people he also had to put into stasis."

Dwayne wiped his hand over his mouth. "Captain, that sort of confirms what I wanted to discuss with you."

"And that is?"

"We've used more fuel at this stage than I had accounted for. I've been going over my calculations and haven't been able to understand them. It seems to indicate we have more mass on board than I originally accounted for."

Luke nudged Dwayne to get his attention. "What's the discrepancy?"

"Several metric tons."

Abrams's eyes widened. "*What?*"

Luke nodded. "OK, let me see if this correlates. If there's an additional fifty individuals on board, that would be approximately three and a half metric tons. Then, there would be an additional twenty-five stasis chambers in use. Each likely weighs about half a metric ton, so that would be an addition twelve and a half metric tons. That's . . . nearly sixteen extra metric tons total."

"That's pretty close to my calculations." Dwayne shook his head, then looked at the captain. "Sir, compared to the whole ship, that's not a lot, but we were very tight on our fuel calculations. This will put us short." He took a heavy breath. "We rely upon both liquid fuel and ion propulsion. The former for initial thrust, course corrections, and periodic microbursts to counteract the small pull from the other ships. The second for acceleration to cut down the time to Mars. This combination has cut our time down to four months." He shook his head. "This unexpected mass will add up over time. I'm not sure we have enough to get back to Earth—or at least not in four months."

"How long, then?"

"I'm unsure, Captain. But now that I know this isn't a discrepancy, I can calculate that more accurately."

Abrams nodded. He clearly had a worried look on his face, but went on. "Now for the other part."

Luke pushed his cup away. The remainder of his coffee was cold. "What do you mean?"

He turned his head. "Well, to hear René tell it, you're the most wanted person on Earth. And you were sent to Mars to pay your penance."

Luke laughed. "Yeah, I guess he would say that."

"But, both you and your wife have been extremely helpful, kind, and considerate about everything we have asked of you. And you even point out issues and help try and solve them." He shook his head. "Not what I would classify as a dissident in my book."

Luke smiled. "Thank you, sir."

Abrams paused. "So what gives?"

"It's like I said earlier. We were trying to expose the Mauchards and their plan to everyone, and they didn't like that, so they wanted to shut us up. It was difficult for them because we were immune to the Invocation wafer. Therefore, they devised an alternate plan. But, as I stated, it wasn't successful due to our countermeasures."

"I get the feeling there's more."

Luke smiled and nodded. "What I stated about the Messiah—what Scripture states about him, his reason for coming to Earth, and his promise of return . . . I believe all of it."

Abrams sat back in his seat. "But you're a scientist. How can you believe in something so . . . unscientific?"

"Once you know all the facts, it's more scientific than you might think."

"So, you think this . . . Messiah will come back and take those who believe in him away with him?"

Luke nodded. "I'm pretty sure of it. We've uncovered a lot of evidence to support such a belief. I'd be happy to share that with you sometime."

Abrams nodded. "Maybe. I need to think about that."

"Understandable." Luke slowly turned toward Dwayne.

Dwayne held up his palm. "Let me think twice."

Luke chuckled. "Sure. No problem."

Luke turned back to Abrams. "Can I now ask you what I was going to ask you tomorrow?"

Abrams nodded. "Sure. What is it?"

"I want to contact Houston and see if they can simulate the meteoroid shower that hit this ship."

Abrams shrugged. "Sure. But why? How will that help?"

"It will let us know if our early detection system is working properly, and will also let us know if this was in the wake of an asteroid or the prelude to one. And knowing that could be critical."

Abrams's eyes widened. "Prelude? Please don't tell me that."

"That's why I want to contact Houston."

"Absolutely. Just let me know when." Abrams looked at his watch. "I've kept you guys up long enough. Get some rest."

THIRTY-TWO

PLANS GO AWRY

Philippe started to knock on Simone's door, but he heard her groan and then pound on something. He assumed it to be her desk. He opened the door rather than knocking.

"Simone, are you all right?"

She looked up with a frown on her face. "No." She gestured for him to sit.

"What's . . . what's so wrong that it's got you this upset?"

She handed him her tablet. "I just received this message from René."

Philippe quickly took the tablet. He hoped René was OK. He glanced back at Simone. What could have her so upset? He read the note—and couldn't believe what he was seeing.

He pointed at the tablet. "How . . . how could Drs. Loughton and Morgan not be under the influence of your chemical once brought out of stasis?"

Simone shrugged. "I don't know." She stood and began to pace. "Those two have been the bane of our existence for far too long. And now . . . " She gestured toward the tablet Philippe was holding. "They continue to be that—while millions of miles away."

"But the Invocation wafers contain your compound . . . "

Simone gave him a smirk with her cold stare.

"Don't they?"

She shook her head. "I just got off the phone with Marta Pentapolous."

Philippe looked confused. "I thought she was now the chef at Pangea's restaurant here in Paris."

Simone nodded. "Yes, but creating the wafers for the Mars mission was her last job in making the Invocation wafers, and she used the older recipe Mr. Pangea had come up with."

Philippe shook his head. "Why?"

Simone sighed. "She said she was given the older recipe to make for the Mars mission. I was suspicious until I checked." She shook her head. "Somehow, she was given the wrong recipe." She cradled her forehead with her hand and shook it slightly. "We're surrounded by idiots!"

Philippe stood and put his hand on her shoulder. "Don't forget, we still have the upper hand." He tried to put his arms around her shoulders for comfort, but Simone took a step away instead. That stung Philippe.

She took another step and turned. "That 'upper hand' is still sitting in the shuttle loading dock!" She put one arm across her abdomen, propped the other elbow onto it and rubbed her forehead. "I can't *believe* the stupidity of some of those who work for us."

Philippe turned up his brow. "What are you talking about, Simone? You're saying none of the drug you manufactured got on *any* of the ships?"

Simone looked up and nodded. "That's exactly what I'm saying." She gestured toward him. "Except for that which got put into the stasis tanks." She shook her head. "But all of it for making Invocation wafers and to use once they get to the colony . . . " She raised her hands and flopped them back to her side. "We're surrounded by idiots!"

Philippe sat on the edge of her desk. "How did this happen?"

Simone gave a bitter laugh. "Oh, get this. Our brilliant loading dock expert didn't load them because there was no more room in storage."

Philippe's eyes widened. "What? He was supposed to remove a crate from each ship and put the compound crate in its place."

Simone thrust her hand toward Philippe. "'Supposed to'— those are the key words here." She paced again. "The fool didn't look at the instructions that came with the crate containing the compound." She turned, her eyes filled with fury. "He assumed them to be more supplies and unneeded since there was no more storage space."

Philippe shook his head. "Unbelievable. After all the precautions we went through to ensure they got onboard undetected."

Simone pushed out another sarcasm-filled laugh. "I guess we were too good. Even the dock superintendent didn't detect them." She plopped onto the other side of her desk.

Philippe read René's note again. He looked over at Simone. "What do we do now?"

Simone threw up her hands. "What *can* we do? Those two rogues will tout their sedition rhetoric to anyone and everyone on the ship who will listen to them."

"Who would believe them?"

Simone's gaze shot to Philippe. "Why would anyone on Earth with a brain believe them? But many did. I would think most on the ship would think them crazy." She shook her head. "But, for some reason, they're so good at brainwashing people."

Philippe stood and came over to her. He held out his arms.

She looked up at him without responding. He continued to hold out his arms and motioned with his fingers for her to come to him. He was determined to console her even if she didn't want it. She slowly responded and came into his arms. He wrapped his arms around her. He felt her muscles slowly relax. He smiled. This was the response he wanted.

"It's all right, Simone. Everything will still work out. They're off the Earth, so nothing can happen. We will send the compound to Mars on a future ship, or we'll send instructions of how those on Mars can synthesize the compound if, or when, the need arises. Either way, we're still successful."

Simone returned the hug and looked up at him. "You really know how to make a bad situation seem like a victory." She smiled. "That's what I love about you. And that's why you've always been a better leader than your brother." She reached up and gave him a kiss.

Philippe was surprised. This kiss felt different than most of her others. He reciprocated, and she pressed in more. He saw her pick up something from her desk as she led him over to the sofa, then watched her hit a button. He heard the doors click and realized she had installed remote-activated locks.

He pulled away from her kiss and smiled. "Neat toy you've got there."

She smiled back. "I thought it would come in handy sometime." She laid it on the table next to the sofa.

"Seems like it just did."

She pushed him down onto the sofa and leaned into him with a smile. "Indeed."

THIRTY-THREE

Earth Communication

Luke wasn't sure why he was so nervous. After all, he was meeting with two of his best friends. His hands were shaking lightly. He interlocked his fingers to keep his hands steady.

Captain Abrams came over. "OK, Luke, your message will go first. Even though we're only three-quarters of the way to Mars and we're using laser communication, there will be about a nine-second delay." He smiled. "It will be a bit annoying, but better than a delay of many minutes using other technology."

Luke nodded. The downside was he would not be able to see their expressions in real time. On the other hand, it would give him time to formulate an appropriate response. "I understand, sir." He took a deep breath and breathed out slowly. He adjusted himself in his chair. "I'm ready."

Abrams nodded and stepped to the side. One of the technicians pointed to Luke.

He gave a big smile and a slight wave. "Hi, Scott, Brian, and Larry. It's me." With nervous laughter he held up his palms, arms wide. "Surprise!" he said in a sing-song tone. He cleared his throat. "I know this is not where you expected me to be."

He shook his head. "It's a long story, but one I told you about. Remember that, Brian? Just remember what I told you."

He looked over at Abrams, who had his arm in a rolling motion. Luke gave a slight nod. He had to speed things along. Every second was precious.

"Anyway," Luke said. "On to our issue. You will be receiving some video footage of a meteoroid shower that occurred earlier. Most of them were no bigger than the size of a pea. Knowing these are from a larger asteroid, I need to know if they would be from the wake of an asteroid or the prelude to one. We are hoping you can look into this area of space and see, based on the trajectory of these small ones, if any larger asteroids are in the vicinity. A second thing: I need you to set up a simulation to trick our early warning system that a threat is imminent so we can be sure it is working. The internal diagnostics say it is, but I need to know for sure. Let us know how soon all of this can be done."

Luke stopped talking and nodded to the technician. He sat back in his chair and breathed out slowly. He looked over at Abrams.

"All we can do now is wait," Abrams said. "It will take nine seconds for the message to get to Houston. They have to respond, and then we wait another nine seconds to receive the message." He shrugged. "If they talk no longer than you did, then I think we should expect something back within three minutes."

Luke nodded and looked at his watch. This was the hard part: just sitting and waiting. While he badly wanted to know about the potential asteroid and the early warning system, he really wanted to know if Brian, seeing him in space and remembering everything he had said, would now believe. He certainly hoped so. Luke was immersed in thought when the monitor came to life.

"Luke, my man." It was Scott. "You are a sight for sore eyes." He cocked his head. "Or, is that one sorry sight for my eyes?" He laughed at his own joke.

Luke chuckled. Leave it to Scott to lighten the mood. He noticed Brian was quiet.

Larry jumped in. "Hey, Luke. Glad you're at least OK. We'll take a look at the videos and work up a simulation model to detect the trajectory and then see what's there. Dr. Cohen was our best asteroid specialist. We don't know where he is either. If he's with you, it would be good to get his perspective on our findings." He put his hand on Brian's shoulder. "Brian here will work on the simulation to test the early warning system."

Brian gave a smile, but didn't say anything.

Scott waved. "We'll be in touch soon, Luke. Say hi to Sarah, assuming she's with you."

The video cut off. Luke nodded and looked at Abrams. "Thank you, sir. We should get some answers soon."

The captain nodded. He took a few steps toward the door of the room and turned back. "Walk with me, Dr. Loughton."

Luke walked with him down several different corridors. "Where are we going, sir?"

Abrams smiled. "I need a walk through the arboretum. Talking to Earth makes me yearn for something green."

Luke smiled and gave a slight nod. It would be good to see vegetation again.

"So, Luke, who is this Dr. Cohen? He's also in stasis?"

Luke nodded.

Abrams shook his head. "And I suppose he was part of this contingency group you mentioned that René had placed in stasis?"

Luke gave a forced smile. "I'm afraid so, sir."

Abrams briefly closed his eyes and shook his head. "Mauchard is going to go ballistic if I bring another person out of stasis."

Before Luke could respond, one of the crew approached; he was walking quickly. Seeing Luke's gaze at something behind him, Abrams turned. The crewman came to attention.

"Yes, Lieutenant."

"You have another . . . message from Mrs. Conway." The lieutenant handed Abrams a handwritten note.

Abrams took the message. "You can call a spade a spade, son. It's another complaint."

The officer gave a slight smile. "Yes, sir." He came to attention again, gave a slight bow with his head, turned, and walked away.

They entered the arboretum as Abrams read the note. While he did, Luke looked around him and found the place amazing. Someone had gone to a lot of trouble to make this place spectacular. Others were also walking about the place. It produced such a peaceful state. There were trees, shrubbery, and all sorts of flowers, seemingly everywhere. There was a walking/jogging path between all the lush vegetation. Every so often there was a seating area consisting of either benches or stone, usually next to a pond or small waterfall. A few sat in these places reading or just relaxing. He noticed several of the ponds contained koi, which some people were feeding. He even saw several species of birds and a squirrel or rabbit every once in a while.

"Wow, this place is amazing."

Abrams looked up from his note. "This is probably the most visited part of the ship." He chuckled. "And probably requires the largest percentage of crew to take care of it." He pointed to a man in dark purple scrubs. "Anyone dressed like that works in this area."

Abrams turned back to his reading. The note looked rather long; Abrams turned the page over and continued to read.

He kept shaking his head, and every so often rubbed his hand across his mouth.

"Everything OK?"

Abrams looked over and gave a half chuckle. "Not according to Mrs. Conway."

"Mind if I ask the problem?"

He laughed. "Bottom line: she doesn't feel pampered enough."

Luke was unsure what that meant or how to respond.

Abrams, evidently seeing the confused look on his face, laughed as he turned in Luke's direction. "You don't happen to have a gourmet chef in stasis, do you?" He laughed again. "That's about the only thing that would get that woman off my case."

Luke stopped and just stared at Abrams.

The captain gave him a double take. "What? You mean . . . "

Luke nodded and smiled. "Ever heard of Jeremy Pangea?"

Abrams's jaw dropped. "Mr. Pangea, owner of the famous Continental Drift restaurant? *He's* in stasis?"

Luke nodded.

"Why?"

Luke shrugged. "Same reason Sarah and I were placed in stasis."

Abrams shook his head. "Just how convoluted is this whole thing?"

Luke gestured for Abrams to have a seat. They sat next to one of the small ponds. Luke noticed the koi swimming toward them, congregating, expecting to be fed. Luke smiled. They would be disappointed this time.

He turned to Abrams. "It's pretty simple, really. Those who control the Illumi-Alliance tried to stop us from spreading the truth of Scripture, and they felt the best way to do that was to send us to Mars and reprogram our minds while in stasis."

Abrams leaned back and sighed. "That still seems so far-fetched." He held up a hand. "I'm not questioning that you believe it. But you have to admit, it sounds like the plot from a conspiracy novel."

Luke nodded. "I'm sure it does. But it's the truth." He gestured toward Abrams. "If not, then why would René Mauchard be so upset about me coming out of stasis?"

Abrams nodded. "That is one of the troubling aspects in all of this. He is acting very strange."

"So what now?"

Abrams scratched his head. "First, I'm going to ponder this some more. Then, I'm going to convince Mauchard to get Cohen and Pangea out of stasis."

He sat quietly for a few more minutes before responding again. "I think I'm also going to take someone you don't know out of stasis and see if they respond as you did—or as René originally said those in stasis would."

"In other words, you need a control subject," Luke said.

Abrams nodded. "Exactly."

THIRTY-FOUR

CULINARY CRISIS

Luke waited with Sarah in the conference room. "I'm so excited some of our friends will be able to join us."

Sarah nodded. "Excited and sad at the same time."

Luke turned his head. "What do you mean?"

She shrugged. "Well, they'll come out of stasis and still be treated as suspicious insurrectionists."

Luke took her hand and rubbed his thumb over her index finger. "Captain Abrams is coming around. It's really only René with whom we have a problem."

She nodded. "He and all his Illumi-Alliance soldiers."

Sarah had a point, but there was nothing any of them could do about that at this moment. He considered Abrams being doubtful about René's motives a win in his book. He decided to change the subject. "So how is your patient, Commander Denning, doing?"

She nodded. "Pretty good, actually." She shook her head. "Not out of the woods. Not by a long shot." She gave a slight smile. "But he's improving each day." She nodded her head. "A few setbacks now and then, but mostly improving. It's a step in the right direction."

Luke patted her hand. "All because of you. See, by being out of stasis, you've done so much good, in spite of what René Mauchard claims." He nodded. "It will be the same for the rest. Let's not let the delusional rantings of one person destroy what we know we bring to the table."

She smiled, reached over, and gave him a kiss. "Thanks. Nice pep talk."

"Anytime. You've done it for me many times. Happy to return the favor."

The door opened and in walked their friends: Jeremy, Natalia, Maher, and Paul. Everyone hugged. Luke was so happy to see everyone. As they all settled into seats around the conference table, in walked Captain Abrams, René Mauchard, and a man and woman Luke had never seen before.

Abrams motioned for the couple to sit at the table. Luke felt sorry for them. They looked like they were about to jump from their own skin. They both kept looking around as if everything was completely foreign to them.

Abrams gave a warm smile as he addressed the couple. "Now, Mr. and Mrs. McElhaney, do you know where you are?"

Both shook their head. Mr. McElhaney replied, "It looks like some type of space station."

"Do you remember being put into stasis?"

Again, each shook their head.

"Where are you from?"

Mr. McElhaney furrowed his brow as if not believing someone would ask such a question. "We're from Mars." He smiled. "We both work in hydroponics."

Mrs. McElhaney looked from her husband to Abrams. "That's where you're taking us, right? Back to Mars?"

Abrams suddenly looked quite confused. "You're from Mars?" He shook his head. "You're not from Earth?"

McElhaney laughed and his wife smiled as she held onto her husband's arm. He shook his head. "Oh, no. Of course not. That was just a visit. We're going back home."

His wife nodded. "It will be so good to get back home."

Abrams looked at Luke, his eyes going wide for a second. Luke agreed with that sentiment. These two had been influenced by the chemical and mind reprogramming. Luke looked over at Mauchard, who was beaming. *Oh, if only I could knock that smugness off his face,* Luke thought.

Abrams smiled at the couple. "Well, it won't be too long before you'll be home." He gestured for one of the guards to enter. "Just follow this gentleman and he'll show you to your quarters."

Both smiled and then stood. McElhaney stuck out his hand to Abrams, but then retracted it quickly, as if unsure of the proper way to thank a captain. He gave a small bow. "Thank you, Captain." He left the room with his arm around his wife's shoulders.

Mauchard looked at Abrams and nodded. "That's the response all should have."

Abrams didn't respond to René's comment. He turned to the others. "And do you know where you are?"

All nodded. Jeremy spoke first. "We're on the North American ship to Mars . . . " He glanced at René. "Not of our own free will, I might add. We were forced into stasis." The others agreed.

Abrams nodded. "I see all of your memories are still intact."

René interjected. "Captain, these are insurrectionists. You're talking to them like they are your . . . friends."

Abrams again ignored René.

"Dr. Cohen, your assistance is needed to help resolve an asteroid incident."

Maher had a look of complete surprise.

"Dr. Loughton will fill you in later."

René pounded the table. "Captain, I insist."

Captain Abrams slowly turned toward René. "Mr. Mauchard, perhaps it's best you leave us. You are too emotionally charged to help us at this moment. I have a ship to get to Mars, unscathed—hopefully. And I have dignitaries to please." He pointed to Luke's friends. "These individuals are able to help me achieve that goal. I will use whatever resources are at my disposal to make this mission a success."

René stood, looked around as if unsure what to do, then walked out in a huff.

Abrams closed his eyes and shook his head slightly. He opened his eyes and looked at Sarah. "Dr. Morgan, can a stasis chamber be used for only a brief time?"

Sarah laughed quietly. "Usually, no. But it's not impossible."

He smiled. "I'll keep that in mind."

Sarah nodded. "Yes, sir." She couldn't stop smiling. She looked at Luke and shook her head.

Abrams turned to Jeremy. "Mr. Pangea, it's really an honor to have you onboard."

Jeremy nodded but didn't say anything. Luke assumed, since Jeremy didn't know Abrams, he hadn't yet made up his mind about him. But the banter Abrams had just shared with Sarah would surely help put Jeremy's mind at ease.

Abrams smiled, then cleared his throat. "I have a . . . culinary crisis."

Jeremy's eyes went up. "And how may I help?"

"I have certain people on board who, as they so often like to remind me, have paid to be treated with elite status on this voyage." He smiled again. "And that includes wonderful and elegant meals." He gestured toward Jeremy. "A person of your reputation, I am sure, could help accomplish that for us."

Luke looked from Abrams to Jeremy and back. He knew

Jeremy would take the challenge. He smiled to himself. Now that Jeremy was awake, one bite of the food served on this ship and he would be in the kitchen telling the cooks what to do anyway. Luke wasn't going to tell the captain that, though. He was sure Jeremy would milk this for all he could.

Jeremy put his hand to his chin. "That depends on what tools and spices I have to work with. Tell me, is the food here equivalent to what we had on the Space Station?"

Abrams nodded. "Pretty much."

Jeremy shook his head. "I'm surprised you haven't already had a mutiny on your hands."

Abrams raised his eyebrows but didn't say anything.

"May I see your kitchen?"

"Now?"

Jeremy nodded. "Preferably before I have to eat a meal."

Abrams raised his eyebrows again, but motioned for another guard to enter. "Please escort Mr. Pangea to the galley. Instruct whoever is there that he has free reign and they should obey whatever orders he gives them about preparing the food."

The guard looked surprised, but he nodded. "Yes, sir."

Jeremy stood, gave a wink to Luke, and followed the guard out. Luke smiled. He could tell Jeremy was going to have fun.

Abrams addressed the other two in the room. "Mrs. Pangea, I understand you are an architect?"

Natalia nodded.

"Are you good at maximizing space?"

She nodded again. "I consider it one of my specialties, yes. Why?"

Abrams gave a small shrug. "Well, we've had a mishap in one of our exercise facilities. We need to move the equipment into a functioning part of the ship, but we also need to keep all the other spaces just as functional as before."

"If I can see the blueprints of where you are considering the relocation, I can certainly come up with a plan I think you would find satisfactory," Natalia said.

Abrams nodded. "I will be sure the plans get to your quarters."

Natalia smiled. "I will work on them as soon as they arrive."

Abrams smiled back. "Thank you." He turned to Paul next. "And who might you be?"

"I'm Paul."

"Well . . . Paul. What do you do?"

Paul shrugged. "I guess you could call me a jack-of-all-trades. I've been known to help increase efficiency of existing computer systems."

"Care to help out our communications team? Luke and Dr. Cohen will need to continue communicating with Houston."

Paul smiled and nodded. "Why not? I'm here. Might as well be useful."

Abrams looked pleased once more. "Wonderful. I'll put you in contact with one of our technicians."

Jeremy walked back in shaking his head. Abrams furrowed a brow. "What's the matter, Mr. Pangea?"

"Sorry, Captain, but your galley crew are highly untrained."

Luke leaned forward. "What did you find?"

He raised his hands in disgust. "They're *cooking* with microwave ovens."

Luke laughed; he thought he did so under his breath. Abrams looked from Jeremy to Luke. "What's so funny, Dr. Loughton?"

Luke waved his hands. "Nothing. He gets this way sometimes."

Jeremy put his hands on his hips. "This is really no laughing matter, Luke. I'm really serious."

Luke nodded. "Absolutely." He looked down, working hard

to suppress another smile.

Abrams kept his puzzled look. "So, what's the problem with microwave ovens, Mr. Pangea?"

Jeremy's eyes widened. "What's *wrong*? Microwave ovens are for popcorn and cold pizza." He pointed toward the door. "They have four—four, mind you—oven simulators. All never used."

Abrams cocked his head. "But isn't it all the same technology?"

Jeremy opened his mouth, but no sound came out. He closed his mouth and mumbled something while shaking his head. It was all Luke could do to keep from laughing. Jeremy was in one of his "chef moments."

Jeremy turned to the captain. Luke could hear Jeremy's teaching voice coming out. It was a little condescending—not quite enough for one to feel insulted, but enough to know they were being lectured. "Although the technology is the same, oven simulators are called that for a reason. They simulate the results of how an oven works, just in less time. A microwave cooks faster, but often yields results not favorable." He raised his hand. "Like the . . . " He did air quotes. " . . . meat loaf I had on the Space Station."

Abrams shrugged. "Well, do whatever you see fit. If I get a positive note from Mrs. Conway, I'll know you were successful."

"Trust me, Captain. You'll get a positive note from more than just Mrs. Conway, whoever she is, or my name isn't Jeremy Pangea."

Luke chuckled lightly. The gauntlet had been thrown.

THIRTY-FIVE

CHANGE IN FLIGHT PLAN

Luke leaned forward in disbelief. "Maher, are you sure?"

Maher pushed the papers toward him. "This is what Scott presented to us."

Luke scanned the paper and ran his hand over his mouth and chin. "This . . . this is not what I expected."

Maher shrugged. "Who would? It's not every day one asteroid knocks two others out of their orbit."

Luke looked at the report again. "So, a large asteroid smashed into a smaller asteroid, which hit an even smaller asteroid, causing it to crumble into bits?" Luke shook his head. "That's just . . . highly unusual, to say the least."

"Absolutely, but the trajectory of those bits which hit the ship led Scott and Brian back to this point in the asteroid belt. Now he's found these two other asteroids along the same trajectory. Through simulation, this is the only explanation of what could have occurred to allow them to be in their current position."

"And one is now headed our way?"

Maher nodded. "And one is headed for Mars."

Luke's eyes widened. "When will the second one hit?"

"Tomorrow."

"Do they know that?"

Before Maher could answer, Paul walked into the conference room and threw a photo on the table. Maher picked it up. His eyebrows raised as he pointed to the photo. "Where did you get this?"

"From Scott and Brian."

"This looks exactly like asteroid XPT-110." Maher shook his head. "But how did you get it so clear? I would have expected the transmission of something like this from Earth to be much grainier."

Paul smiled. "I sent them my newly developed data compression software." His smile turned to a grin. "Pretty neat, huh?"

"Incredible." Maher looked at the picture again and then back at Paul. "How did you do it?"

Paul shrugged. "It's something I've been working on for quite some time. Just hadn't had the time to complete it, and demonstrate it, until now."

Maher pushed the photo over to Luke. He turned back to Paul. "Wait. What did you mean by 'demonstrating it'?"

Paul had a light smile, but a somewhat sheepish one. "Don't be mad."

Maher paused. "Mad about what?"

Luke looked from Maher to Paul. "What did you do?"

Paul shrugged. "Well, I couldn't be sure if the Illumi-Alliance shut down all the websites or not."

Luke shook his head. "Come again? What does that have to do with Maher's question?"

"I keep all of the posts on a flash drive. I still have it." He gave a light shrug. "Within the compressed file, I sent not only the compression software code, but all the posts in hidden files—along with a replicating virus."

"What if you get caught?" Maher sat on the edge of the table with a thud. "Was that wise?"

"But that's the beauty of this. They're expecting a specific thing. When they decompress the file, they will only see the compression software. The virus will take the hidden files and upload them to the nearest server and then replicate them continuously from server to server. It continuously checks the next server. If the posts are not there, it will copy them." He grinned. "So, even if they delete them . . . they get copied again." He chuckled. "About the only way to stop it is to delete all servers simultaneously." He shook his head. "Not totally impossible, but as far as I know, no one has ever tried to do that."

Maher turned up his brow. "But won't they see the difference in file size and realize something is off?"

Paul raised his index finger. "Only *if* they know what they're looking for. But I also embedded some photos as well. Since different compression software handles the white space of photos differently, they won't really know the difference is not this white space and won't go looking for the hidden files." He shrugged. "Yeah, it can be detected, but likely won't since they're not looking for it."

Luke laughed. "Paul, I don't know if you're a genius or insane."

Paul laughed along with him. "They're not mutually exclusive, you know."

Luke laughed even harder.

Maher shook his head. "I'm leaning toward the latter."

Paul threw a phantom punch in Maher's direction. "You know you like the idea. Besides, isn't the message more important than our safety?"

Maher nodded and shook his head. "As usual, you're right." He turned back to Luke. "So, back to business. Do you recognize the asteroid in the picture?"

Luke looked more closely. "I think so. Isn't this one of the ones we picked out for terraforming?"

Maher nodded. "I don't know if you remember, but we chose it because it was likely to stand up to Mars's thin atmosphere upon entry but break apart very easily upon impact."

Luke nodded. "Where is it projected to hit? Maybe we can chalk it up to early terraforming." He chuckled.

Both men looked at Paul. He wasn't laughing.

Luke laid the photo down. "What have you not told us, Paul?"

"Uh, the trajectory puts its hit pretty close to the settlement." Paul grimaced. "A report just came back from Scott. It may be as close as seventy-five kilometers."

Luke's eyes widened. He looked at Maher, who had the same look. Luke shook his head. "And the other one?"

"It seems to be larger—and is headed our way."

Luke nodded. "Is Earth in danger?"

Paul shrugged and looked at Maher.

Maher shook his head. "No, it will be far from Earth by the time it gets there."

Luke let out the breath he realized he had been holding. "Well, that's at least some good news. How long do we have before it gets to us?"

Maher tilted his head a bit. "I would say in about a week to a week and a half."

"What's the captain's plans?" Luke asked.

"I'm not sure," Paul said. "He was in the room when we got the last message. He walked out without saying anything. That's when I came here."

Luke stood. "Well, let's go find out the plan."

He turned to exit at the same time Abrams was quickly entering the conference room. Luke had to stop in his tracks or he would have run directly into him. "Captain, we were just coming to see you."

Abrams motioned for all of them to sit. "I went to get Dr. Campbell."

Dwayne nodded as he sat. "Looks like we have a dilemma on our hands," he said.

Luke looked from Dwayne to Abrams and back. "What do you mean?"

Dwayne opened his hands slightly. "As you know, we're already tight with fuel. Getting out of the asteroid's way will use up even more fuel—really, more than we have in reserve for such maneuvering." He shook his head. "Very perplexing."

Abrams hit a button on the table and a monitor came to life. After typing in something, an image displayed on the monitor. "Here's our scheduled flight path." A line moved across the monitor from where their ship was located and went directly to Mars. "And here is the path of the asteroid."

Luke shook his head. "That's not good. We meet it almost head-on."

Abrams nodded.

Dwayne showed another projection. "Here is what I would like to do." The flight path morphed into another trajectory. "This puts us going around the planet to get to the settlement—rather than directly to it." He pointed to the screen. "You see, if we change our trajectory toward Mars now, it has us miss the asteroid completely." He bobbed his head. "Well, almost completely."

Maher leaned in. "That sounds ominous."

Dwayne turned to Maher and nodded. "It normally wouldn't be a big deal. We would only get hit with minute fragments, if any."

Paul shifted in his seat. "And what's bad about that? I heard someone say this ship is designed to withstand that degree of abuse."

The captain nodded. "Normally, that is the case." He cocked his head. "But we have some faulty windows to take into consideration."

Luke turned to Abrams. "What are you saying? I thought you said the one that imploded was the only one."

The captain nodded. "That's the way it was looking, but the investigative team just found two more."

Luke looked worried, confused. "So what do you plan to do?"

Abrams gestured to Dwayne. "Care to show them?"

Dwayne nodded and pressed another button. The screen display changed. "If we go in the opposite direction, we can avoid the asteroid. Then we can go straight toward Mars and meet the others just above the Martian settlement." He shrugged. "It puts us on a different course than the others, but we should arrive at approximately the same time, or slightly after them."

Luke still looked concerned. "What about fuel consumption?"

"We will have fewer course corrections and we can utilize the momentum of the initial burst to propel us to Mars. We will go a little slower but conserve fuel at the same time."

Abrams smiled. "The only person to be disappointed by this will likely be René Mauchard. The lead ship will not be the first in orbit around Mars."

Luke smiled as well. He could almost see René's face turning deep red as he imagined Abrams telling him the news. "He'll probably ask to be transferred to the European ship."

Abrams's smile vanished. "I certainly hope not. We don't have time for such an endeavor. Actually . . . " He turned to Dwayne. "We need to get everyone on the new course trajectory as quickly as possible."

Dwayne nodded and headed out the door. "I'll go alert everyone now." He almost ran over one of Abrams's lieutenants entering, but turned to the side just in time, gave a sideways glance at the lieutenant, and continued his exit.

The lieutenant came to attention. "Excuse me, sir."

"Yes, Lieutenant. What is it?"

He handed a note to the captain. "Another note from Mrs. Conway, sir."

Abrams rolled his eyes. "What is it now?"

"Don't know, sir. But she said to give it to you since you were not at dinner."

He looked at his watch. "Yes, I guess it is getting late." He nodded. "Thank you, Lieutenant. You are dismissed."

The officer saluted. "Thank you, sir." He turned and left.

Abrams opened the note. His frown turned to a smile and then he was letting out a slight chuckle.

Luke looked at Maher with raised eyebrows and turned back to Abrams. "Good news, sir?"

The captain looked up and smiled. "You could say that. Listen to this:

Dear Captain Abrams. You missed one of the best dinners ever. I have never had meat loaf so wonderful. We all groaned when we saw the menu, but everyone is only giving accolades now. I didn't know Jeremy Pangea was on board! Where have you been keeping him? In stasis or something? This doesn't make up for all my previous complaints, but it's definitely a start."

Luke laughed. "Looks like Jeremy came through as usual."

Abrams nodded. "At least one of my problems is solved." He folded the letter and put it in his pocket. "Now, let me go solve a few more."

Luke nodded as the captain left the conference room. He turned to Maher. "So dinner is saved, and the ships are saved—we think, or hope. I just hope the settlement is as lucky."

Maher nodded. "I sure hope so." He grabbed his stomach as it growled. "Now let's go see Jeremy and save my stomach."

THIRTY-SIX

TROUBLE ON MARTIAN COLONY

Luke peeked into Astrophysics. Jayne sat at a console staring at a monitor. "Hey, have you heard anything?"

Jayne looked up and nodded. "Looking at the footage now."

Luke walked over to where Jayne sat and looked over her shoulder.

"I've slowed it down somewhat."

Luke nodded and continued to watch. The asteroid went from a tiny spec to more easily identifiable as an asteroid. It looked oblong and uneven and appeared to wobble as it approached the planet.

Unfortunately, the impact zone was below the horizon from the point of view from which they were looking, but spray from impact was visible.

Luke's eyebrows went up. "Wow. That must have been quite the impact."

Jayne nodded.

"Any word from the Martian colony?"

Jayne looked up and shook her head. "Not yet. Derek went to see if Communications had any information."

Luke stood and patted Jayne on her shoulder. "I think I'll go and see as well."

She nodded but kept staring at the monitor. It seemed this had shaken her quite a bit.

"Don't think the worst, until you know for sure," Luke said.

She glanced up briefly and nodded, but kept looking at the footage.

He gave her a quick look in the eyes. "Don't forget. Higher powers are in control."

She returned a blank stare. Luke smiled, turned, and left. He hoped his comment would at least become an icebreaker for he and Sarah to talk deeper with her about what she actually believed.

On the way to Communications, Luke met Derek.

"Find out anything?"

Derek nodded. "Yeah, it seems everyone is all right, but one of the structures that is supposed to house many of us got damaged."

Luke eyes widened. "What's the plan?"

Derek shrugged. "Don't know. But the captain is looking for you."

Luke looked at Derek intently. "What does he want?"

Derek shrugged. "Also don't know, but he seemed pretty agitated. He asked you to meet him in the conference room you met in yesterday."

Luke nodded. He was unsure what Abrams would want from him. He looked at Derek and tapped his shoulder. "OK, thanks."

Derek moved on. Luke watched him for a few seconds before he turned the corner out of sight. He hoped he could influence both Derek and Jayne. He really liked them.

Once Luke reached the conference room, Abrams and two other men he had not met were at the table. They wore scrubs; the color was something between a brown and orange. Abrams motioned for Luke to enter and take a seat.

"Dr. Loughton, these two men are engineers who are part of our crew."

Luke nodded. They nodded in return, but neither introduced himself.

Luke looked back at the captain. "So, what do you want with me, sir?"

"There's been structural damage to one of the buildings designed to house many of us."

Luke nodded. "I just ran into Derek—I mean, Mr . Foster—who told me the same." He shook his head. "But I still don't see what you want from me. I'm not a structural engineer."

Abrams nodded. "And neither are these men."

Luke raised his eyebrows. Before he could think much further, the two men chimed in.

"I'm an electrical engineer."

"And I'm a mechanical engineer. We're . . . " He motioned to both of them. "Not well trained in structural engineering."

Luke nodded. "I see." He turned his gaze back to Abrams. "So, you want to know if I know a structural engineer?"

Abrams nodded. "Sort of. I just took a structural engineer out of stasis and he's pretty useless to me right now." He bobbed his head. "At least until Dr. Layne is through with him. And I don't know how long that is going to take." He cleared his throat. "I wanted to know if you know a structural engineer personally. One who would . . . remember things . . . like you and your friends."

Luke gave a slight smile and nodded. "I see." He shook his head. "I don't know a structural engineer, but I do know Natalia can help."

Abrams squinted. "I thought Mrs. Pangea was an architect."

Luke nodded. "The structure in question is a dome, right?"

The captain nodded. "Yes, but . . . "

"The last restaurant Natalia designed was a domed structure, in China. It was built in record time, mainly because she did all the structural calculations herself." Luke turned his head. "Yes, licensed structural engineers had to sign off on her plans, but they barely even tweaked her work before signing. Trust me, Captain, she's the best one for this job." He glanced at the other two men. "No offense."

Each held up a palm. "None taken," one said.

The other turned to Abrams. "Sir, we can assist, but if Mrs. Pangea has the most recent and relevant experience, I would use her as your starting point."

The other man nodded. "It seems the fastest and most prudent thing to do. Otherwise, we'll be there, people will need someplace to live, and the structure won't be repaired and ready."

Abrams was deep in thought and stared straight ahead for a few seconds. His gaze turned to Luke. "OK. I'll take your word."

"You'll . . . what?" René Mauchard had just entered the conference room. He pointed at Luke. "Captain, you can't take this man's word for anything." He put a big emphasis on the last word, then added, "He's . . . he's an insurrectionist."

Abrams closed his eyes, took a deep breath, and let it out quickly through his nose. His gaze turned to René. "Mr. Mauchard, I don't know what Dr. Loughton was before he arrived on this ship, and I don't know the history between the two of you. But I have found him and his friends to be extremely helpful." He stood and turned toward René. "And as I stated to you before . . . " His index finger hit the table with nearly every other word. "I will use whatever resource is available to me to ensure this mission is a complete success. You can either get on board with me . . . " He pointed to the door. "Or go pout in your room like last time."

René's face turned beet red. Luke nearly laughed, but refrained, wiping his hand slowly over his mouth to cover his smile.

René turned and faced Luke. "You may think you have everyone snowed, but I know you and your tactics. You will not remain in the captain's good graces forever." He turned and stormed out.

Abrams looked at Luke with eyes wide. "Was it something I said?"

Luke couldn't help himself; a laugh came tumbling out. The other men were laughing as well.

Abrams smiled. "Would you please ask Mrs. Pangea to come see me?"

Luke stood and nodded. "Yes, sir. I'll do that right now."

THIRTY-SEVEN

INTERNET POSTS PROLIFERATE

Philippe looked up from his reading. Who was that yelling? He paused to listen more intently. It sounded like Simone. Was she in her office? *Wow, she must be literally screaming,* he thought. He got up, opened his office door to the conference room, and walked through that room and into her office. He didn't have to open her door to hear her clearly. Each phrase seemed to get louder and louder.

"I'm not asking for excuses . . . I don't care! . . . I expect you to do your job and shut it down . . . just shut it *down!*"

Philippe knocked and opened the door without waiting for a response. Simone was at her desk, face red, breathing heavily.

"Simone, are you OK? I don't think there's anyone on this floor who can't hear you."

Simone sighed and rubbed her forehead with her fingertips, her elbow propped on her desk. After a few seconds, she looked up. "I'm sorry, Philippe, but it was just so infuriating."

"What? What's happened?"

She motioned for him to sit. "All of the insurrectionists' posts that we finally got rid of . . . are now, all of a sudden, everywhere—more prolific than ever."

Philippe's jaw dropped. He shook his head. How was that even possible? "That's . . . that's . . . *how*?"

Simone gestured in his direction. "That was my sentiment exactly."

"Who's behind it?"

Simone shook her head. "No one knows. As soon as the posts get deleted, next thing you know, they're right back up again." She clenched her fists. "It's so infuriating."

There was a knock on Simone's office door.

"Yes?" Simone's answer was clearly one of irritation.

Sonja opened the door and stuck her head in. "Sorry for the interruption, but I thought you'd want to see the news program."

"Which one?"

Sonja shook her head. "Doesn't matter. It's on all of them."

Simone reached for her remote and turned on the monitor. Philippe saw Sonja hang at the door as if waiting for a response, but upon not receiving one, she shrugged and stepped out, closing the door. Philippe turned his attention to the program.

"This is unprecedented. These posts seem to proliferate everywhere. Some are dubbing them, 'Messiah Wedding Posts.'" She laughed. "Adrianne, these posts are apparently about someone coming back from what is sometimes called Heaven to receive a select few. There will then be some type of cosmic marriage in the sky." She shook her head. "Believe it or not, some are buying into these messages. Hoax or fact?" She shrugged. "You decide. Back to you, Adrianne."

Simone turned the monitor off. She shook her head. "This just gets better and better." She looked at Philippe. "We have to contain this somehow."

Philippe nodded toward the monitor. "Did you hear what the reporter said? She doesn't believe them and challenged anyone else to believe such drivel."

Simone nodded. "Yes, but she said some are buying into these messages."

Philippe gave a small shrug. "Can it really be that many?"

Simone looked shocked at the question. "Even one is too many." She sat back in her chair. "Philippe, I'm just trying to fulfill your father's wishes, the same as you. No one can believe in the prophecy, or there is a chance it could come true." She gestured toward him. "Isn't this what he would want us to do?"

Philippe nodded. "You're right. But it shouldn't have to be your job."

Simone sat upright in her chair, arms on her desk. "Philippe, I'm on your side. Your job is my job. I want us to be united."

Philippe smiled. "We are. But don't worry. Let me take care of it."

Simone's head jerked upward a bit, meeting Philippe's eyes. "How?"

He smiled. "Oh, I know some people who know some people. By the end of the week, everyone will be calling it all a hoax. And by the end of next week . . . " He shrugged again. "No one will even remember."

Simone sat back in her chair. A smile slowly formed. Her expression softened. "Philippe, have I told you just how wonderful you are?"

Philippe chuckled. "Yes, but not recently."

She stood and walked around her desk to where he was sitting. She sat in his lap and wrapped her arms around his neck. Leaning in, she kissed his earlobe. The warmth sent electricity through him. He turned his head and gave her a kiss, and she reciprocated.

Simone released her kiss and cocked her head. "You take me to my favorite restaurant with my favorite meal, take me back to your place for a nightcap, and I'll show you some real appreciation."

Philippe felt heat shoot through his body. He smiled. "Let me make one phone call and we can be on our way."

Simone stood and Philippe followed suit. He headed toward his office with a bounce in his step. He loved being able to move Simone from being highly upset to ecstatic. He was amazed at how quickly she could undergo these mood swings. He was just glad he could put her in the happy category. He smiled. Happy usually led to fringe benefits.

THIRTY-EIGHT

CONTEMPLATING MARS

Luke looked around the table in the galley. These weren't all of his friends, as some important ones were still in stasis, but these were special. He thought about a future on Mars. Could it really be that bad if these friends were there with him?

He looked up and saw Captain Abrams approaching their table. "Hey, Cap. Everything OK?"

"Mind if I sit?"

Luke gestured to the chair at the end of their table. "Please do."

Abrams leaned forward with hands interlocked on the table. "First of all, I want to thank each of you for your service." He shook his head. "I don't know why there's such bad blood between you and René, but from my standpoint, you guys are outstanding."

Luke smiled. "Thanks, Captain. That means a lot."

Everyone nodded in agreement.

"Mrs. Pangea . . . "

"Natalia, please."

Abrams smiled. "Natalia, the building supervisor of the

Martian colony wanted me to extend his thanks for all of your help. Everything is holding up to your specifications." He held up his palms. "They have a ways to go, but should be done by the time we get there." He swept his hand across the galley. "Everyone here may never know what you did, but each and every one, including René, owes you a debt of gratitude."

Natalia smiled. "Thank you, Captain. That's sweet of you to say." She shrugged. "I just did what my skills allowed me to contribute." She pointed her index finger at him. "But if you get René to admit that, you're more magician than captain."

Abrams laughed. "You're probably right." He paused. "And Jeremy, what can I say?" He put his hand to his chest. "You've made Mrs. Conway my biggest fan." He paused again. "Well, second to you, of course."

Jeremy laughed. "She is sweet. Opinionated, but sweet."

Abrams nodded. "Tell me about it." He laughed. "She is such a fan of yours she took René's dinner plate from him the other night, saying if he was going to be critical of you then he didn't deserve to eat your food."

Jeremy gave a small grimace. "That must have made him angry." He held up his palms. "I don't like the guy any more than anyone else, but I don't want him to hate me more than he already does."

Abrams raised his eyebrows. "Mrs. Conway can be a little irritating, or quite charming. All she needs is a little schmoozing."

Luke laughed. "Believe me, Jeremy can schmooze."

Jeremy gave him a stern look. "You make that sound like a bad thing." He shook his head. "It isn't."

Natalia nodded. "Politicians do it all the time."

Abrams laughed. "Jeremy, you think you could be a politician?"

Jeremy's eyes widened. "I'm a businessman. There's only

two things separating me from a politician."

"Oh really?" Abrams smiled. "And what would those be?"

Jeremy used his fingers to list them. "One. I have to know what I'm talking about. And, two. At the end of the day, my financial books have to balance."

Abrams threw his head back and laughed once more. "So true, Jeremy. So true."

Maher got Jeremy's attention and pointed. "There's Mrs. Conway now."

Jeremy nodded. "OK. It's time to schmooze. I'm going to introduce Mrs. Conway to Mr. and Mrs. McElhaney and get them to schmooze René Mauchard into creating a great place for people to eat in the colony."

Luke's eyes widened. "Uh, Jeremy, you do know the McElhaneys are on their way to Mars for the first time, just like the rest of us?"

"Yes, but they are in hydroponics and know a lot about raising herbs."

Luke chuckled. "And you know that how?"

Jeremy smiled as he stood. "From schmoozing."

Luke laughed as he watched Jeremy go over and start talking to Mrs. Conway. She gave him a hug, and, in just a few minutes, Jeremy had her talking with the McElhaneys. After several minutes, Mrs. Conway walked over to René's table with the McElhaneys as Jeremy walked back to the table with the others.

Jeremy sat with a big grin. "Schmoozing 101 accomplished."

Luke put his palms up and bowed toward him. "Oh, great master, please teach me your ways."

Jeremy gave him a silly grin. "Just remember we have to live with that guy in much closer proximity than before. Anything we can do to ease tension is a good thing in my book."

Luke sighed. "Why do you always make sense and spoil my fun?"

Jeremy laughed. "What are friends for?"

Luke shook his head. He glanced at Mauchard's table. René seemed to be very engaged in the conversation. Apparently a little schmoozing and a little niceness had gone a long way.

"My turn." Abrams stood and smiled. "Jeremy, I'll capitalize on what you've started."

Jeremy laughed. "Go for it." Abrams walked over to René's table.

Luke looked over and saw Paul had a pensive look. "Hey, Paul. You OK?"

Paul looked up and smiled. "Yeah. I was just thinking."

"About what?"

"I knew you all were friends, but you're more than that. You're all so tight."

Luke smiled and gave Paul a friendly shove. "We are, but we think of you as one of us."

Natalia nodded. "It's just we haven't had as much experience with you—yet." She smiled. "But from what I've heard from Maher and Luke, you're making up for lost time."

Paul laughed. "Maher's rubbing off on me."

Maher's eyes went wide. "How did I get involved in this?"

Paul shrugged. "You're sitting next to me."

"Oh, so guilt by association?"

Luke laughed. "That's how it always works, Maher. You know that."

Sarah stood. "Well, I'm going to go check on my patient."

Natalia looked up. "How's he doing, anyway?"

Sarah nodded her head. "Pretty good. He's improving nicely. I just have to keep him from overdoing things and making himself go backward." She laughed. "It's nice for him to be so positive, but he has to let his body catch up with his enthusiasm."

Luke grabbed her arm and pulled her down for a kiss. "I'll

see you back in the room."

She nodded and headed out.

Natalia looked at Jeremy. "Let's take a walk through the arboretum."

"OK. Sounds good." He looked at the others. "Want to come?"

Luke glanced at Natalia. He wanted to know if she wanted time alone with Jeremy, but she gave a slight nod. Luke shrugged. "Sure. I'm in."

The others agreed as well.

Luke, Paul, and Maher let Jeremy and Natalia walk ahead of them. Enjoying this sprawling lushness was a nice contrast to the rest of the ship. It amazed Luke how calming walking through the arboretum and hearing the sounds of running water and the periodic chirping of birds was for him. He wished Sarah was by his side. He would have to make sure he could come back here with her.

They caught up with Jeremy and Natalia at the lookout area, which had plush seating and huge viewing windows. On one side was a view of Mars. It reminded Luke of the size of a harvest moon on earth, only redder.

"Wow." Paul walked to the window and stared. He turned. "It's beautiful."

Maher nodded. "Yeah, but it still feels surreal that we'll be living there."

Luke agreed. He was just happy he had so many friends with him for this huge change in life.

"Hey, Lukey."

He looked over at Natalia.

"I'm assuming this other window points toward Earth. Which star is it?"

Because they were so close to Mars, Earth had shrunk in visibility to become just another star. He looked out the window and scanned the view. He wasn't used to looking at the stars from this angle, but he mentally put things in their proper perspective. He pointed to one of the larger stars.

Natalia shook her head. "It's just so weird to think our home has been reduced to the size of a star."

Jeremy rubbed her back. "At least we're all together and we all have our complete memories intact."

She looked at him and nodded. "Putting everything in perspective, we are truly blessed." She looked at each of them and smiled. "I really mean that."

Luke smiled. "We all feel the same way." Paul and Maher nodded as well.

Natalia looked at Paul. "And I'm very happy you are with us, Paul. Would you mind saying a prayer to mark this phase of our lives?"

Paul nodded and bowed his head. "Our heavenly Father, while we aren't really happy with our state, we have to admit we can see your hand at work and the blessings you have given us. You have allowed us to continue to be with wonderful friends and you've allowed our memories to be intact. Please continue to use us to bring you glory, and may our lives, even on Mars, help others to discover you and your love for them. Amen."

Natalia smiled. "Thanks, Paul. I couldn't have said it better."

She stood and kissed him on his cheek. "I feel closer to you already."

THIRTY-NINE

CAPTAIN ABRAMS'S DECISION

Luke smiled. "Aren't you glad I insisted we come here?"

Sarah put her head on his shoulder. "Absolutely. It's so tranquil here. If I close my eyes and focus on the water tumbling over the rocks, it's almost like being back on earth at the park near our apartment." She sighed. "I could stay here forever."

"That could be a problem."

Luke looked up and saw Captain Abrams standing before them.

Sarah laughed. "You can't just circle Mars forever?"

Luke gestured for the captain to have a seat.

"Unfortunately, René and his alliance fund what we do."

Sarah sat up and frowned. "Yeah, I try to forget that part."

"And honestly, that's why I'm here," Abrams said. "That's one of the things I want to understand from you two."

Luke furrowed a brow. "What do you mean?"

Abrams leaned over, propping his elbows on his knees. "Well, I've seen how positive you and your friends have been in spite of being placed in stasis against your will. Most would have come out very bitter and confrontational. Yet, you didn't." He glanced between the two of them. "I want to understand why."

Luke smiled. "Captain, I've already told you."

Abrams nodded. "I know, but . . . it can't be just that. I mean, some invisible entity helping you to have a positive attitude no matter what happens to you?" He shook his head. "What am I missing?"

Luke chuckled. "Well, God may be an invisible entity, but he's certainly more than a positive attitude."

Abrams shook his head. "So how does he work?"

Sarah reached over and touched his arm. Abrams looked at her.

She smiled. "He works by changing this . . . " She touched his chest. "And this." She reached up and lightly touched his head.

Abrams looked more confused than before. "What do you mean?"

Sarah looked down as if thinking. After a couple of seconds, she looked back up. "Are you good?"

Abrams's head snapped back just a bit, as if the question caught him totally off guard. "Excuse me?"

"Are you *good*?"

He thought harder. "I . . . think so. Or, at least I try to be." He squinted at Sarah.

She nodded. "But are you perfect?"

"Perfect? As in flawless?"

Sarah nodded.

Abrams laughed. "Hardly."

"So, what if you had to bank your entire eternity on being perfect from this point on?"

He shook his head. "Impossible."

"Exactly. But that's what God requires."

Abrams took a deep breath. "I've never been religious, but I remember hearing somewhere that God is loving."

Sarah nodded again. "That's very true, but there's more to him than love. He's also a God of justice."

The captain still seemed quite confused. "That seems a little . . . dichotomous."

Luke smiled. "That's why God's unique. He can be both things simultaneously."

Abrams shook his head. "H . . . how?"

"He knew we could never be perfect, so rather than changing his requirement, he fulfilled it instead. He died in our place. That was the penalty for our imperfection."

Abrams held up a hand. "Wait. You're saying God *died*." He shook his head. "That doesn't make any sense."

Sarah touched his arm again. "God is unique because he is Trinity. God, the first part of the Godhead, who we call God the Father, sent the second part of the Godhead to identify with us; he was God the Son. God was able to instill the verdict of death for our disobedience, and God the Son was able to pay that price and overcome that penalty by rising from the dead. His victory now becomes our victory because, if we believe, accept what he did for us, and trust in him for our future, we can be with him forever."

She reached up toward him and very gently touched his head once more. "So take what you learned . . . " She touched his chest. " . . . and trust with your heart. Then the third part of the Godhead, called the Holy Spirit, will also dwell in you and lead you to become more and more like him."

Abrams swallowed hard. "I . . . I need to think about all of this. That's quite a lot to take in."

Luke shook his head. "Captain, that's what you said last time."

Abrams became tense, his tone defensive. "And your point?"

"Captain." Luke tried not to match his tone, but instead to be caring. "My point is, you're avoiding. Why?"

Abrams shook his head. "It's just too much to take in."

"Captain, I think you know what we've been telling you is true. Don't you?"

Luke could see sweat forming on the captain's forehead. He kept rubbing his palms along his pants legs. Luke knew Abrams was dealing with an internal struggle.

Sarah turned to look Abrams in the eyes. "Captain . . . " Her voice was low and calm. "Both Luke and I have gone through exactly what you are now. We had doubt—serious doubt—about all we just told you. We were wanting to believe, but afraid to at the same time. Is that what you're going through?"

Abrams gave a slight nod. "So, what did you do?"

"I just talked to him," Sarah answered.

"Talked? How? How did you do that?"

"Captain . . . " It was Luke now getting his attention.

"He's here. Maybe you can't see him, but he's here and everywhere. Picture him sitting right here with us. Just talk to him like you would to Sarah or to me."

Abrams rubbed the back of his neck. He shook his head and let out a light laugh. He looked back at Luke. "Just talk, huh?"

Luke nodded and smiled.

Abrams gave a quick nod. "OK." He cleared his throat. "God, this is Cap– . . . I mean, Timotheus Abrams." He gave a soft chuckle and looked at Luke.

Luke nodded. "Go ahead. He's listening."

Abrams nodded. "God, I don't know exactly what I'm doing, but I know I'm not perfect and never could be. I know that's what you require. I trust in what God the Son did on my behalf, and I trust in you for my future, because only you can provide that. I trust in your perfection and not mine."

He glanced between Luke and Sarah. "Is that it?"

Luke smiled. "How do you feel?"

Abrams shrugged. "How am I supposed to feel?"

Sarah turned to him gently once more. "Captain, everyone is different. You don't have to feel any special way. You just have to know you did the right thing if you truly believe what you said."

The captain nodded, sat back, and sighed. After several seconds, he wiped his brow and smiled. He sat there for what seemed like several silent minutes.

"You know, I do feel different." He nodded again. "Well, different may not be the right word. I feel freer . . . somehow." He turned to both of them. "Does that make sense?"

Luke nodded and smiled. "Captain, believe it or not, it makes perfect sense."

Abrams stood. He held out his hand to Luke. "Thanks, Luke."

Luke took his hand and shook it. Sarah stood and gave him a hug. She took a step back. "I hope that was OK to do."

Abrams smiled. "Perfect for this situation."

Sarah laughed. Her eyes watered. "Congratulations, sir."

He nodded. "I will be forever grateful to you both." He turned. "Now, I have something to do."

Luke nodded. "Heading back to the bridge, sir?"

He turned and smiled. "No, I have to go see Commander Denning. I need to tell him that God spared his life. I think an introduction is in order."

Luke looked at Sarah. She smiled back.

Their witness for God had now reached even beyond Earth.

FORTY

AG BALL

Luke looked in on Jayne and Derek. He hadn't seen them since the ship had averted the doom posed by the asteroids. As Luke entered, Jayne looked at him but put her index finger to her lips to motion for complete quiet.

Luke raised his eyebrows. Derek sat at his console with his back to the door. Jayne slowly eased herself over to where Derek sat while being careful not to make a sound. He suppressed a laugh as she stayed low and gently placed a dead bee on Derek's shoulder. Derek didn't notice. She then took a feather and gently touched his cheek. She must have found both these things in the arboretum. Derek brushed at his cheek with his hand, but stayed focused on what he was doing. Jayne tickled his cheek again. This time, Derek turned his head. Seeing the bee, he jerked, brushing at the insect in a rapid motion.

"Whoa . . . oh-oh." His jerk made the chair, which was on wheels, turn and roll backward. Derek quickly stood and looked around to see if the bee was gone.

Jayne nearly fell on the floor in laughter.

A scowl draped its way across Derek's face. "Ha ha. Very funny."

Jayne stood, still laughing. "I thought it was."

Luke stepped forward. "I thought you said Jayne didn't have a sense of humor."

Derek turned to him, annoyance on his face. "That's not humor. That's being a pest."

Luke laughed. "It looks like the two of you have too much time on your hands."

Derek shrugged. "Well, it has been a little slow since the asteroid scare."

"How would you like to get back at her, Derek?"

Derek grinned and nodded. "What do you have in mind?"

"Hey, whose side are you on?" Jayne folded her arms across her midsection.

Luke smiled. "Actually, yours."

Her eyebrows went up.

Luke laughed. "Has either of you played AG ball?"

They looked at each other and then back at Luke, shaking their heads.

"Would you like to?"

Derek nodded with enthusiasm. "Yeah." He looked over at Jayne and back to Luke. "We were talking about anti-gravity ball just the other day. But it takes four to play, and we don't know anyone who is daring enough to play with us."

Luke gave a short bow. "Well, look no further. My wife and I would love to play with you guys." He pointed to the console. "Put the alert on to contact you in case of an emergency, and let's go."

Derek's eyes widened. "Right now?"

Luke shrugged. "Sure. As long as you're kept on alert, what do you need to be here personally for? Do you have anything else going on?"

Derek shook his head. "No, it's been pretty dead."

Luke looked between them. "Ready to go, then?"

Jayne looked out the door. "Where's your wife?"

"She's checking on her patient and will meet us there."

They walked toward the end of the arch. Here, there was still gravity, but it was pretty weak. They found Sarah waiting for them.

Luke introduced them to Sarah. "I thought Jayne and I would take on you and Derek."

Sarah looked at Derek. "OK with you, Derek?"

Derek nodded. "Sure. Since we're all green at this, I think it'll be fun."

They went to the changing room and donned clothing; it was tight-fitting but padded where there wasn't a joint. It allowed for range of motion and yet helped provide protection in case one hit the walls. Before exiting, they donned gravity boots; these kept them grounded until they entered the arena.

Once they turned the corner from the arch and were at the center of the ship, gravity no longer existed. They stepped forward; their boots anchored them to the floor as they approached the arena. It was a little disorienting as Jayne and Sarah stood on one wall and Luke and Derek stood on one perpendicular to their position. Then, one by one, they slipped from their boots and entered the arena.

As each entered the playing area, they let out a "Wow."

The wall attached to the ship, as well as the remainder of the arena, was transparent. From this perspective, they had a great view of Mars between the turning arches. Luke wanted to pinch himself. Never in his wildest dreams did he think he would experience something like this.

As they floated, each tried to get his or her bearing and understand how Newton's third law of motion could be used in their favor. As he tried to push on someone, Luke found, it made him go backward as the other person went forward. Before they even began, everyone was giggling while just trying to stop moving around unintentionally.

Eventually, Luke got everyone together. "OK, from what I was told, the goal is for each team to get the ball through the opposite opening." He pointed to the far clear wall, which had a blue circle around an opening. "A hollow tube connects the two goal openings. If the shot is ideal, the ball will go all the way through the tube and come out the opposite goal." He pointed to the tube as it went along the outside wall. The tube also had a blue line along its path for easier tracking. "On the bottom side of the tube is a slit where one can block the ball, and if it comes back out the goal it went in, the point is nullified. There are two red-colored stops along the tube on the outside wall you can push to stop the ball. You can then take it out of the tube and continue to keep it in play."

Jayne pointed to the top. "What's the opening up there for?"

Luke smiled. "That's where the ball is deposited. You just shout 'ball!'—and out it comes." He looked at the other three. "Ready to start?"

Everyone nodded. Luke shouted: "Ball!"

The blue circle surrounding the opening lit up, the ball came out, went straight down, and bounced off the opposite wall. Luke caught it on the rebound. It sent him to the ceiling. He pushed off toward his team's goal. He threw the ball to Jayne. Luke went backward and so did Jayne when she caught it. She pushed off from the wall, and when she came in line with the goal, she threw the ball toward it. It went in, causing the blue circle surrounding the goal to light up and the scoreboard to register. Jayne's body flew in the opposite direction of her throw.

As the ball traveled through the tube along the outside wall, the blue line lit up, keeping track of the ball's position.

Derek flew across the arena ahead of the ball and inserted his fist into the slit of the tube. The ball bounced off his fist and flew back toward the goal. Everyone's eyes widened when they saw the ball come back out the goal opening and head straight to the other goal. Before Luke could get there, the ball flew into the other goal.

Derek threw up his arms and yelled, "Score!"

"Hey!" Jayne came flying by and bumped into Derek. He went flying across the arena. They both roared in laughter.

The scoreboard took the point away from Luke and Jayne and gave a point to Sarah and Derek.

Seeing the ball now heading through the tube back toward their goal, Luke pushed off and made it to the stop before the ball got there. The stop glowed red as he pressed it. The ball hit the stop and headed back to Sarah and Derek's goal. Out of the corner of his eye, he saw Sarah head straight for their goal. Before the ball could exit back into the arena, Sarah inserted her fist through the goal opening to propel the ball back through and secure their point. The ball went back through the tube toward Luke and Jayne's goal as it sent Sarah flying backward. She accidently hit Derek and they both went sprawling backward even farther.

Luke yelled at Jayne. "Hit the second stop as soon as the ball passes the first one. I'll hit the first one after that."

Jayne pushed off from the opposite wall, just missing Sarah and Derek as they passed. As soon as the ball passed the first stop, she pressed the second one. Luke then pressed the first stop before the ball ricocheted off Jayne's stop and hit his. It ricocheted back toward Jayne's stop and then bounced back again. With the stops pushed in, Luke and Jayne dragged them together. The ball bounced back and forth between the two stops until the ball finally quit moving as the stops came together. Luke was then able to pull the ball from the tube. Once each let go of their stops, they went back to their original positions. Jayne shot off the wall toward their goal. Positioning himself against the wall, Luke threw the ball toward Jayne and then pushed himself off toward their goal.

As he was traveling, he saw Derek heading toward the ball. "Jayne, watch out for Derek!"

Jayne turned, but too late. Derek didn't catch the ball, but was able to deflect it. It headed straight toward Sarah. She was able to turn her body over and kick it. Her body then shot in the opposite direction, but the ball headed straight for the goal. Luke managed to get between the ball and the goal. He caught the ball, but it projected his body toward the goal. Before he could turn and brace himself, his body hit the wall—hard. He let out an "Umph."

"Are you OK?" It was nice to hear Sarah concerned for him.

"Yeah, I'm fine."

He threw the ball toward Jayne, who headed for their goal. For the next several minutes, all four of them went here and there in a chaotic manner with no one able to make a goal.

Finally, Luke got the ball. He looked at the clock. There were only two minutes left.

He yelled at Jayne. "Head for the goal. I'm coming your way."

Luke pushed off as hard as he could. He turned and was ready to throw the ball to Jayne, but Derek flew by in the opposite direction and knocked the ball from his hand. It went straight to Sarah, who was next to their goal. She threw it in just as the buzzer for time went off.

Luke saw the ball head for their goal through the tube, but when it got halfway, another stop opened, and this one sucked the ball down another tube and out of play. The contest was over.

Derek flew to Sarah and they spun in triumph. They had

won two to zero.

Luke pushed off and headed to Jayne. They grabbed each other and spun. "Good game, Jayne."

"You too. Man, forty-five minutes went by so fast." She smiled. "I had fun, though."

Luke nodded. He aimed Jayne toward the door of the arena and pushed. She headed forward and Luke backward. When he hit the back wall, he pushed himself off toward the door. He looked over and saw Derek do the same.

They reached the door at the same time. Once through and in their boots, Luke patted Derek on the back. "Nice game, Derek. Thanks for playing."

Derek smiled. "Anytime. You play pretty good for an old man."

Everyone laughed. Derek displayed a big grin.

"Just remember you wouldn't have won without my wife."

Derek just smiled again.

They headed to the changing rooms. Sweaty from head to toe, Luke had to peel the suit off his body. He noticed Derek doing the same.

"Quite the workout, huh?" Luke said.

Derek nodded. "I bet you'll be sorer than me tomorrow."

Luke laughed. "That's one bet I'm not taking." Derek laughed again.

They headed to the showers. Because the gravity in this part of the ship was minimal, the water felt strange. The shower, while effective, left the water lingering longer wherever it touched the body.

After drying off and getting dressed, they all met outside and headed back up the arch to normal gravity.

Derek patted Luke on his back. "That was really fun. Thanks. But man, I'm hungry now."

Luke nodded. "Why don't you and Jayne join us and our

friends for dinner at the galley?"

"Sounds good to me." Derek looked at Jayne. She nodded. "See you there in, say, twenty minutes? We should check the lab before we leave—just in case."

Luke nodded. Derek and Jayne went in one direction, he and Sarah in the other.

Sarah squeezed Luke's arm. "That was a great idea to get to know your new friends better. Plus, it was really fun."

"Yeah, of course it was. You won."

She swatted at Luke. "Spoilsport."

Luke laughed as he wrapped his arm around Sarah's shoulders and rubbed her arm. "The only bad thing is, you'll never let me live it down."

Sarah patted his chest. "Oh, I'll only bring it up occasionally."

"Uh-huh. Yeah. Let's call a truce and get some dinner."

Sarah laughed. "Deal."

FORTY-ONE

JAYNE'S REACTION

Jeremy, Natalia, Maher, and Paul were already seated when Luke and Sarah joined them in the galley. Luke felt stiffness already setting in as he took his seat gingerly at the table.

Jeremy laughed. "Getting old there, Luke? Or did Sarah beat you? I'm sure you deserved it."

Luke gave Jeremy a halfhearted grin. "We played AG ball. I didn't realize it would make me use muscles so differently than normal."

Jeremy's eyebrows raised. "Really? I've heard that's not an easy game."

"It's definitely different." He looked at Sarah. She nodded.

Jeremy took a drink of water. "So, Sarah, why aren't you complaining?"

Sarah shrugged. "I guess the yoga Natalia and I have been doing helped."

Natalia smiled. "Lukey, you can join us if you want."

Luke gave a weak smile. "We'll see."

He looked up and saw Derek and Jayne getting their food. He waved them over. "Everyone, this is Derek and Jayne.

They helped us avoid the asteroids." He pointed to Jeremy and Natalia and introduced them. He then did the same with Maher and Paul.

Friendly greetings were exchanged.

Luke gestured for Derek and Jayne to sit. They acted a little nervous. Luke tried to think of something to break the tension and begin a conversation. "So, Derek. How did you play so well? You had some good moves out there in the arena."

Derek chuckled. "First-time luck, I guess." He looked at Sarah. "You had some pretty wicked moves out there yourself."

Luke laughed and turned to Jayne. "That must have been our problem, Jayne. Sarah and Natalia have been doing yoga. I can tell Derek works out."

Jayne nodded and smiled. "I used to do yoga. I guess I'm stiffer than I used to be."

Sarah perked up. "You can join us, Jayne, if you want."

Natalia nodded. "It would be good to have someone else join us. I'm sure you could show us old gals a thing or two."

Jayne laughed. "I'm not so sure of that. Sarah was pretty nimble in the arena. Maybe it would be you guys showing me something."

Sarah smiled. "Join us tomorrow and we can help each other. It'll be fun."

Jayne nodded. "Maybe."

Derek looked at Luke. "You're welcome to join me in the gym, if you want. It usually isn't very crowded."

Luke nodded. "OK. I really should get back into working out."

"Maybe I'll join you guys," Paul said, joining in. "I miss exercising."

Derek grinned. "Great. It's so much more motivating working out with other people." He took a drink of water. "The food has really been good the last couple of weeks. I hear that's thanks to you, Mr. Pangea."

Jeremy smiled. "I try. Thanks for the compliment."

Derek shook his head. "Oh, not so much a compliment as a fact."

Jayne nodded. "I wasn't sure I could have survived much longer on the food they were serving. How did you make it taste so much better?" She shrugged. "It's not like you have something different than they already had."

Jeremy smiled. "Sometimes, how you make a dish is just as important as the ingredients you use."

Jayne's eyes got wide. "You mean you didn't change anything except how the food is prepared?"

Jeremy nodded. "Well, I probably changed a few spices, but the main thing was using the oven simulators. Before that, they had just been using the microwave ovens. That alone can make a big difference."

"Well, this casserole is wonderful," Jayne said as she enjoyed another large bite.

Jeremy smiled. "Thanks. I'm glad you like it."

Derek finished the last portion of his meal. "Uh, Luke. I know why you were taken out of stasis. But what about all of your friends?"

Luke swallowed a bite and cleared his throat. "Well, the order was like this: Sarah was needed to do surgery on Commander Denning. Captain Abrams asked me to check out the asteroid fragments. He then jokingly asked me if I knew anyone in stasis who was a chef. That's when Jeremy and Natalia were brought out of stasis. As you just said, Jeremy has made some wonderful improvements. Natalia, being an architect, then helped the Martian colony understand what repairs were needed after the asteroid struck near them. Maher, here, helped us with the asteroid trajectory, and Paul helped enhance the transmission to earth."

Derek nodded. "It seems we were fortunate to have you all on board."

Jayne cocked her head and pointed with her fork across the table. "So, you all are friends?"

Everyone simply smiled.

"And you each were selected for the lottery? The odds of that are . . . " She shook her head. "Astronomical."

Luke shook his head. "Jayne, none of us were selected by the lottery."

Jayne just stared at Luke, confused.

Derek turned his head slightly. "So you were recruited for your special talents just in case something like what happened, happened?"

Luke shook his head again. "Believe it or not, each ship has fifty extra people placed in stasis who were not part of the original lottery. We were part of one of those groups."

Both Derek and Jayne looked shocked. This was complete news to them.

"Wh—Why?" Derek seemed dumbfounded.

Jayne nodded. "That makes no sense."

Luke chuckled. "I can't argue with you there."

Jayne squinted. "So what gives?"

"Do you want the real, complete truth?"

Jayne nodded. Luke looked at Derek. He nodded as well.

"OK." Luke began and told both of them everything he had told Captain Abrams and Dwayne earlier. He didn't hold anything back; he really wanted his new friends to understand their world and the possibility for their future.

"Wait." Jayne held up her hands. "You're saying *you're* the ones who put all those heretical posts on the Internet?"

Luke nodded. "Well . . . "

Maher interjected. "I wouldn't go with the word 'heretical'— that implies something is incorrect."

Jayne's jaw dropped. She shook her head. "But your spreading information from a seventy-year-old, outdated, banned book. How is *heretical* not the correct word?"

"You're implying what we said is wrong," Maher calmly answered. "But we believe it to be true."

"You can believe what you want, but you're putting Mr. Mauchard in a bad light." Jayne breathed hard through her nose; she was staunch in her position on this. "You should feel bad about that."

Natalia leaned forward. She reached out her hand to place on Jayne's, but Jayne quickly pulled her hand back. Natalia gave a forced smile. "Jayne, we have nothing against René Mauchard as a person. However, his tactics against immunes put us at odds philosophically."

"What are you trying to achieve?"

Sarah turned to Jayne. "The only thing we're trying to achieve is to get the truth out to everyone so they can make an informed decision and realize there is another option to consider."

Jayne stood and held up her hands. "I'm not sure I can go along with any of this."

Luke turned to face her. "Jayne, I think if you talk to the McElhaneys that will help you see there is truth to what we have told you."

Derek gave a short chuckle. "I've talked to them. They're definitely strange. They think they're going home to Mars." He shook his head. "No one on this ship has ever been to Mars."

Jayne had a blank stare on her face as she listened to Derek. "So, what are you saying, Derek?"

He shrugged. "I think I have to at least consider what Luke is saying."

Jayne cocked her head and closed her eyes for a few seconds, inhaling a deep breath. She shook her head as she slowly breathed out. "I don't know. I . . . I just can't get behind this." She picked up her plate and walked away.

Derek looked at Luke and shook his head. "She gets like this sometimes." He pushed his chair back and stood. "Let me talk to her and see what she's thinking."

Luke nodded.

Derek picked up his plate and turned to walk away. He turned back. "We're still on for tomorrow, right?"

Luke's eyebrows raised. "Oh, absolutely."

Derek smiled. "Oh-seven-hundred?"

Luke looked at Paul. He nodded. Luke smiled. "We'll see you there."

"Super."

As Derek stepped away, Sarah gave a small laugh. "What do you want to bet Jayne doesn't join us for yoga?"

"Oh, I don't think that's even worth betting on," Natalia said. "She's a definite no-show." She nodded her head. "Unless . . . unless Derek is able to begin to make some sense with her."

Luke raised his eyebrows. "Well, let's pray to that effect."

Natalia and Sarah nodded their agreement.

Maher laughed.

"What's so funny, Maher?" Luke asked.

He shook his head. "I was just thinking about what she'll likely do next week."

Luke furrowed his brow. "What do you mean?"

Maher gestured to Paul.

Paul smiled. "The first inter-ship post goes live."

Maher nodded. "Everyone, including Jayne, will get an e-mail with the first post I did with Clarity of The Way."

FORTY-TWO

INTERROGATION

Luke drummed his fingers on the table. "Does anyone know why we're here?"

He knew it was probably not good since Jeremy, Natalia, Maher, and Paul had been called to this room with him and Sarah. He had a feeling some kind of lecture was in their future.

Paul looked over at Natalia. "Have you had any luck with Jayne? Luke and I have had a couple of good talks with Derek, usually after cooling down from our workouts."

Natalia shook her head. "We've not been able to get her to come to our yoga session."

Sarah nodded. "And not due to a lack of trying." She shook her head. "We've invited her for the past couple of weeks, but she's just turned us off completely."

"Paul, what time are your workouts again?" Jeremy asked.

Paul turned to Jeremy. "Oh-seven-hundred. Why? You plan to join us? You want to become the buff chef or something?"

Jeremy laughed. "That does have a ring to it." He turned to Luke. "What do you think, buddy? Maybe a new image on

Mars would be good."

Luke chuckled and shook his head. "Well, don't expect me to call you buff chef. Not unless you get more buff than Derek."

Maher laughed. "That would be quite a feat."

"Hey." Jeremy gave a shocked look. "I resemble that remark." That brought a few laughs.

The conference room door opened and Derek walked in. He stopped dead in his tracks, eyebrows raised. "Hello." He looked at each of them. "Am . . . I . . . in the right . . . place?"

Luke smiled. "I don't know. Let's find out. Why did you come?"

Derek took a seat. "Jayne said to meet her here." He pointed at everyone else at the table with a quick sweep of his hand. "You too?"

Luke shook his head. "Captain Abrams asked us to come."

Derek turned his head. "Why?"

Luke shrugged. "No idea, but . . . "

Derek raised an eyebrow. "But?"

Luke shook his head. "It can't be good."

Sarah put her hand on Luke's shoulder. "Luke, you don't know that yet."

"True, but—"

The door opened. In walked Captain Abrams, Jayne, and . . . René Mauchard.

Luke looked back at Sarah and cocked his head as if to say, "Told you so."

They each sat quietly as the three approached the table and also sat.

Captain Abrams cleared his throat. "It seems Mr. Mauchard and Ensign Ewing, here, have some information to share."

René shot Abrams a hot stare. "Information to share? This isn't show-and-tell time." René appeared agitated—and didn't try to hide it.

Abrams remained calm. It amazed Luke how the captain always seemed to manage to do that. He had a lot to learn from this man, Luke thought.

"Now, René, I'm simply not trying to draw implications until the facts are truly known," Abrams said.

"Humph." René turned up his nose. "And I thought *I* was the politician." He pointed his finger at each person—Luke and his friends—on the opposite side of the table from him. "It's entirely obvious they are behind all of this. You can't deny that." René's face turned red. He pointed to Jayne. "Ms. Ewing, please tell everyone."

"Well . . . " Jayne wasn't making eye contact. She was clearly uncomfortable yet seemed determined to continue.

She nodded toward Derek. He sat up straighter in his chair. It was obvious he didn't know why he had been brought into the conversation.

"Derek and I had dinner with Drs. Loughton and Morgan after playing AG ball with them. Their friends were also present." She cleared her throat. "They, uh, told us about God and how Scripture supports the belief that he is coming back for those who believe in him. A few days later . . . " She pulled something out of a folder she had brought in with her. "I found this." She shoved it along the table and in front of Captain Abrams.

The captain's eyebrows went up. His only words were, "I see."

"You see *what*?" René was turning red again. "This is clearly proof that these . . . insurrectionists . . . "

The captain looked a bit stunned as he looked at Rene, but continued to listen.

" . . . are once again conspiring to do what is forbidden. They are terrorists and should be arrested."

Abrams again remained calm. Luke was so impressed with

what he saw in this man. He could see how he made the rank of captain: remaining calm when others around him became so heated. He picked up the piece of paper. "René, I concede this is evidence, but it hardly constitutes proof."

"But, sir." It was Jayne.

Abrams looked her way. "Yes, Ensign?"

"It, uh . . . it has to at least be circumstantially incriminating."

Abrams put the paper back on the table and placed his palms flat. "OK, let's get our terminology straight before we all say something we regret." He patted the table with his palms on top of the paper. "This . . . this is evidence that is circumstantial, similar to what Ensign Ewing has stated. But it is not at this point incriminating without additional evidence."

René rolled his eyes. "Oh, for crying out loud. The law states—"

Abrams held up his palm to halt René in mid-sentence.

Mauchard stopped, but it was obvious he wasn't happy with the interruption.

"Before you go further, let's get another thing straight," Abrams said. "Law on Earth doesn't necessarily apply here—or on Mars—unless it is specifically worded for that implication."

René sucked in a deep breath and breathed it out—hard—as he pursed his lips. "You're going to stand on technicalities?"

"Mr. Mauchard, you of all people should realize that law always stands on technicalities."

"Yes, but—"

Abrams held up his palm again.

René sat back in his seat and folded his arms across his chest. Luke wanted to laugh but suppressed any urge. He had never seen anyone put René Mauchard in his place like that.

Abrams interlocked his fingers and placed his hands on the table. "Now, this is worth further investigation."

René sat up straighter.

Abrams looked over at Derek. "Ensign Foster, you heard the same information as Ensign Ewing, correct?"

Derek nodded. "Yes, sir."

"This undoubtedly offended Ensign Ewing, yet you don't seem offended. Want to explain?"

Derek looked from Abrams to Jayne and then to everyone else around the table. "Sir, I . . . I, uh, don't really know how to answer that. I considered it just a conversation. One person telling how they feel. I can choose to agree or disagree with them."

Abrams gave a slight nod. "So, you didn't find the information offensive?"

Derek shook his head. "No, sir." He gave a half-laugh. "I was on the debate team at the Academy. We debated far more controversial topics."

Abrams's eyebrows went up. "Care to elaborate?"

Derek's face flushed slightly. "No, sir. Not really."

The captain cocked his head. "Humor me."

Derek swallowed hard. "Yes . . . yes, sir. Uh, may I preface this with the fact that these were topics for debate and not necessarily beliefs?" He gave a weak smile. "We, uh, debated about the existence of God, if aliens exist, was the Mauchard family really human . . . "

A few snickers could be heard seeping out. Luke did his best to keep from doing so, biting both his upper and lower lips. He noticed Abrams did the same. René gave a glaring stare. Derek's face turned beet red.

"Sorry, sir. But as I said, these were all just topics to practice our debating skills."

Mauchard leaned forward, clearly extremely irritated. "And just what was your position on the last one?"

Derek looked from Mauchard to the captain with a look

that said: Please don't make me answer that one.

Abrams slowly nodded his head.

Derek shook his head just a bit and sighed. "Sorry, Mr. Mauchard. I was on the con side of that one."

"Humph." René sat back in his seat and scowled while folding his arms across his chest.

Abrams gave a small smile. "Thank you, Ensign. I think we get the picture. So, you didn't take what was said as something these people were forcing you to believe?"

Derek shook his head. "No, sir." He looked from Abrams to Luke. "I do . . . think they believe in what they said. But I, uh, didn't get the feeling I was being forced to believe it for myself."

René shot straight up in his seat. Derek actually flinched.

Mauchard leaned forward. "So, you weren't forced to believe it. But do you?"

"Sir?"

"Believe it." He pointed at Luke. "Do you believe what Dr. Loughton told you?"

"It's, uh, intriguing, sir."

René gestured toward Derek as he faced Abrams. "You can see they are having an effect on others with their insurrectionist ideals."

Abrams looked back at René. "Do I need to remind you the difference between rules and laws on Earth and those in space?"

René shot to his feet. "Oh, this is pointless." He waved toward Jayne. "Come on, Ms. Ewing. Let's get out of here. I know a snow job when I see one."

"Mr. Mauchard—"

This time René held up a hand; it was clear he didn't want to hear more. Abrams raised his eyebrows but stopped. René and Jayne left the conference room.

Abrams shook his head. He looked at Derek. "Thank you, Ensign, for being honest in your answers. You may leave if you wish."

Derek nodded. "Thank you, Captain." He stood, then paused.

Abrams looked up. "Anything else, Ensign?"

"Uh, sir. If you want, I could discard that for you."

Abrams paused, but then smiled and handed the paper to Derek. "That's very considerate of you, son."

Derek glanced at the paper and then at Luke. He gave the slightest hint of a smile. He folded it and stuffed it in his pocket as he left.

Luke wasn't sure why Abrams let Derek have the printout, but he now knew Derek was on the verge of a decision. He would definitely have to follow up with him. Maybe tomorrow after their workout. He turned his attention back to the captain.

Abrams sat silently for a couple of minutes after Derek had stepped out. He finally turned his focus to Paul. "Mr. Samuels, mind telling me how Ensign Ewing got a printout of a post off the inter-ship communications network?"

Paul's countenance went pale. "I'm sorry, sir. I'm not . . . really sure. I blocked the printing function." He gestured into the air. "And I made sure the post deletes itself after giving someone time to slowly read it. It was supposed to help avoid just this type of thing from occurring."

Maher raised his hand slowly. "I think I may know."

Abrams's eyebrows went up.

Maher glanced at Paul. "Did you also block the ability to print screen?"

Paul put his palm to his forehead and tapped it. He looked up and shook his head. "No, I completely forgot to do that." He looked at Abrams. "I'll take care of it immediately, sir."

The captain nodded. "Please do."

"Consider it done," Paul said.

Abrams then looked at each of them. He put his hand to his chest. "I can never tell you how appreciative I am for your influence on me. You made me think of things I had never allowed myself to think about. I don't want you to stop. In spite of Mr. Mauchard's ire, what you share is too vital to keep quiet. But we have to be careful. I have a lot of clout on this ship, but not ultimate clout. Mr. Mauchard can stir up a lot of controversy and make things difficult for all of us. So let's be careful. And vigilant."

Everyone nodded.

Abrams smiled. "Now go influence. But keep it under René's radar."

FORTY-THREE

Simone Honored

Philippe looked over at Simone. He couldn't get over how stunning she looked tonight. Her golden evening gown practically twinkled with the light as she moved. She had been right. The two of them now seemed able to do no wrong. Everything they touched seemed to turn to gold.

Seated at the table with them were Valerie and Bradley, Simone's graduate students. They looked amazed at the evening they were a part of and everything going on around them.

Valerie smiled. "Simone, thanks for inviting Bradley and me to this gala to honor your achievements." She looked around again. "It's . . . exciting." Bradley nodded his agreement.

Simone patted her hand. "Of course I invited you. All your work has helped lead to all of this."

Valerie blushed slightly. "That's kind of you to say, but all the credit goes to you."

Simone shook her head. She looked over at Philippe. "Valerie has not yet graduated, but almost every pharmaceutical company in the world is clamoring for her to work with them." She put her hand on Bradley's shoulder. "And Bradley here has already won a distinguished paper award at the recent molecular biology conference held here in Paris."

Philippe grinned and gave a slight nod. "Well, congratulations to you both."

Each smiled. "Thank you, Mr. Mauchard," Bradley said. "I know you were the one to open up another graduate student slot, which allowed me to work for Professor Mercure. I feel honored."

Philippe nodded. "You're welcome."

Simone smiled. "Both of you may have been given an opportunity, but you both seized it, and now others are recognizing the quality of your work."

Philippe held up his champagne glass. "A toast to Valerie and Bradley."

All raised their glasses and clinked them together in one motion.

Valerie raised her glass again. "And to Professor Mercure. After all, this is her night."

They repeated the ritual.

Simone grinned. "Thanks, Valerie. I have to admit, it is rather exciting."

Philippe nodded. "I should think so. You're being put on the board of directors of the hospital where you used to work, your Neuroscience Center and your work are being recognized for groundbreaking brain research, and you're receiving an award as one of the most influential people in our world today." He grinned. "Can't get much more exciting than that."

Simone blushed slightly as she smiled back. Philippe knew she thrived on such accolades even though she tried to act modest about it. But he too was proud of her. This wouldn't have happened for Simone if she hadn't taken René's place at the company; the reality is the move gave her far more influence and power. A lot of the awards came from that influence, but she also was one smart cookie, and a lot of her achievement came from her own hard work. No one could say it wasn't well deserved.

They heard a clinking of glass from the podium. Everyone in the room focused their attention on the front. The first to speak was the chairman of the hospital's board. He had glowing remarks about Simone and a few anecdotes of her time as a resident. Philippe was impressed. Even if he didn't already know Simone, he told himself, he would find himself loving her after that presentation. Then came one of the leading neuroscientists, who again praised her for her breakthrough research. Philippe smiled to himself. Little did they know the research actually enhanced the memory reprogramming which he and Simone now controlled through the Illumi-Alliance. Next came some big shot from Hollywood, in the U.S. Philippe wasn't sure why this man was here, as he really didn't know her. Yet the audience knew the speaker since he often appeared on television. Simply through this association, Simone's status was raised several notches in everyone's eyes.

The speaker invited Simone to the podium. As she stood and walked to the front, everyone stood and applauded loudly. Philippe found her mesmerizing. She looked extremely sophisticated with her hair in some type of an updo with a fancy name he couldn't remember. Some of the pins in her hair twinkled as the light hit them in a certain way, and her dress shimmered gold as she walked. He was happy for her, but also happy that he now played such a big role in her life.

Philippe knew Simone had practiced her speech a great deal. Yet, to hear her talk now, the words came off as almost spontaneous, and certainly genuine. She barely looked at her notes. She thanked all those giving her the awards and accolades, she thanked Philippe and recognized all he had done for her, and she thanked her graduate students. Surprisingly, she even thanked Anton for his work at the Neuroscience Center. She came across as modest, as someone who puts others in the limelight, yet does so in a way that sets herself above and beyond others in a most subtle way. Her speech was extremely well-crafted, Philippe had to admit. He wondered how long it took her to put it together.

At the end of her talk, there was silence for a few seconds as everyone remained spellbound. Then a thunderous round of applause began to rise; Simone was showered with a standing ovation. Bradley whistled. Valerie looked over at him and grinned as she nodded.

Simone looked just as mesmerizing walking back to their table as she had approaching the dais. Yet this time it took her much longer as many people congratulated her and wanted pictures with her. The paparazzi were taking pictures and doing so at a furious pace. In a word, this woman was now suddenly world famous.

Once she got back to their table, Simone sat and took a big breath. "Whew. That was something else."

Philippe smiled. "You were something else."

Simone grinned. "So the speech sounded OK?"

Bradley laughed. "It was spectacular."

Valerie nodded. "Everyone was spellbound. I didn't know you could deliver a speech like that."

Simone smiled. "Well, I spent more time on that speech than I have on just about anything else."

The waiters came with their food, first setting a gorgeous salad in front of them. "All I know is, that speech will go down in history as one of the most well-crafted speeches of the century," Philippe gushed.

Simone chuckled. "I don't know about that."

Philippe swallowed a bite of salad. He pointed with his fork in hand. "You just watch. Those covering this event will be talking about your speech."

Simone smiled and shook her head as she began her salad. That smile remained on her face for many more minutes.

* * * * *

Once dinner was over, there was dancing and more kibitzing. But the dancing took a back seat to everyone wanting to talk with Simone and have their picture taken with her. Everyone seemed to be trying to launch themselves off of Simone's now assured fame. Philippe began to find this a little irritating, but Simone seemed to glory in it. Somehow he knew this would turn in her favor as well.

It was early morning before they made it to their limo. Once inside, Philippe could see Simone's muscles slowly relax.

"You OK?"

She nodded. "Oh, I'm fine. It's just nice to be able to decompress from all of the adrenaline surges."

Philippe chuckled. "Well, you not only had those, but caused a lot of them as well. Everyone was clamoring for your attention."

Simone sat up straighter. "They did, didn't they?" She chuckled. "I know it's selfish, but I really enjoyed it."

Philippe leaned over and kissed her on her cheek. "I know you did, but you deserve the reverie."

Simone leaned back into the leather seat and smiled. "Thank you, Philippe." She took his hand. "Thanks for being there for me."

"Of course."

They sat in silence for a few minutes. And then he began to notice her expression gradually turning from her state of reverie to one of business. He shook his head. Simone could never bask in anything for too long.

"I got word from René," she suddenly said.

Philippe raised an eyebrow. "Oh, when?"

"Earlier today." She sat up. "I didn't want to think about it until tonight's event was over." She shrugged. "Yet, I'm not sure what we can do about it."

Philippe had curiosity plastered across his face. "What did he say?"

"The new wave of e-mail posts likely came from the North American ship."

Philippe repositioned himself to face Simone directly. "What? How is that even possible?"

Simone gave a tiny shrug. "Evidently, when they communicated with Houston about the asteroid, they piggybacked a replicating virus that contained the posts. It then duplicated itself every time it hit another server."

"So that's why we had a sudden surge of activity."

Simone nodded and sighed. "I thought for sure once we got those radicals off the earth, that would be the end to their meddling." She shook her head. "Evidently, their reach has no bounds."

Philippe rubbed her arm. "Don't worry. I've got it under control."

Simone tilted her head and closed her eyes. "I know you're trying to make me feel better, but how can you possibly do that?"

Philippe smiled. "Well, I can't control what's going on in space, but I can control things here. The number of posts is already on the decline."

Simone sat up straighter; tired as she was, she appeared genuinely interested. "What do you mean?"

He held her hand. "I mean, they're on the decline. You think these radicals are the only ones who can develop a replicating virus?"

Simone leaned in and smiled. "What did you do?"

"I had a replicating virus start finding and deleting their posts." He nodded. "It's kind of a cyberwar, so to speak." He smiled. "And we're winning."

"We should celebrate."

"I have a party for two waiting at my place."

Simone's eyes got bigger. "Does that include fluffy scrambled eggs and strawberries?"

Philippe laughed. "It definitely could." He turned his head. "You know, we could have breakfast, watch you on the morning news, and then take a nap." He smiled as he did air quotes upon using the word 'nap.'

Simone raised her eyebrows. "That depends on if the eggs are fluffy or not."

"Believe me. They will be fluffy."

Simone giggled, reached over, and gave Philippe a kiss. "And how do you know I'll be on the news?"

"Are you kidding me? With that many cameras at this event? It's guaranteed."

The limo pulled up to Philippe's mansion. He led Simone to the kitchen. As he prepared breakfast, she excused herself to freshen up. He turned on the monitor to watch the early morning news.

When Simone returned to the kitchen, Philippe was placing the eggs on their plates. He gestured for her to sit at the counter. He picked up a fork and fed her a bite. He raised his eyebrows, anticipating her response. "Fluffy?"

Simone smiled. "Very fluffy."

Philippe gave her a kiss. He knew that was a sign of good things to come. He sat beside Simone and turned up the monitor as the newscaster came onscreen.

" . . . And locally, the big news is the gala held last night at the Hôtel d'Evreux, where Mademoiselle Simone Mercure was bestowed with several honors for her work in brain research. But it's her speech that seems to have become the subject of many in circles of influence. Even our very own President said in response that someone who can deliver a speech like that deserves to represent France in broader circles." The newscaster smiled. "It is likely this is not the last time we will hear of Dr. Mercure."

Philippe turned to her. "See, I told you."

Simone beamed. "I had no idea."

Philippe reach over and kissed her. She kissed back.

"Philippe, a lot of this is due to you."

He smiled. "It's like you told Valerie. You took advantage of what was given you, but it's you and your talent that put you in the limelight." He took her hand. "Simone, you are becoming someone very special to me."

She gave a coy smile. "And you to me as well."

He kissed her hand. "Ready for a nap?"

She gave a light, sensual laugh. "Absolutely."

FORTY-FOUR

THE ULTIMATE LIBERATION EVENT

Luke looked over at René, who was scowling in return. Luke chuckled inwardly. He knew René was furious Captain Abrams had allowed him and Sarah to be on the bridge to watch their spacecraft join the rest of the ships, which were now orbiting Mars above the colony site.

Captain Abrams walked over. "Like the view?"

Sarah nodded. "Captain, this is spectacular."

Luke nodded. "Best view on the ship."

"The planet looks so large from this angle." She looked back at the captain. "Can you tell us where the colony is? I'm not sure where to look."

Abrams pointed. "See the European ship?"

Both nodded.

"The colony will be just off to the left of its bridge. If you look closely, you'll see a slight glimmer once in a while as the huge solar panel arrays reflect the sunlight."

Both Luke and Sarah focused on the spot Abrams had

indicated. Sarah suddenly jumped. "I see it." She looked over at Luke. "This is really exciting."

Luke smiled and nodded. He once again glanced sideways at René. Very softly, almost under his breath, he said, "Captain, are you sure it's OK for us to be here? René Mauchard hasn't stopped scowling at us since we arrived."

Abrams patted Luke's shoulder. "You as well as he are my guests on this bridge." He glanced over at René and looked back at Luke. "He's just jealous because I invited someone besides him. It makes him feel . . . less special."

Luke smiled. "Well, he may never let you live this down."

Abrams just smiled. "You may be right, Dr. Loughton. You may be right."

Luke put his arm around Sarah's shoulders. She scooted closer to him.

"Well, it looks like my dream of us glove in glove on Mars going out on a rover together will actually come true."

She looked at him with a weak smile. "I guess I can concede now that, yes, it was indeed a prophetic dream." She shook her head. "But if we're together, I'll be happy."

He kissed her forehead. "Me too."

From a reflection in the glass, Luke saw Commander Denning approaching. He was using a cane for assistance in walking. Luke turned and stuck out his hand. "Commander Denning, it's good to see you up and about."

He shook Luke's hand and smiled. "Not back to one hundred percent, but thanks to your wife here, I'm at least back to my post."

Sarah gave a weak smile. "I'm not sure you should really be here."

Commander Denning held up his palm. "I know you were skeptical, but this was much too historic to miss."

Sarah nodded and pointed her finger at him. "And that's

the only reason I'm allowing this. That and the fact you need to start using your leg to rebuild its strength."

Commander Denning gave a small smile in return. "Oh, I thought it was your idea to keep a close watch on me so the two of you can have a great view of us joining orbit with the other ships."

Sarah smiled. "Well, I do need to be sure you don't overdo things. Being here helps me do that." She paused and smiled. "But I concede there may be some possibility to what you're implying."

Commander Denning chuckled. "How about you keep to your story and I'll keep to mine?"

Sarah nodded and gave a light laugh herself. "Deal. We'll stick to our nonbiased stories."

He put his hand on her shoulder and smiled. Denning turned and went back to his post.

Luke turned back and looked at Mars as it became larger the closer the ship got to the others. Sarah whispered in his ear, "Don't look now. But here comes your favorite Mauchard."

Luke closed his eyes and shook his head lightly. "Favorite is not the word I would use."

"Dr. Loughton. Dr. Morgan. Interesting you both are on the bridge to see us enter Martian orbit."

Luke smiled. "Yes, isn't it?"

It looked like Sarah was forcing a smile. "I needed to keep an eye on Commander Denning. He wanted to be part of this historic occasion, but his leg is still weak and he's not fully recovered from all his internal injuries."

René returned a forced smile. "Yes, it's generous of you to make yourself so available." His tone quickly turned condescending. "And you, Dr. Loughton? Just here to give moral support to your wife? Or are you going to assist with ECG and temperature strips if they become necessary?"

Luke knew René was trying to goad him, yet he couldn't resist the urge to be a little condescending himself. It was his turn to give a forced smile. "If the need arises. Then you can be here and give me moral support."

The forced smile faded from René's face. He practically spit out his words. "I am the face of this mission, so it is only fitting I'm here for everyone to see. It adds morale for everyone."

Luke nodded. "I see." He forced another smile. "I feel better already."

René turned up his nose and walked away.

Luke breathed out through his nose quickly, sighing. It was so difficult being around that man.

Luke gave an irritated shake of his head. He looked at Sarah, who was looking intently back at him. He gave a slight shrug. Sarah gave a light laugh. "You'd better be careful. The Martian colony is not that large. You'll be running into him quite often."

Luke nodded. "You're right. I'll have to remember to keep a barf bag with me at all times."

She elbowed him in his side. "You're impossible." Luke could only smile.

She shook her head. "I'm serious. You're going to have to make peace with the guy."

Luke's eyebrows raised. "Oh, so you're now a René Mauchard supporter?"

"No, of course not." Sarah looked ahead for a couple of seconds and then turned back to him. "All I'm saying is, with the Martian colony not being that big, we have to find a way to get along with the guy." She shook her head. "We don't have to support him, just not be openly antagonistic. What's the old adage? You catch more flies with honey than vinegar."

Luke nodded. "Yeah, I know you're right." He shook his head. "He just gets under my skin. It's hard to be nice."

Sarah scooted closer and patted his chest. "But isn't that why you have the Holy Spirit in there? Let him work."

He put his arm around her shoulders. "You're right . . . again."

She bumped her hip into his.

Luke laughed. "Hey, I'm just saying you're almost always right and I should listen to you more."

She looked up and him and smiled. "Well, when you say it like that . . . "

He looked up. "Hey, look. We've almost reached the other ships. We should be in orbit with the rest of them soon."

The ships looked like they were part of some gigantic game of follow-the-leader. They were in a line; the North American ship would soon turn and be in the front of the others.

Sarah scooted in closer to Luke. "This part makes me nervous. It looks like we're going to ram the other ships."

Luke smiled. "The captain will give new headings shortly and the ship will turn and then glide right in front of the others. Then we'll be in the same orbit trajectory."

Luke looked at the crew. All were at consoles touching various icons or buttons and talking to others to ensure the ship performed as it should. Captain Abrams sat and turned in his chair, giving orders and answering questions. Commander Denning stood behind the captain reviewing various reports being handed to him and also giving out instructions.

It was then that it happened . . .

Luke heard what sounded like an enormous trumpet blast. Before he could even turn this over in his mind, he heard a distinct voice. He couldn't be sure if it was audible or just in his head.

Yet it was very clear: "Luke Loughton, come to your bridegroom." He had an overwhelming desire to do just what the voice said. He felt his body rise. As he did so, he looked down and saw . . . a pile of clothes. *Are those mine?* He then looked at his body; his skin seemed to have a glow to it, and he seemed to be dressed in *light* rather than . . . in clothes. He couldn't explain how that was possible. Also, no one seemed to see him; he would expect others to be startled by such an event.

Although he floated between the floor and the ceiling, it was a different feeling than the one he got being in the AG ball arena. There he felt out of control. Here, he felt in control, completely rejuvenated.

Looking back down, next to his clothes were another pair of clothes. He looked over and saw Sarah next to him, also aglow.

"Sarah, it's . . . happening. Just what Maher stated about Scripture . . . is coming true."

"Luke, let's go. He's calling. I can't wait to see Him."

Luke nodded. His body rose even more. He heard a commotion below him. As he looked down, he saw two more pairs of clothes. A cane was lying on top of one pair. He looked over and saw two more people rising. He could tell it was Captain Abrams and Commander Denning. He saw them rise and pass directly through the ceiling of the bridge.

He looked back down. René was yelling. "Change course! Change course! The ship is going to ram the others!"

A lieutenant was running around—seemingly nearly in tears, in complete frustration—trying to make course corrections, but unable to do so. "We need the captain's authorization code." She banged on the console. "I can't change course without it."

"Well, who else has it? He can't have been the only one!" René yelled.

The lieutenant pointed to the other pair of clothes, the ones with the cane lying on top. "Commander Denning." She closed her eyes for a brief second, likely trying to maintain her composure. "What's happened to them? Where did they go?" She looked at René with panic in her eyes. "Were they abducted by aliens or . . . what?"

Luke knew René knew the answer. What he had been trying to prevent from happening . . . was now happening. The Messiah had come back for His own, and it didn't matter if they were on Earth or not. He had come for His bride, and all those who had accepted Him were responding.

René simply shook his head. "How the heck should I know what happened?" he blurted out in abject frustration. He pointed toward the door at the back of the bridge. "Just go find someone—quickly—who can put the right coordinates into the computer."

The lieutenant simply remained in place and shook her head. "Sir, there is no one else. It's just the captain and one person as backup—and that was Commander Denning." She once again pointed to the clothes. "And . . . they're . . . both . . . *gone!*" Her voice, volume, and force increased with each word, ending in what was nearly a scream.

She looked up at the scene before them.

René turned and looked as well. He shook his head. "We're going to crash." His voice got nearly inaudible. "We're going to crash."

Luke felt his body stay in place as the ship continued on its collision course. Luke's new body simply passed directly through the walls of the ship. In a matter of moments, he found himself outside the ship entirely, watching it descend on its collision course.

From this vantage point, he could see more people drifting toward him, and all were dressed in a bright light. They seemed to be coming from nearly every one of the ships. He knew there were too many to be only from those who were awake. Many of these were people who had been in stasis.

Apparently, not being conscious or awake had no bearing on them hearing the trumpet blast and their Master's voice. There must have been hundreds who flew near or by him as he watched the scene below him unfold . . .

. . . The North American ship, now unpiloted, never changed course. It smashed into the European ship, rupturing the fuel compartments on both. An enormous explosion erupted. No sound could be heard; there was nothing for sound waves to travel through. But that didn't prevent the destructive force from throwing shards of metal and other composites in all directions. The sight of the light and combustive force lasted as long as the oxygen from the fuel lasted.

The explosion from the two ships set off a chain reaction. The debris from the explosion went in all directions. Fuel compartments on the other ships were penetrated, once again causing explosions and more debris traveling in all directions. Parts of the ships were ripped open. Luke could see bodies now floating away—some by themselves and others amidst all the debris. It looked as though not a single ship was going to survive these impacts and explosions.

The North American ship continued on its course, undeterred, though much of the ship no longer remained intact. He wasn't sure if the ship was still running on its own power or if its inertia was thrusting it toward the Martian surface. If nothing changed its course, the destruction would include the colony itself.

Luke now had a compelling—no, overwhelming—urge to go to his Messiah. He turned. Sarah was still next to him. Luke thought of being where his bridegroom was waiting for him, and his body responded. It seemed as if space folded around him and he passed through the same distance the ship had gone—and that had taken four months—in just a matter of seconds. He passed so close to the asteroid their ship had avoided that he felt he could literally reach out and touch it. Then, in what seemed like just a couple of seconds, he flew past the moon. Earth, which they had left so long ago, now loomed before him. It looked as beautiful as ever with its blue oceans and white, wispy clouds.

His attention then turned to an iridescently bright One who everyone was gathering around. He appeared so much brighter than everyone or anything else.

Luke knew this had to be his Messiah exhibiting His Shekinah glory that Luke had heard Maher speaking about. He saw thousands of people rising from Earth, joining those already gathered around their Messiah, their bridegroom.

As he and Sarah arrived, his other friends were already there—including Oliver and Viktoria, whom he hadn't seen in months. They both smiled at him. Luke knew they were thinking the same thoughts he was.

There were no words for the feeling, the complete joy.

Luke then noticed another group of people. To one side of the Messiah were others who looked different than he and his friends. He wanted to ask Maher a question about them, but wasn't sure if his voice would travel in space. He had to remind himself he wasn't really functioning in the natural world. He looked over at Maher. "What's going on there?"

Maher smiled. "Those are the ones who have returned with our Messiah."

"You mean those who previously died and believed in Him?"

Maher nodded. "Their spirits are now uniting with their glorified bodies."

Luke watched in amazement as their spirits met their new bodies and then glowed, now looking just like Luke, the rest of his friends, and the innumerable others.

Once the last person arrived, all looked at this One they

had each put their belief, faith, and hope in for their future. Their Messiah smiled and stretched out His hands. Luke saw . . . scars on those hands. He gasped loudly as he realized the sacrifice this One, this beautiful One, had paid for him. His love and admiration for his Messiah skyrocketed even further, if that was possible.

"You are my bride. You have made yourselves ready for this moment. I have looked forward to this time for such a long time. My Father has decreed this is now the time to gather you to Myself." A large smile swept across His face. "Come, see the place I have prepared for you. Come, enter your marriage supper, which my Father has prepared."

Luke smiled. This was truly . . . The Ultimate Liberation Event. Now he was experiencing it. His future, now secure, could be nothing short of wonderful. He felt his body tingle. His mind focused on where his Master dwelled, and he saw Earth and everything before him fade and vanish from his view.

His new life had begun.

FORTY-FIVE

He's Here

Philippe sat at his desk reading the news on his tablet. He was amazed Simone was still such a hot topic. Commentators were now predicting the French president would ask her to speak to the United Nations. Philippe smiled as he shook his head. Simone would so much enjoy reading this.

The door from the conference room flew open and Simone stormed in.

Philippe flinched. "Simone, you startled me." He waved her over. "I'm glad you're here. Come look at this."

She shook her head and held up her tablet. "No, you've got to see *this*."

He looked up. She seemed tense, almost panicked. "What's wrong, Simone?"

She handed him her tablet. "I just received this."

Philippe furrowed his brow as he took the tablet. He saw René in freeze frame. "Another report from René?"

He looked at Simone, but she just looked back, lips pulled in, eyes watering.

He knew this was something serious. He hit the play button.

René was screaming, asking someone to "change course!" The viewport was visible and the European ship was getting closer and closer. He heard screams—and then all went dark, quiet.

He looked up at Simone. "What . . . what just happened? Did they crash?"

Simone nodded. "As far as we can tell, they did. And we haven't been able to reach any ship."

"You're saying all the ships crashed? How is that even possible?"

Simone shook her head.

"What about the colony? Can't we reach them to see what happened?"

Simone continued to shake her head. "We can't reach them either."

Philippe stood and came from behind his desk. He began to pace. "I . . . I can't believe this." He ran his hand across his mouth. "What are we going to do?" He turned back to Simone. "We have to at least confirm this . . . somehow. Let's get Mauna Kea to look via telescope."

Simone picked up her tablet. "Let me e-mail them now."

Philippe saw Simone start scrolling on her tablet. Her eyes got wider and wider as her mouth opened slightly wider as well.

"Simone? What is wrong?"

She looked up with the same expression. She pointed to his large monitor. "Turn on the news."

"What, is the Mars mission on the news? But there hasn't been enough time that they would know of news from space yet!"

Simone shook her head. "It's not the Mars mission." She paused, looked pale. "But it may explain what happened."

Philippe looked confused. He had no idea what she was trying to say . . . but really wasn't. He opened his desk drawer and pulled out his remote. He pressed the button and the monitor came to life.

The news channel was on. The newscaster was in the middle of his report. " . . . it's incredible. It seems people have disappeared—everywhere. There are so many deaths from all types of transportation accidents. It seems in all of these incidents, the consistent telltale sign of something amiss is that clothes remain behind. All those found dead are fully clothed. No one knows what happened. Some are speculating alien abduction." The man looked frightened, pale, his words now raspy. "Any idea seems valid at this point."

Philippe pressed mute. He turned to Simone. "This can't be happening. Is this really meaning what . . . I think it means?"

Simone nodded. "I . . . I think it does." She picked up her tablet and played the footage again.

"What are you doing?"

"Looking for some . . . *there!*" She pointed, tapping the tablet. "See that?"

Philippe looked closer. "Are those clothes on the floor?"

Simone nodded.

"But, we . . . we put safeguards in place." He began to pace again. "How . . . how could they have failed us?"

Simone pulled him to the sofa and sat. She held his hand. "Philippe, I don't know how they failed. But we need to know what these insurrectionists were actually touting."

Philippe shook his head. "Why? What good does that do us?"

She squeezed his hand. "I don't like this any more than you, but now that our belief has failed, we need to know what is now likely to happen. Reading their posts is the fastest way to understand that."

Philippe stood and began to wring his hands. "I'm not sure there are any . . . left."

Simone squinted. "None? You mean your replicating destructive virus actually defeated their replicating virus?"

Philippe looked pale. "Well, that was what we wanted, wasn't it?"

Simone nodded her head. "Yes. But I didn't think it would be that efficient."

"We could do another sweep of the servers. We have sometimes seen the posts pop up periodically." He rubbed the back of his neck. "We could get lucky . . . " He chuckled softly, but there was no joy in his voice. "I never thought I'd be saying this. We could get lucky and find they've reappeared."

Simone stood. "So, what do we need to do to find out?"

"We first need to get our cyberhacker to shut down his virus." He walked to his desk and hit a button for Sonja. "Sonja, get me Henri Moreau."

Simone walked in his direction. "You mean the infamous hacker we've put in prison three times?"

Philippe smiled. "The one and only. If you want the best, you have to use the best."

"And he just . . . agreed to help you?"

"Well, he had a few requests."

She put her hands on her hips. "Yeah, I bet."

He shrugged. "Well, it was only money, and he gave us exactly what we asked for."

"Yeah, I guess he did."

He turned and buzzed Sonja again. "Sonja! Have you reached Henri?"

There was no answer.

"Sonja!"

Philippe sighed. "She must be on break or something." He shook his head. "Let me go find her."

He opened the door and walked past Sonja's desk, storming toward the break room. Simone, following him out, grabbed his arm. "Philippe."

He turned. "What is it?"

She pointed toward Sonja's desk. She didn't have to say anything.

He looked at her and then at the desk. He walked closer and then saw what Simone had wanted him to see. He ran his hands through his hair. He couldn't believe what he was looking at. There on her chair were . . . Sonja's clothes. Her shoes were in front of the chair.

"I had no idea she was . . . was . . . a follower of Clarity of The Way." He shook his head. "Only Sonja had Henri's contact information."

"I don't think you need it."

"Why?"

Simone pointed to Sonja's screen. It was one of the posts. He read the words in front of him.

Think about it. The Creator of the Universe is asking you to become his bride because He loves you so much. How can anyone say no to such an offer? In a Jewish wedding, the bridegroom comes to receive his bride and takes her back to his home. There is a celebration and a wedding feast. It won't be long before God says, "It's time." Will you be ready? Take Him up on His offer. He's coming.

Philippe glanced down at Sonja's desk. She had started to write something. It looked incomplete—there was a jagged mark after the last letter, like a pen haphazardly pulled down the paper. It was clear, though, she had been attempting to leave a message for those left behind:

He's here.

I hope you've enjoyed this book and series. Letting others know of your enjoyment of these books is a way to help others share your experience. Please consider posting an honest review. You can post a review at Amazon, Barnes & Noble, Goodreads, or other places you wish. Reviews can be posted at more than one site!

This author, and other readers, appreciate your engagement. Also, check out my next series coming soon!

—RANDY DOCKENS

MERCY OF THE
IRON SCEPTER

CHAPTER 1

Friends. Enemies. Those lines could get blurred tonight.

Kalem hugged the shadows as he made his way through the town. His town. This was where he grew up, but the fewer people who saw him tonight, the better. He scurried into the small park on the edge of town. It would likely be deserted at this hour. The contents of his backpack dug into his shoulder blade. That pain equaled the pain his heart had borne for more than a decade. He was now old enough to correct the injustice that had been done.

He climbed into the gazebo on the edge of the park. The Town Square was just ahead. Beyond the long-range teleporter was the Civic Center. The main part of town lay to his right. His destination was to his left. He only had to scurry across the square undetected and head back into the shadows.

He started to jump over the gazebo railing and dart across the Square when suddenly the light above the teleporter came on. Kalem ducked and peered through the latticework of the gazebo. Having dark brown hair should be helpful tonight. Still, he pulled the hood over his head in case the light caught his auburn highlights. Two men appeared at the teleporter. He squinted in an attempt to see who they were, but didn't recognize them. Who were these men? They wore nothing distinguishing. Just pullovers and khakis. Visitors to this part of mid-America were a rarity. Hopefully, this had nothing to do with his mission tonight. He shook his head. Couldn't be. No one else knew.

Kalem held his breath until he knew which direction these two strangers would go. They seemed to talk among themselves for a few minutes and look around, and then they headed toward the town itself. Kalem slowly let out his breath. His plans could go forward. Once he knew the two strangers were out of sight, he jumped over the gazebo railing and hurried to the opposite end of the Town Square before the teleporter light turned off. This solved the problem of how to avoid its motion-activated sensor. He turned left and headed back into the cover of darkness.

In just a few minutes, Kalem came to his destination. This was the lodge his parents had helped build to hold Family Nights for all the farmers in the area to gather and for their kids to play together. It looked centuries old, but it was likely no more than a half century since it was constructed. Ever since he could remember, everyone considered this lodge the showplace for the town. It sat by itself, nestled in the trees. Lights had been installed to highlight its red metal roof, which matched some of the reddish hues in the stones composing its outside wall, now highlighted with lights shining down from the eaves. The front door was made of clear glass—the only modern-looking part of the building. There were also lights along the fieldstone sidewalk going up to the entrance.

As Kalem opened the door to enter, he stopped and read the bronze plaque:

We have raised our Ebenezer (1 Sa 7:12). This building demarks the change from pre-Refreshing to our current Refreshing, and from whom our help comes. Let us give glory and honor to our King.

Kalem shook his head. No, he wasn't here to honor anyone tonight. He had no desire to give glory to this king—this false king. What he had in his backpack was all the proof he needed to bring down this one who took his brother. In this time of earth's history, death did not occur unless it came by the hand of the King. Kalem shook his head. The King had no right.

Kalem opened the door and entered. The light smoky scent from the fireplace brought back so many childhood memories. Glancing around, everything looked the same except for newer trophies lining the mantel of the huge stone fireplace forming the back wall of the room. He walked around small wooden tables scattered throughout the room and around the large wooden table near the fireplace. How long had it been since he had been here? While his friends stayed and became farmers like their dads, he had become an archeologist, a path to better understand what happened so many years ago. He had found what he needed. Now he just needed his friends on his side.

Kalem ran his hand along the stones. Memories of happy times with his friends and with his older brother, Peter, came flooding back. Peter always ensured, to all the kids' delight, that a fire would be awaiting them in the fireplace for roasting marshmallows. This memory only heightened Kalem's desire to understand the why behind Peter's banishment at the hand of the King—his banishment to the place of lost souls. He still missed his older brother terribly.

Kalem lit a few candles to supply light, but not too much light. He hoped the dimmer the lights inside, the more the bright lights outside would disguise anyone inside the building. He pulled out a chair from the long table and sat with his back to the fireplace so he could see his friends enter.

He touched the T-band on his wrist. It displayed the time. He debated whether to use the holo-communicator in his T-band to call his friends. He shook his head. No, he wanted to see which of them were loyal enough to show up. He kept looking at the time. His heart rate increased and his palms became sweaty. This would be a lot to ask of his friends, but they admired Peter as much as he did. They would surely be supportive.

The door opened. Kalem stood. Five of his friends entered. The largest of the group gave a wave. "Hello, Kalem."

Kalem smiled. They had come—all of them. He went around the table and gave each a handshake and quick hug. "Welcome. Have a seat."

For a further look at Randy's exciting next series,
please turn the page!

THE
STELE
PROPHECY
PENTALOGY

Do you know your future? Come see the possibilities in a world God creates. Is it perfect? Human nature is still involved, so not all rough edges are smoothed. Come read about an archeologist exploring what happened to his older brother and how that search colors his view of the world; how a utopian society rises from an apocalypse and plunges toward another apocalypse; how a priest finds renewed excitement in his destiny; how a princess finds love in an unexpected way that changes her life; and how a headstrong commodities analyst seems to not understand the perfection of the world into which she is born.

Come explore a world you've hoped for but may not have understood!

*The series is coming from Randy Dockens
beginning February 2019!*

www.ingramcontent.com/pod-product-compliance
Lightning Source LLC
Chambersburg PA
CBHW071102250626

47159CB00002B/570